Terry Pratchett is one of the most popular authors writing today. He lives behind a keyboard in Wiltshire and says he 'doesn't want to get a life, because it feels as though he's trying to lead three already'. He was appointed OBE in 1998 and his first Discworld novel for children, *The Amazing Maurice and His Educated Rodents*, was awarded the 2001 Carnegie Medal.

EQUAL RITES is the third novel in his phenomenally successful Discworld series.

Register to receive
news from Discworld!

Simply email: news@discworld.co.uk

www.booksattransworld.co.uk/terrypratchett

BOOKS BY TERRY PRATCHETT

For Younger Readers

THE BROMELIAD TRILOGY
(containing *Truckers*, *Diggers*
and *Wings*)

TRUCKERS ✧

DIGGERS ✧

WINGS ✧

THE CARPET PEOPLE ✧

ONLY YOU CAN
SAVE MANKIND ✧

JOHNNY AND THE DEAD ✧

JOHNNY AND THE BOMB ✧

THE JOHNNY MAXWELL
TRILOGY
(containing *Only You Can Save Mankind*,
Johnny and the Dead and *Johnny and
the Bomb*)

JOHNNY AND THE DEAD
playscript (adapted by Stephen Briggs) ★

Discworld for Younger Readers

THE AMAZING MAURICE AND HIS
EDUCATED RODENTS ✧

THE AMAZING MAURICE AND HIS
EDUCATED RODENTS playscript
(adapted by Stephen Briggs) ★

THE WEE FREE MEN ✧

A HAT FULL OF SKY

For Adults of All Ages

The Discworld® series

THE COLOUR OF MAGIC ✧

THE LIGHT FANTASTIC ✧

EQUAL RITES ✧

MORT ✧

SOURCERY ✧

WYRD SISTERS ✧

PYRAMIDS ✧

GUARDS! GUARDS! ✧

ERIC ✧ ●

MOVING PICTURES ✧

REAPER MAN ✧

WITCHES ABROAD ✧

SMALL GODS ✧

LORDS AND LADIES ✧

MEN AT ARMS ✧

SOUL MUSIC ✧

INTERESTING TIMES ✧

MASKERADE ✧

FEET OF CLAY ✧

HOGFATHER ✧

JINGO ✧

THE LAST CONTINENT ✧

CARPE JUGULUM ✧

THE FIFTH ELEPHANT ✧

THE TRUTH ✧

THIEF OF TIME ✧

NIGHT WATCH ✧

MONSTROUS REGIMENT ✧

GOING POSTAL ✧

THE COLOUR OF MAGIC –
GRAPHIC NOVEL

THE LIGHT FANTASTIC –
GRAPHIC NOVEL

MORT: A DISCWORLD BIG COMIC
(illustrated by Graham Higgins) ●

GUARDS! GUARDS!: A DISCWORLD
BIG COMIC
(adapted by Stephen Briggs,
illustrated by Graham Higgins) ●

EQUAL RITES

Terry Pratchett

CORGI BOOKS

EQUAL RITES

A CORGI BOOK: 0 552 15260 9

Originally published in Great Britain by Victor Gollancz Ltd in
association with Colin Smythe Ltd

PRINTING HISTORY
Victor Gollancz edition published 1987
Corgi edition published 1987

23 25 27 29 30 28 26 24

Set in Minion by Falcon Oast Graphic Art Ltd.

Corgi Books are published by Transworld Publishers,
61-63 Uxbridge Road, London W5 5SA,
a division of The Random House Group Ltd,
in Australia by Random House Australia (Pty) Ltd,
20 Alfred Street, Milsons Point, Sydney, NSW 2061, Australia,
in New Zealand by Random House New Zealand Ltd,
18 Poland Road, Glenfield, Auckland 10, New Zealand
and in South Africa by Random House (Pty) Ltd,
Endulini, 5a Jubilee Road, Parktown 2193, South Africa.

Printed and bound in Great Britain by
Cox & Wyman Ltd, Reading, Berkshire.

Papers used by Transworld Publishers are natural, recyclable
products made from wood grown in sustainable forests.
The manufacturing processes conform to the environmental
regulations of the country of origin.

Thanks to Neil Gaiman, who loaned us the last surviving copy of the Liber Paginarum Fulvarum, *and a big hallo to all the kids at the H.P. Lovecraft Holiday Fun Club.*

I would like it to be clearly understood that this book is not wacky. Only dumb redheads in Fifties' sitcoms are wacky.

No, it's not zany either.

EQUAL RITES

THIS IS A STORY ABOUT magic and where it goes and perhaps more importantly where it comes from and why, although it doesn't pretend to answer all or any of these questions.

It may, however, help to explain why Gandalf never got married and why Merlin was a man. Because this is also a story about sex, although probably not in the athletic, tumbling, count-the-legs-and-divide-by-two sense unless the characters get totally beyond the author's control. They might.

However, it is primarily a story about a world. Here it comes now. Watch closely, the special effects are quite expensive.

A bass note sounds. It is a deep, vibrating chord that hints that the brass section may break in at any moment with a fanfare for the cosmos, because the scene is the blackness of deep space with a few stars glittering like the dandruff on the shoulders of God.

Then it comes into view overhead, bigger than the biggest, most unpleasantly-armed starcruiser in the imagination of a three-ring film-maker: a turtle, ten thousand miles long. It is Great A'Tuin, one of the rare astrochelonians from a universe where things are less as they are and more like people imagine them to be, and it carries on its meteor-pocked shell four giant elephants who bear on their enormous shoulders the great round wheel of the Discworld.

As the viewpoint swings around, the whole of the world can be seen by the light of its tiny orbiting sun. There are continents, archipelagos, seas, deserts, mountain ranges and even a tiny central ice cap. The inhabitants of this place, it is obvious, won't have any truck with global theories. Their world, bounded by an encircling ocean that falls forever into space in one long waterfall, is as round and flat as a geological pizza, although without the anchovies.

A world like that, which exists only because the gods enjoy a joke, must be a place where magic can survive. And sex too, of course.

He came walking through the thunderstorm and you could tell he was a wizard, partly because of the long cloak and carven staff but mainly because the raindrops were stopping several feet from his head, and steaming.

It was good thunderstorm country, up here in the Ramtop Mountains, a country of jagged peaks, dense forests and little river valleys so deep the daylight had no sooner reached the bottom than it was time to leave again. Ragged wisps of cloud clung to the lesser peaks below the mountain trail along which the wizard slithered and slid. A few slot-eyed goats watched him with mild interest. It doesn't take a lot to interest goats.

Sometimes he would stop and throw his heavy staff into the air. It always came down pointing the same way and the wizard would sigh, pick it up, and continue his squelchy progress.

The storm walked around the hills on legs of lightning, shouting and grumbling.

The wizard disappeared around the bend in the track and the goats went back to their damp grazing.

Until something else caused them to look up. They stiffened, their eyes widening, their nostrils flaring.

This was strange, because there was nothing on the path. But the goats still watched it pass by until it was out of sight.

There was a village tucked in a narrow valley between steep woods. It wasn't a large village, and wouldn't have shown up on a map of the mountains. It barely showed up on a map of the village.

It was, in fact, one of those places that exist merely so that people can have come from them. The universe is littered with them: hidden villages, windswept little towns under wide skies, isolated cabins on chilly mountains, whose only mark on history is to be the incredibly ordinary place where something extraordinary started to happen. Often there is no more than a little plaque to reveal that, against all gynaecological probability, someone very famous was born halfway up a wall.

Mist curled between the houses as the wizard crossed a narrow bridge over the swollen stream and made his way to the village smithy, although the two facts had nothing to do with one another. The mist would have curled anyway: it was experienced mist and had got curling down to a fine art.

The smithy was fairly crowded, of course. A smithy is one place where you can depend on finding a good fire and someone to talk to. Several villagers were lounging in the warm shadows but, as the wizard approached, they sat up expectantly and tried to look intelligent, generally with indifferent success.

The smith didn't feel the need to be quite so sub-servient. He nodded at the wizard, but it was a greeting between equals, or at least between equals as far as the smith was concerned. After all, any halfway competent blacksmith has more than a nodding acquaintance with magic, or at least likes to think he has.

The wizard bowed. A white cat that had been sleeping by the furnace woke up and watched him carefully.

'What is the name of this place, sir?' said the wizard.

The blacksmith shrugged.

'Bad Ass,' he said.

'Bad—?'

'Ass,' repeated the blacksmith, his tone defying any-one to make something of it.

The wizard considered this.

'A name with a story behind it,' he said at last, 'which were circumstances otherwise I would be pleased to hear. But I would like to speak to you, smith, about your son.'

'Which one?' said the smith, and the hangers-on sniggered. The wizard smiled.

'You have seven sons, do you not? And you yourself were an eighth son?'

The smith's face stiffened. He turned to the other villagers.

'All right, the rain's stopping,' he said. 'Piss off, the lot of you. Me and—' he looked at the wizard with raised eyebrows.

'Drum Billet,' said the wizard.

'Me and Mr Billet have things to talk about.' He waved his hammer vaguely and, one after another, craning over their shoulders in case the wizard did anything interesting, the audience departed.

The smith drew a couple of stools from under a bench. He took a bottle out of a cupboard by the water tank and poured a couple of very small glasses of clear liquid.

The two men sat and watched the rain and the mist rolling over the bridge. Then the smith said: 'I know what son you mean. Old Granny is up with my wife now. Eighth son of an eighth son, of course. It did cross my mind but I never gave it much thought, to be honest. Well, well. A wizard in the family, eh?'

'You catch on very quickly,' said Billet. The white cat jumped down from its perch, sauntered across the floor and vaulted into the wizard's lap, where it curled up. His thin fingers stroked it absent-mindedly.

'Well, well,' said the smith again. 'A wizard in Bad Ass, eh?'

'Possibly, possibly,' said Billet. 'Of course, he'll have

to go to University first. He may do very well, of course.'

The smith considered the idea from all angles, and decided he liked it a lot. A thought struck him.

'Hang on,' he said. 'I'm trying to remember what my father told me. A wizard who knows he's going to die can sort of pass on his sort of wizardness to a sort of successor, right?'

'I have never heard it put so succinctly, yes,' said the wizard.

'So you're going to sort of die?'

'Oh yes.' The cat purred as the fingers tickled it behind the ear.

The smith looked embarrassed. 'When?'

The wizard thought for a moment. 'In about six minutes time.'

'Oh.'

'Don't worry,' said the wizard. 'I'm quite looking forward to it, to tell you the truth. I've heard it's quite painless.'

The blacksmith considered this. 'Who told you?' he said at last.

The wizard pretended not to hear him. He was watching the bridge, looking for tell-tale turbulence in the mist.

'Look,' said the smith. 'You'd better tell me how we go about bringing up a wizard, you see, because there isn't a wizard in these parts and—'

'It will all sort itself out,' said Billet pleasantly. 'The magic has guided me to you and the magic will take care of everything. It usually does. Did I hear a cry?'

The blacksmith looked at the ceiling. Above the splash of the rain he could make out the sound of a pair of new lungs at full bore.

The wizard smiled. 'Have him brought down here,' he said.

The cat sat up and looked interestedly at the forge's wide doorway. As the smith called excitedly up the stairs it jumped down and padded slowly across the floor, purring like a bandsaw.

A tall white-haired woman appeared at the bottom of the stairs, clutching a bundle in a blanket. The smith hurried her over to where the wizard sat.

'But—' she began.

'This is very important,' said the smith importantly. 'What do we do now, sir?'

The wizard held up his staff. It was man-high and nearly as thick as his wrist, and covered with carvings that seemed to change as the smith looked at them, exactly as if they didn't want him to see what they were.

'The child must hold it,' said Drum Billet. The smith nodded and fumbled in the blanket until he located a tiny pink hand. He guided it gently to the wood. It gripped it tightly

'But—' said the midwife.

'It's all right, Granny, I know what I'm about. She's a witch, sir, don't mind her. Right,' said the smith. 'Now what?'

The wizard was silent.

'What do we do n—' the smith began, and stopped. He leaned down to look at the old wizard's face. Billet was smiling, but it was anyone's guess what the joke was.

The smith pushed the baby back into the arms of the frantic midwife. Then, as respectfully as possible, he unpried the thin, pale fingers from the staff.

It had a strange, greasy feel, like static electricity. The wood itself was almost black, but the carvings were slightly lighter, and hurt the eyes if you tried to make out precisely what they were supposed to be.

'Are you pleased with yourself?' said the midwife.

'Eh? Oh. Yes. As a matter of fact, yes. Why?'

She twitched aside a fold of the blanket. The smith looked down, and swallowed.

'No,' he whispered. 'He said—'

'And what would *he* know about it?' sneered Granny.

'But he said it would be a son!'

'Doesn't look like a son to me, laddie.'

The smith flopped down on his stool, his head in his hands.

'What have I done?' he moaned.

'You've given the world its first female wizard,' said the midwife. 'Whosa itsywitsy, den?'

'What?'

'I was talking to the *baby*.'

The white cat purred and arched its back as if it was rubbing up against the legs of an old friend. Which was odd, because there was no one there.

* * *

'I was foolish,' said a voice in tones no mortal could hear. 'I assumed the magic would know what it was doing.'

PERHAPS IT DOES.

'If only I could do something . . .'

THERE IS NO GOING BACK. THERE IS NO GOING BACK, said the deep, heavy voice like the closing of crypt doors.

The wisp of nothingness that was Drum Billet thought for a while.

'But she's going to have a lot of problems.'

THAT'S WHAT LIFE IS ALL ABOUT. SO I'M TOLD. I WOULDN'T KNOW, OF COURSE.

'What about reincarnation?'

Death hesitated.

YOU WOULDN'T LIKE IT, he said. TAKE IT FROM ME.

'I've heard that some people do it all the time.'

YOU'VE GOT TO BE TRAINED TO IT. YOU'VE GOT TO START OFF SMALL AND WORK UP. YOU'VE NO IDEA HOW HORRIBLE IT IS TO BE AN ANT.

'It's bad?'

YOU WOULDN'T BELIEVE IT. AND WITH YOUR KARMA AN ANT IS TOO MUCH TO EXPECT.

The baby had been taken back to its mother and the smith sat disconsolately watching the rain.

Drum Billet scratched the cat behind its ears and thought about his life. It had been a long one, that was one of the advantages of being a wizard, and he'd done a lot of things he hadn't always felt good about. It was about time that . . .

I HAVEN'T GOT ALL DAY, YOU KNOW, said Death, reproachfully.

The wizard looked down at the cat and realized for the first time how odd it looked now.

The living often don't appreciate how complicated the world looks when you are dead, because while death frees the mind from the straitjacket of three dimensions it also cuts it away from Time, which is only another dimension. So while the cat that rubbed up against his invisible legs was undoubtedly the same cat that he had seen a few minutes before, it was also quite clearly a tiny kitten and a fat, half-blind old moggy and every stage in between. All at once. Since it had started off small it looked like a white, cat-shaped carrot, a description that will have to do until people invent proper four-dimensional adjectives.

Death's skeletal hand tapped Billet gently on the shoulder.

COME AWAY, MY SON.

'There's nothing I can do?'

LIFE IS FOR THE LIVING. ANYWAY, YOU'VE GIVEN HER YOUR STAFF.

'Yes. There is that.'

The midwife's name was Granny Weatherwax. She was a witch. That was quite acceptable in the Ramtops, and no one had a bad word to say about witches. At least, not if he wanted to wake up in the morning the same shape as he went to bed.

The smith was still staring gloomily at the rain

when she came back down the stairs and clapped a warty hand on his shoulder.

He looked up at her.

'What shall I do, Granny?' he said, unable to keep the pleading out of his voice.

'What have you done with the wizard?'

'I put him out in the fuel store. Was that right?'

'It'll do for now,' she said briskly. 'And now you must burn the staff.'

They both turned to stare at the heavy staff, which the smith had propped in the forge's darkest corner. It almost appeared to be looking back at them.

'But it's magical,' he whispered.

'Well?'

'Will it burn?'

'Never knew wood that didn't.'

'It doesn't seem right!'

Granny Weatherwax swung shut the big doors and turned to him angrily.

'Now you listen to me, Gordo Smith!' she said. 'Female wizards aren't right either! It's the wrong kind of magic for women, is wizard magic, it's all books and stars and jommetry. She'd never grasp it. Whoever heard of a female wizard?'

'There's witches,' said the smith uncertainly. 'And enchantresses too, I've heard.'

'Witches is a different thing altogether,' snapped Granny Weatherwax. 'It's magic out of the ground, not out of the sky, and men never could get the hang of it. As for enchantresses,' she added. 'They're no better than they should be. You take it from me, just burn the staff, bury the body and don't let on it ever happened.'

Smith nodded reluctantly, crossed over to the forge, and pumped the bellows until the sparks flew. He went back for the staff.

It wouldn't move.

'It won't move!'

Sweat stood out on his brow as he tugged at the wood. It remained unco-operatively immobile.

'Here, let me try,' said Granny, and reached past him. There was a snap and a smell of scorched tin.

Smith ran across the forge, whimpering slightly, to where Granny had landed upside down against the opposite wall.

'Are you all right?'

She opened two eyes like angry diamonds and said, 'I see. That's the way of it, is it?'

'The way of what?' said Smith, totally bewildered.

'Help me up, you fool. And fetch me a chopper.'

The tone of her voice suggested that it would be a very good idea not to disobey. Smith rummaged desperately among the junk at the back of the forge until he found an old double-headed axe.

'Right. Now take off your apron.'

'Why? What do you intend to do?' said the smith, who was beginning to lose his grip on events. Granny gave an exasperated sigh.

'It's leather, you idiot. I'm going to wrap it around the handle. It'll not catch me the same way twice!'

Smith struggled out of the heavy leather apron and handed it to her very gingerly. She wrapped it around the axe and made one or two passes in the air. Then, a spiderlike figure in the glow of the nearly incandescent furnace, she stalked across the room and with a grunt of triumph and effort brought the heavy blade sweeping down right in the centre of the staff.

There was a click. There was a noise like a partridge. There was a thud.

There was silence.

Smith reached up very slowly, without moving his head, and touched the axe blade. It wasn't on the axe any more. It had buried itself in the door by his head, taking a tiny nick out of his ear.

Granny stood looking slightly blurred from hitting an absolutely immovable object, and stared at the stub of wood in her hands.

'Rrrrighttt,' she stuttered. 'Iiiinnn tthhatttt cccasseee—'

'No,' said Smith firmly, rubbing his ear. 'Whatever it is you're going to suggest, no. Leave it. I'll pile some stuff around it. No one'll notice. Leave it. It's just a stick.'

'*Just a stick?*'

'Have you got any better ideas? Ones that won't take my head off?'

She glared at the staff, which appeared not to notice.

'Not right now,' she admitted. 'But you just give me time—'

'All right, all right. Anyway, I've got things to do, wizards to bury, you know how it is.'

Smith took a spade from beside the back door and hesitated.

'Granny.'

'What?'

'Do you know how wizards like to be buried?'

'Yes!'

'Well, how?'

Granny Weatherwax paused at the bottom of the stairs.

'Reluctantly.'

Later, night fell gently as the last of the world's slow light flowed out of the valley, and a pale, rain-washed moon shone down in a night studded with stars. And in a shadowy orchard behind the forge there was the occasional clink of a spade or a muffled curse.

In the cradle upstairs the world's first female wizard dreamed of nothing much.

The white cat lay half-asleep on its private ledge near the furnace. The only sound in the warm dark forge was the crackle of the coals as they settled down under the ash.

The staff stood in the corner, where it wanted to be, wrapped in shadows that were slightly blacker than shadows normally are.

Time passed, which, basically, is its job.

There was a faint tinkle, and a swish of air. After a while the cat sat up and watched with interest.

Dawn came. Up here in the Ramtops dawn was always impressive, especially when a storm had cleared the air. The valley occupied by Bad Ass overlooked a panorama of lesser mountains and foothills, coloured purple and orange in the early morning light that flowed gently over them (because light travels at a dilatory pace in the Disc's vast magical field) and far off the great plains were still a puddle of shadows. Even further off the sea gave an occasional distant sparkle.

In fact, from here you could see right to the edge of the world.

That wasn't poetic imagery but plain fact, since the world was quite definitely flat and was, furthermore, known to be carried through space on the backs of four elephants that in turn stood on the shell of Great A'Tuin, the Great Sky Turtle.

Back down there in Bad Ass the village is waking up. The smith has just gone into the forge and found it tidier than it has been for the last hundred years, with all the tools back in their right places, the floor swept and a new fire laid in the furnace. He is sitting on the anvil, which has been moved right across the room, and is watching the staff and is trying to think.

Nothing much happened for seven years, except that one of the apple trees in the smithy orchard grew perceptibly taller than the others and was frequently climbed by a small girl with brown hair, a gap in her front teeth, and the sort of features that promised to become, if not beautiful, then at least attractively interesting.

She was named Eskarina, for no particular reason other than that her mother liked the sound of the word, and although Granny Weatherwax kept a careful watch on her she failed to spot any signs of magic whatsoever. It was true that the girl spent more time climbing trees and running around shouting than little girls normally did, but a girl with four older brothers still at home can be excused a lot of things. In fact, the witch began to relax and started to think the magic had not taken hold after all.

But magic has a habit of lying low, like a rake in the grass.

Winter came round again, and it was a bad one. The clouds hung around the Ramtops like big fat sheep, filling the gulleys with snow and turning the forests into silent, gloomy caverns. The high passes were closed and the caravans wouldn't come again until spring. Bad Ass became a little island of heat and light.

Over breakfast Esk's mother said: 'I'm worried about Granny Weatherwax. She hasn't been around lately.'

Smith looked at her over his porridge spoon.

'I'm not complaining,' he said. 'She—'

'She's got a long nose,' said Esk.

Her parents glared at her.

'There's no call to make that kind of remark,' said her mother sternly.

'But father said she's always poking her—'

26

'Eskarina!'

'But he said—'

'I said—'

'Yes, but, he *did* say that she had—'

Smith reached down and slapped her. It wasn't very hard, and he regretted it instantly. The boys got the flat of his hand and occasionally the length of his belt whenever they deserved it. The trouble with his daughter, though, was not ordinary naughtiness but the infuriating way she had of relentlessly pursuing the thread of an argument long after she should have put it down. It always flustered him.

She burst into tears. Smith stood up, angry and embarrassed at himself, and stumped off to the forge.

There was a loud crack, and a thud.

They found him out cold on the floor. Afterwards *he* always maintained that he'd hit his head on the doorway. Which was odd, because he wasn't very tall and there had always been plenty of room before, but he was certain that whatever happened had nothing to do with the blur of movement from the forge's darkest corner.

Somehow the events set the seal on the day. It became a broken crockery day, a day of people getting under each other's feet and being peevish. Esk's mother dropped a jug that had belonged to her grandmother and a whole box of apples in the loft turned out to be mouldy. In the forge the furnace went sullen and refused to draw. Jaims, the oldest son, slipped on the packed ice in the road and hurt his arm. The white cat, or possibly one of its descendants, since the cats led a private and complicated life of their own in the hayloft next to the forge, went and climbed up the chimney in the scullery and refused to come down. Even the sky pressed in like an old mattress, and the air felt stuffy, despite the snow.

Frayed nerves and boredom and bad temper made the air hum like thunderstorm weather.

'Right! That's it. That's just about enough!' shouted Esk's mother. 'Cern, you and Gulta and Esk can go and see how Granny is and – where's Esk?'

The two youngest boys looked up from where they were halfheartedly fighting under the table.

'She went out to the orchard,' said Gulta. 'Again.'

'Go and fetch her in, then, and be off.'

'But it's cold!'

'It's going to snow again!'

'It's only a mile and the road is clear enough and who was so keen to be out in it when we had the first snowfall? Go on with you, and don't come back till you're in a better temper.'

They found Esk sitting in a fork of the big apple tree. The boys didn't like the tree much. For one thing, it was so covered in mistletoe that it looked green even in midwinter, its fruit was small and went from stomach-twisting sourness to wasp-filled rottenness overnight, and although it looked easy enough to climb it had a habit of breaking twigs and dislodging feet at inconvenient moments. Cern once swore that a branch had twisted just to spill him off. But it tolerated Esk, who used to go and sit in it if she was annoyed or fed up or just wanted to be by herself, and the boys sensed that every brother's right to gently torture his sister ended at the foot of its trunk. So they threw a snowball at her. It missed.

'We're going to see old Weatherwax.'

'But you don't have to come.'

'Because you'll just slow us down and probably cry anyway.'

Esk looked down at them solemnly. She didn't cry a lot, it never seemed to achieve much.

'If you don't want me to come then I'll come,' she said. This sort of thing passes for logic among siblings.

'Oh, we want you to come,' said Gulta quickly.

'Very pleased to hear it,' said Esk, dropping on to the packed snow.

They had a basket containing smoked sausages, preserved eggs and – because their mother was prudent as well as generous – a large jar of peach preserve that no one in the family liked very much. She still made it every year when the little wild peaches were ripe, anyway.

The people of Bad Ass had learned to live with the long winter snows and the roads out of the village were lined with boards to reduce drifting and, more important, stop travellers from straying. If they lived locally it wouldn't matter too much if they did, because an unsung genius on the village council several generations previously had come up with the idea of carving markers in every tenth tree in the forest around the village, out to a distance of nearly two miles. It had taken ages, and re-cutting markers

29

was always a job for any man with spare time, but in winters where a blizzard could lose a man within yards of his home many a life had been saved by the pattern of notches found by probing fingers under the clinging snow.

It was snowing again when they left the road and started up the track where, in summer, the witch's house nestled in a riot of raspberry thickets and weird witch-growth.

'No footprints,' said Cern.

'Except for foxes,' said Gulta. 'They say she can turn herself into a fox. Or anything. A bird, even. Anything. That's how she always knows what's going on.'

They looked around cautiously. A scruffy crow was indeed watching them from a distant tree stump.

'They say there's a whole family over Crack Peak way that can turn themselves into wolves,' said Gulta, who wasn't one to leave a promising subject, 'because one night someone shot a wolf and next day their auntie was limping with an arrow wound in her leg, and . . .'

'I don't think people can turn themselves into animals,' said Esk, slowly.

'Oh yes, Miss Clever?'

'Granny is quite big. If she turned herself into a fox what would happen to all the bits that wouldn't fit?'

'She'd just magic them away,' said Cern.

'I don't think magic works like that,' said Esk. 'You can't just make things happen, there's a sort of – like a seesaw thing, if you push one end down, the other end goes up . . .' Her voice trailed off.

They gave her a look.

'I can't see Granny on a seesaw,' said Gulta. Cern giggled.

'No, I mean every time something happens, something else has to happen too – I think,' said Esk uncertainly, picking her way around a deeper than usual snowdrift. 'Only in the . . . opposite direction.'

'That's silly,' said Gulta, 'because, look, you remember when that fair came last summer and there was a wizard with it and he made all those birds and things appear out of nothing? I mean it just happened, he just said these words and waved his hands, and it just happened. There weren't any seesaws.'

'There was a swing,' said Cern. 'And a thing where you had to throw things at things to win things.'

'And you didn't hit anything, Cern.'

'Nor did you, you said the things were stuck to the things so you couldn't knock them off, you said . . .'

Their conversation wandered away like a couple of puppies. Esk listened with half an ear. I know what I mean, she told herself. Magic's easy, you just find the place where everything is balanced and push. Anyone could do it. There's nothing magical about it. All the funny words and waving the hands is just . . . it's only for . . .

She stopped, surprised at herself. She knew what she meant. The idea was right up there in the front of her mind. But she didn't know how to say it in words, even to herself.

It was a horrible feeling to find things in your head and not know how they fitted. It . . .

'Come on, we'll be all day.'

She shook her head and hurried after her brothers.

The witch's cottage consisted of so many extensions and lean-tos that it was difficult to see what the original building had looked like, or even if there had ever been one. In the summer it was surrounded by dense beds of what Granny loosely called 'the Herbs' – strange plants, hairy or squat or twining, with curious flowers or vivid fruits or unpleasantly bulging pods. Only Granny knew what they were all for, and any wood-pigeon hungry enough to attack them generally emerged giggling to itself and bumping into things (or, sometimes, never emerged at all).

Now everything was deep under the snow. A forlorn windsock flapped against its pole. Granny didn't hold with flying but some of her friends still used broomsticks.

'It looks deserted,' said Cern.

'No smoke,' said Gulta.

The windows look like eyes, thought Esk, but kept it to herself.

'It's only Granny's house,' she said. 'There's nothing wrong.'

The cottage radiated emptiness. They could feel it. The windows *did* look like eyes, black and menacing against the snow. And no one in the Ramtops let their fire go out in the winter, as a matter of pride.

Esk wanted to say 'Let's go home,' but she knew that if she did the boys would run for it. Instead she said, 'Mother says there's a key on a nail in the privy,' and that was nearly as bad. Even an ordinary unknown privy held minor terrors like wasps' nests, large spiders, mysterious rustling things in the roof and, one very bad winter, a small hibernating bear that caused acute constipation in the family until it was persuaded to bed down in the haybarn. A witch's privy could contain *anything*.

'I'll go and look, shall I?' she added.

'If you like,' said Gulta airily, almost successfully concealing his relief.

In fact, when she managed to get the door open against the piled snow, it was neat and clean and contained nothing more sinister than an old almanack, or more precisely about half an old almanack, carefully hung on a nail. Granny had a philosophical objection to reading, but she'd be the last to say that books, especially books with nice thin pages, didn't have their uses.

The key shared a ledge by the door with a chrysalis and the stump of a candle. Esk took it gingerly, trying not to disturb the chrysalis, and hurried back to the boys.

It was no use trying the front door. Front doors in Bad Ass were used only by brides and corpses, and Granny had always avoided becoming either. Around the back the snow was piled in front of the door and no one had broken the ice on the water butt.

The light was starting to pour out of the sky by the time they dug through to the door and managed to persuade the key to turn.

Inside, the big kitchen was dark and chilly and smelled only of snow. It was *always* dark, but they were used to seeing a big fire in the wide chimney and smelling the thick fumes of whatever it was she was boiling up this time, which sometimes gave you a headache or made you see things.

They wandered around uncertainly, calling, until Esk decided they couldn't put off going upstairs any longer. The clonk of the thumb-latch on the door to the cramped staircase sounded a lot louder than it ought to.

Granny was on the bed, with her arms tightly folded across her chest. The tiny window had blown open. Fine snow had blown in across the floor and over the bed.

Esk stared at the patchwork quilt under the old woman, because there were times when a little detail could expand and fill the whole world. She barely heard Cern start to cry: she remembered her father, strangely enough, making the quilt two winters before when the snow was almost as bad and there wasn't much to do in the forge, and how he'd used all kinds of rags that had found their way to Bad Ass from every part of the world, like silk, dilemma leather, water cotton and tharga wool and, of course, since he wasn't much good at sewing either, the result was a rather strange lumpy thing more like a flat tortoise than a quilt, and her mother had generously decided to give it to Granny last Hogswatchnight, and . . .

'Is she dead?' asked Gulta, as if Esk was an expert in these things.

Esk stared up at Granny Weatherwax. The old woman's face looked thin and grey. Was that how dead people looked? Shouldn't her chest be going up and down?

Gulta pulled himself together.

'We ought to go and get someone and we ought to go now because it will get dark in a minute,' he said flatly. 'But Cern will stay here.'

His brother looked at him in horror.

'What for?' he said.

'Someone has got to stay with dead people,' said Gulta. 'Remember when old Uncle Derghart died and Father had to go and sit up with all the candles and things all night? Otherwise something nasty comes and takes your soul off to . . . to somewhere,' he ended lamely. 'And then people come back and haunt you.'

Cern opened his mouth to start to cry again. Esk said hurriedly, 'I'll stay. I don't mind. It's only Granny.'

Gulta looked at her in relief.

'Light some candles or something,' he said. 'I think that's what you're supposed to do. And then—'

There was a scratching from the windowsill. A crow had landed, and stood there blinking suspiciously at them. Gulta shouted and threw his hat at it. It flew off with a reproachful caw and he shut the window.

'I've seen it around here before,' he said. 'I think Granny feeds it. Fed it,' he corrected himself. 'Anyway, we'll be back with people, we'll be hardly any time. Come on, Ce.'

They clattered down the dark stairs. Esk saw them out of the house and bolted the door behind them.

The sun was a red ball above the mountains, and there were already a few early stars out.

She wandered around the dark kitchen until she found a scrap of dip candle and a tinderbox. After a great deal of effort she managed to light the candle and stood it on the table, although it didn't really light the room, it simply peopled the darkness with shadows. Then she found Granny's rocking chair by the cold fireplace, and settled down to wait.

Time passed. Nothing happened.

Then there was a tapping at the window. Esk took up the candle stub and peered through the thick round panes.

A beady yellow eye blinked back at her.

The candle guttered, and went out.

She stood stock still, hardly breathing. The tapping started again, and then stopped. There was a short silence, and then the door-latch rattled.

Something nasty comes, the boys had said.

She felt her way back across the room until she nearly tripped over the rocking chair, and dragged it back and wedged it as best she could in front of the door. The latch gave a final clonk and went silent.

Esk waited, listening until the silence roared in her ears. Then something started to bang against the little window in the scullery, softly but insistently. After a while it stopped. A moment later it started again in the bedroom above her – a faint scrabbling noise, a claw kind of noise.

Esk felt that bravery was called for, but on a night like this bravery lasted only as long as a candle stayed alight. She felt her way back across the dark kitchen, eyes tightly shut, until she reached the door.

There was a thump from the fireplace as a big lump of soot fell down, and when she heard the desperate scratchings coming from the chimney she slipped the bolts, threw open the door and darted out into the night.

The cold struck like a knife. Frost had put a crust on the snow. She didn't care where she was going, but quiet terror gave her a burning determination to get there as fast as she could.

Inside the cottage the crow landed heavily in the fireplace, surrounded by soot and muttering irritably to itself. It hopped into the shadows, and a moment later there was the bang of the latch of the stairway door and the sound of fluttering on the stairs.

Esk reached up as high as she could and felt around the tree for the marker. This time she was lucky, but the pattern of dots and grooves told her she was over a mile from the village and had been running in the wrong direction.

There was a cheese-rind moon and a sprinkling of stars, small and bright and pitiless. The forest around her was a pattern of black shadows and pale snow and, she was aware, not all the shadows were standing still.

Everyone knew there were wolves in the mountains, because on some nights their howls echoed down from the high Tops, but they seldom came near the village – the modern wolves were the offspring of ancestors that had survived because they had learned that human meat had sharp edges.

But the weather was hard, and this pack was hungry enough to forget all about natural selection.

Esk remembered what all the children were told. Climb a tree. Light a fire. When all else fails, find a stick and at least hurt them. Never try to outrun them.

The tree behind her was a beech, smooth and unclimbable.

Esk watched a long shadow detach itself from a pool of darkness in front of her, and move a little closer. She knelt down, tired, frightened, unable to think, and scrabbled under the burning-cold snow for a stick.

Granny Weatherwax opened her eyes and stared at the ceiling, which was cracked and bulged like a tent.

She concentrated on remembering that she had arms, not wings and didn't need to hop. It was always wise to lie down for a bit after a borrow, to let one's mind get used to one's body, but she knew she didn't have the time.

'Drat the child,' she muttered, and tried to fly on to the bedrail. The crow, who had been through all this dozens of times before and who considered, insofar as birds can consider anything, which is a very short distance indeed, that a steady diet of bacon rinds and choice kitchen scraps and a warm roost for the night was well worth the occasional inconvenience of letting Granny share its head, watched her with mild interest.

Granny found her boots and thumped down the stairs, sternly resisting the urge to glide. The door was wide open and there was already a drift of fine snow on the floor.

'Oh, bugger,' she said. She wondered if it was worth trying to find Esk's mind, but human minds were never so sharp and clear as animal minds and anyway the overmind of the forest itself made impromptu searching as hard as listening for a waterfall in a thunderstorm. But even without looking she could feel the packmind of the wolves, a sharp, rank feeling that filled the mouth with the taste of blood.

She could just make out the small footprints in the crust, half filled with fresh snow. Cursing and muttering, Granny Weatherwax pulled her shawl around her and set out.

The white cat awoke from its private ledge in the forge when it heard the sounds coming from the darkest corner. Smith had carefully shut the big doors behind him when he went off with the nearly-hysterical boys, and the cat watched with interest as a thin shadow prodded at the lock and tested the hinges.

The doors were oak, hardened by heat and time, but that didn't prevent them being blown right across the street.

Smith heard a sound in the sky as he hurried along

the track. So did Granny. It was a determined whirring sound, like the flight of geese, and the snow-clouds boiled and twisted as it passed.

The wolves heard it, too, as it spun low over the treetops and hurtled down into the clearing. But they heard it far too late.

Granny Weatherwax didn't have to follow the foot-prints now. She aimed herself for the distant flashes of weird light, the strange swishing and thumping, and the howls of pain and terror. A couple of wolves bolted past her with their ears flattened in grim determination to have it away on their paws no matter what stood in their way.

There was the crackle of breaking branches. Some-thing big and heavy landed in a fir tree by Granny and crashed, whimpering, into the snow. Another wolf passed her in a flat trajectory at about head height and bounced off a tree trunk.

There was silence.

Granny pushed her way between the snow-covered branches.

She could see that the snow was flattened in a white circle. A few wolves lay at its edges, either dead or wisely deciding to make no move.

The staff stood upright in the snow and Granny got the feeling it was turning to face her as she walked carefully past it.

There was also a small heap in the centre of the circle, curled tightly up inside itself. Granny knelt down with some effort and reached out gently.

The staff moved. It was little more than a tremble,

but her hand stopped just before it touched Esk's shoulder. Granny glared up at the wooden carvings, and dared it to move again.

The air thickened. Then the staff seemed to back away while not moving, while at the same time something quite indefinable made it absolutely clear to the old witch that as far as the staff was concerned this wasn't a defeat, it was merely a tactical consideration, and it wouldn't like her to think she had won in any way, because she hadn't.

Esk gave a shudder. Granny patted her vaguely.

'It's me, little one. It's only old Granny.'

The hump didn't uncurl.

Granny bit her lip. She was never quite certain about children, thinking of them — when she thought about them at all — as coming somewhere between animals and people. She understood babies. You put milk in one end and kept the other end as clean as possible. Adults were even easier, because they did the feeding and cleaning themselves. But in between was a world of experience that she had never really enquired about. As far as she was aware, you just tried to stop them catching anything fatal and hoped that it would all turn out all right.

Granny, in fact, was at a loss, but she knew she had to do something.

'Didda nasty wolfie fwiten us, den?' she hazarded.

For quite the wrong reasons, this seemed to work. From the depths of the ball a muffled voice said: 'I *am* eight you know.'

'People who are eight don't curl up in the middle of

the snow,' said Granny, feeling her way through the intricacies of adult-child conversation.

The ball didn't answer.

'I've probably got some milk and biscuits at home,' Granny ventured.

There was no perceptible effect.

'Eskarina Smith, if you don't behave this minute I will give you such a smack!'

Esk poked her head out cautiously.

'There's no need to be like that,' she said.

When Smith reached the cottage Granny had just arrived, leading Esk by the hand. The boys peered around from behind him.

'Um,' said Smith, not quite aware of how to begin a conversation with someone who was supposed to be dead. 'They, um, told me you were – ill.' He turned and glared at his sons.

'I was just having a rest and I must have dozed off. I sleeps very sound.'

'Yes,' said Smith, uncertainly. 'Well. All's well, then. What's up with Esk?'

'She took a bit of a fright,' said Granny, squeezing the girl's hand. 'Shadows and whatnot. She needs a good warm. I was going to put her in my bed, she's a bit mazed, if that's all right with you.'

Smith wasn't absolutely sure that it was all right with him. But he was quite sure that his wife, like every other woman in the village, held Granny Weatherwax in solemn regard, even in awe, and that if he started to object he would rapidly get out of his depth.

'Fine, fine,' he said, 'if it's no trouble. I'll send along for her in the morning, shall I?'

'That's right,' said Granny. 'I'd invite you in, but there's me without a fire—'

'No, no, that's all right,' said Smith hurriedly. 'I've got my supper waiting. Drying up,' he added, looking down at Gulta, who opened his mouth to say something and wisely thought better of it.

When they had gone, with the sound of the two boys' protests ringing out among the trees, Granny opened the door, pushed Esk inside, and bolted it behind them. She took a couple of candles from her store above the dresser and lit them. Then she pulled some old but serviceable wool blankets, still smelling of anti-moth herbs, from an old chest, wrapped Esk in them and sat her in the rocking chair.

She got down on her knees, to an accompaniment of clicks and grunts, and started to lay the fire. It was a complicated business involving dry fungus punk, wood shavings, bits of split twig and much puffing and swearing.

Esk said: 'You don't have to do it like that, Granny.'

Granny stiffened, and looked at the fireback. It was a rather nice one Smith had cast for her, years ago, with an owl-and-bat motif. Currently, though, she wasn't interested in the design.

'Oh yes?' she said, her voice dead-level. 'You know of a better way, do you?'

'You could magic it alight.'

Granny paid great attention to arranging bits of twig on the reluctant flames.

'How would I do that, pray?' she said, apparently addressing her remarks to the fireback.

'Er,' said Esk, 'I . . . I can't remember. But you must know anyway, don't you? Everyone knows you can do magic.'

'There's magic,' said Granny, 'and then again, there's magic. The important thing, my girl, is to know what magic is for and what it isn't for. And you can take it from me, it was never intended for lighting fires, you can be absolutely certain of that. If the Creator had meant us to use magic for lighting fires, then he wouldn't have given us – er, matches.'

'But could you light a fire with magic?' said Esk, as Granny slung an ancient black kettle on its hook. 'I mean, if you wanted to. If it was allowed.'

'Maybe,' said Granny, who couldn't: fire had no mind, it wasn't alive, and they were two of the three reasons.

'You could light it much better.'

'If a thing's worth doing, it's worth doing badly,' said Granny, fleeing into aphorisms, the last refuge of an adult under siege.

'Yes, but—'

'But me no buts.'

Granny rummaged in a dark wooden box on the dresser. She prided herself on her unrivalled knowledge of the properties of Ramtops herbage – none knew better than she the many uses of Earwort, Maiden's Wish and Love-Lies-Oozing – but there were times when she had to resort to her small stock of jealously traded and carefully hoarded medicines from Forn Parts (which as far as she was concerned was anywhere further than a day's journey) to achieve the desired effect.

She shredded some dry red leaves into a mug, topped it up with honey and hot water from the kettle, and pushed it into Esk's hands. Then she put a large round stone under the grate – later on, wrapped in a scrap of blanket, it would make a bedwarmer – and, with a stern injunction to the girl not to stir from the chair, went out into the scullery.

Esk drummed her heels on the chair legs and sipped the drink. It had a strange, peppery taste. She wondered what it was. She'd tasted Granny's brews before, of course, with a greater or lesser amount of honey in them depending on whether she thought you were making too much of a fuss, and Esk knew that she was famous throughout the mountains for special potions for illnesses that her mother – and some young women too, once in a while – just hinted at with raised eyebrows and lowered voices . . .

When Granny came back she was asleep. She didn't remember being put to bed, or Granny bolting the windows.

Granny Weatherwax went back downstairs and pulled her rocking chair closer to the fire.

There was something there, she told herself, lurking away in the child's mind. She didn't like to think about what it was, but she remembered what had happened to the wolves. And all that about lighting fires with magic. Wizards did that, it was one of the first things they learned.

Granny sighed. There was only one way to be sure, and she was getting rather old for this sort of thing.

She picked up the candle and went out through the scullery into the lean-to that housed her goats. They watched her without fear, each sitting in its pen like a furry blob, three mouths working rhythmically on the day's hay. The air smelled warm and slightly flatulent.

Up in the rafters was a small owl, one of a number of creatures who found that living with Granny was worth the occasional inconvenience. It came to her hand at a word, and she stroked its bullet head thoughtfully as she looked for somewhere comfortable to lie. A pile of hay it would have to be.

She blew out the candle and lay back, with the owl perched on her finger.

The goats chewed, burped and swallowed their way through their cosy night. They made the only sound in the building.

Granny's body stilled. The owl felt her enter its mind, and graciously made room. Granny knew she would regret this, Borrowing twice in one day would leave her good for nothing in the morning, and with a terrible desire to eat mice. Of course, when she was younger she thought nothing of it, running with the stags, hunting with the foxes, learning the strange dark ways of the moles, hardly spending a night in her own body. But it was getting harder now, especially coming back. Maybe the time would come when she couldn't get back, maybe the body back home would be so much dead flesh, and maybe that wouldn't be such a bad way of it, at that.

This was the sort of thing wizards could never know. If it occurred to them to enter a creature's mind they'd do it like a thief, not out of wickedness but because it simply wouldn't occur to them to do it any other way, the daft buggers. And what good would it do to take over an owl's body? You couldn't fly, you needed to spend a lifetime learning. But the gentle way was to ride in its mind, steering it as gently as a breeze stirs a leaf.

The owl stirred, fluttered up on to the little windowsill, and glided silently into the night.

The clouds had cleared and the thin moon made the mountains gleam. Granny peered out through owl eyes as she sped silently between the ranks of trees. This was the only way to travel, once a body had the way of it! She liked Borrowing birds best of all, using them to explore the high, hidden valleys where no one went, the secret lakes between black cliffs, the tiny walled fields on the scraps of flat ground, tucked on the sheer rock faces, that were the property of hidden and secretive beings. Once she had ridden with the geese that passed over the mountains every spring and autumn, and had got the shock of her life when she nearly went beyond range of returning.

The owl broke out of the forest and skimmed across the rooftops of the village, alighting in a shower of snow on the biggest apple tree in Smith's orchard. It was heavy with mistletoe.

She knew she was right as soon as her claws touched the bark. The tree resented her, she could feel it trying to push her away.

I'm not going, she thought.

In the silence of the night the tree said, *Bully me, then, just because I'm a tree. Typical woman.*

At least you're useful now, thought Granny. *Better a tree than a wizard, eh?*

It's not such a bad life, thought the tree. *Sun. Fresh air. Time to think. Bees, too, in the spring.*

There was something lascivious about the way the tree said 'bees' that quite put Granny, who had several hives, off the idea of honey. It was like being reminded that eggs were unborn chickens.

I've come about the girl Esk, she hissed.

A promising child, thought the tree, *I'm watching her with interest. She likes apples, too.*

You beast, said Granny, shocked.

What did I say? Pardon me for not breathing, I'm sure.

Granny sidled closer to the trunk.

You must let her go, she thought. *The magic is starting to come through.*

Already? I'm impressed, said the tree.

It's the wrong sort of magic! screeched Granny. *It's wizard magic, not women's magic! She doesn't know what it is yet, but it killed a dozen wolves tonight!*

Great! said the tree. Granny hooted with rage.

Great? Supposing she had been arguing with her brothers and lost her temper, eh?

The tree shrugged. Snowflakes cascaded from its branches.

Then you must train her, it said.

48

Train? What do I know from training wizards!

Then send her to university.

She's female! hooted Granny, bouncing up and down on her branch.

Well? Who says women can't be wizards?

Granny hesitated. The tree might as well have asked why fish couldn't be birds. She drew a deep breath, and started to speak. And stopped. She knew a cutting, incisive, withering and above all a *self-evident* answer existed. It was just that, to her extreme annoyance, she couldn't quite bring it to mind.

Women have never been wizards. It's against nature. You might as well say that witches can be men.

If you define a witch as one who worships the pan-creative urge, that is, venerates the basic – the tree began, and continued for several minutes. Granny Weatherwax listened in impatient annoyance to phrases like *Mother Goddesses* and *primitive moon worship* and told herself that she was well aware of what being a witch was all about, it was about herbs and curses and flying around of nights and generally keeping on the right side of tradition, and it certainly didn't involve mixing with goddesses, mothers or otherwise, who apparently got up to some very questionable tricks. And when the tree started talking about *dancing naked* she tried not to listen, because although she was aware that somewhere under her complicated strata of vests and petticoats there was some skin, that didn't mean to say she approved of it.

The tree finished its monologue.

Granny waited until she was quite sure that it

wasn't going to add anything, and said, *That's witch-craft, is it?*

Its theoretical basis, yes.

You wizards certainly get some funny ideas.

The tree said, *Not a wizard any more, just a tree.*

Granny ruffled her feathers.

Well, just you listen to me, Mr so-called Theoretical Basis Tree, if women were meant to be wizards they'd be able to grow long white beards and she is not going to be a wizard, is that quite clear, wizardry is not the way to use magic, do you hear, it's nothing but lights and fire and meddling with power and she'll be having no part of it and good night to you.

The owl swooped away from the branch. It was only because it would interfere with the flying that Granny wasn't shaking with rage. Wizards! They talked too much and pinned spells down in books like butterflies but, worst of all, they thought theirs was the only magic worth practising.

Granny was absolutely certain of one thing. Women had never been wizards, and they weren't about to start now.

She arrived back at the cottage in the pale shank of the night. Her body, at least, was rested after its slumber in the hay, and Granny had hoped to spend a few hours in the rocking chair, putting her thoughts in order. This was the time, when night wasn't quite over but day hadn't quite begun, when thoughts stood out bright and clear and without disguise. She . . .

The staff was leaning against the wall, by the dresser.

Granny stood quite still.

'I see,' she said at last. 'So that's the way of it, is it? In my own house, too?'

Moving very slowly, she walked over to the inglenook, threw a couple of split logs on to the embers of the fire, and pumped the bellows until the flames roared up the chimney.

When she was satisfied she turned, muttered a few precautionary protective spells under her breath, and grabbed the staff. It didn't resist; she nearly fell over. But now she had it in her hands, and felt the tingle of it, the distinctive thunderstorm crackle of the magic in it, and she laughed.

It was as simple as this, then. There was no fight in it now.

Calling down a curse upon wizards and all their works she raised the staff above her head and brought it down with a clang across the firedogs, over the hottest part of the fire.

Esk screamed. The sound bounced down through the bedroom floorboards and scythed through the dark cottage.

Granny was old and tired and not entirely clear about things after a long day, but to survive as a witch requires an ability to jump to very large conclusions and as she stared at the staff in the flames and heard the scream her hands were already reaching for the big black kettle. She upended it over the fire, dragged the staff out of the cloud of steam, and ran upstairs, dreading what she might see.

Esk was sitting up in the narrow bed, unsinged but shrieking. Granny took the child in her arms and tried to comfort her; she wasn't sure how one went about it, but a distracted patting on the back and vague reassuring noises seemed to work and the screams became wails and, eventually, sobs. Here and there Granny could pick out words like 'fire' and 'hot', and her mouth set in a thin, bitter line.

Finally she settled the child down, tucked her in, and crept quietly downstairs.

The staff was back against the wall. She was not surprised to see that the fire hadn't marked it at all.

Granny turned her rocking chair to face it, and sat down with her chin in her hand and an expression of grim determination.

Presently the chair began to rock, of its own accord. It was the only sound in a silence that thickened and spread and filled the room like a terrible dark fog.

Next morning, before Esk got up, Granny hid the staff in the thatch, well out of harm's way.

Esk ate her breakfast and drank a pint of goat's milk without the least sign of the events of the last twenty-four hours. It was the first time she had been inside Granny's cottage for more than a brief visit, and while the old woman washed the dishes and milked the goats she made the most of her implied licence to explore.

She found that life in the cottage wasn't entirely

straightforward. There was the matter of the goats' names, for example.

'But they've got to have names!' she said. 'Everything's got a name.'

Granny looked at her around the pear-shaped flanks of the head nanny, while the milk squirted into the low pail.

'I dare say they've got names in Goat,' she said vaguely. 'What do they want names in Human for?'

'Well,' said Esk, and stopped. She thought for a bit. 'How do you make them do what you want, then?'

'They just do, and when they want me they holler.'

Esk gravely gave the head goat a wisp of hay. Granny watched her thoughtfully. Goats did have names for themselves, she well knew: there was 'goat who is my kid', 'goat who is my mother', 'goat who is herd leader', and half a dozen other names not least of which was 'goat who is this goat'. They had a complicated herd system and four stomachs and a digestive system that sounded very busy on still nights, and Granny had always felt that calling all this names like Buttercup was an insult to a noble animal.

'Esk?' she said, making up her mind.

'Yes?'

'What would you like to be when you grow up?'

Esk looked blank. 'Don't know.'

'Well,' said Granny, her hands still milking, 'what do you think you will do when you are grown up?'

'Don't know. Get married, I suppose.'

'Do you want to?'

Esk's lips started to shape themselves around the D,

but she caught Granny's eye and stopped, and thought.

'All the grown ups I know are married,' she said at last, and thought some more. 'Except you,' she added, cautiously.

'That's true,' said Granny.

'Didn't you want to get married?'

It was Granny's turn to think.

'Never got around to it,' she said at last. 'Too many other things to do, you see.'

'Father says you're a witch,' said Esk, chancing her arm.

'I am that.'

Esk nodded. In the Ramtops witches were accorded a status similar to that which other cultures gave to nuns, or tax collectors, or cesspit cleaners. That is to say, they were respected, sometimes admired, generally applauded for doing a job which logically had to be done, but people never felt quite comfortable in the same room with them.

Granny said, 'Would you like to learn the witching?'

'Magic, you mean?' asked Esk, her eyes lighting up.

'Yes, magic. But not firework magic. Real magic.'

'Can you fly?'

'There's better things than flying.'

'And I can learn them?'

'If your parents say yes.'

Esk sighed. 'My father won't.'

'Then I shall have a word with him,' said Granny.

* * *

'Now you just listen to me, Gordo Smith!'

Smith backed away across his forge, hands half-raised to ward off the old woman's fury. She advanced on him, one finger stabbing the air righteously.

'I brought you into the world, you stupid man, and you've got no more sense in you now than you had then—'

'But—' Smith tried, dodging around the anvil.

'The magic's found her! Wizard magic! *Wrong* magic, do you understand? It was never intended for her!'

'Yes, but—'

'Have you any idea of what it can do?'

Smith sagged. 'No.'

Granny paused, and deflated a little.

'No,' she repeated, more softly. 'No, you wouldn't.'

She sat down on the anvil and tried to think calm thoughts.

'Look. Magic has a sort of – life of its own. That doesn't matter, because – anyway, you see, wizard magic—' she looked up at his big, blank expression and tried again. 'Well, you know cider?'

Smith nodded. He felt he was on firmer ground here, but he wasn't certain of where it was going to lead.

'And then there's the licker. Applejack,' said the witch. The smith nodded. Everyone in Bad Ass made applejack in the winter, by leaving cider tubs outside overnight and taking out the ice until a tiny core of alcohol was left.

'Well, you can drink lots of cider and you just feel better and that's it, isn't it?'

The smith nodded again.

'But applejack, you drink that in little mugs and you don't drink a lot and you don't drink it often, because it goes right to your head?'

The smith nodded again and, aware that he wasn't making a major contribution to the dialogue, added, 'That's right.'

'That's the difference,' said Granny.

'The difference from what?'

Granny sighed. 'The difference between witch magic and wizard magic,' she said. 'And it's found her, and if she doesn't control it, then there are Those who will control her. Magic can be a sort of door, and there are unpleasant Things on the other side. Do you understand?'

The smith nodded. He didn't really understand, but he correctly surmised that if he revealed this fact Granny would start going into horrible details.

'She's strong in her mind and it might take a while,' said Granny. 'But sooner or later they'll challenge her.'

Smith picked up a hammer from his bench, looked at it as though he had never seen it before, and put it down again.

'But,' he said, 'if it's wizard magic she's got, learning witchery won't be any good, will it? You said they're different.'

'They're both magic. If you can't learn to ride an elephant, you can at least learn to ride a horse.'

'What's an elephant?'

'A kind of badger,' said Granny. She hadn't

maintained forest-credibility for forty years by ever admitting ignorance.

The blacksmith sighed. He knew he was beaten. His wife had made it clear that she favoured the idea and, now that he came to think about it, there were some advantages. After all, Granny wouldn't last for ever, and being father to the area's only witch might not be too bad, at that.

'All right,' he said.

And so, as the winter turned and started the long, reluctant climb towards spring, Esk spent days at a time with Granny Weatherwax, learning witch craft.

It seemed to consist mainly of things to remember.

The lessons were quite practical. There was cleaning the kitchen table and Basic Herbalism. There was mucking out the goats and The Uses of Fungi. There was doing the washing and The Summoning of the Small Gods. And there was always tending the big copper still in the scullery and The Theory and Practice of Distillation. By the time the warm Rim winds were blowing, and the snow remained only as little streaks of slush on the Hub side of trees, Esk knew how to prepare a range of ointments, several medicinal brandies, a score of special infusions, and a number of mysterious potions that Granny said she might learn the use of in good time.

What she hadn't done was any magic at all.

'All in good time,' repeated Granny vaguely.

'But I'm supposed to be a witch!'

'You're not a witch yet. Name me three herbs good for the bowels.'

Esk put her hands behind her back, closed her eyes, and said: 'The flowering tops of Greater Peahane, the root pith of Old Man's Trousers, the stems of the Bloodwater Lily, the seedcases of—'

'All right. Where may water gherkins be found?'

'Peat bogs and stagnant pools, from the months of—'

'Good. You're learning.'

'But it's not magic!'

Granny sat down at the kitchen table.

'Most magic isn't,' she said. 'It's just knowing the right herbs, and learning to watch the weather, and finding out the ways of animals. And the ways of people, too.'

'That's all it is!' said Esk, horrified.

'*All? It's a pretty big all,*' said Granny. 'But no, it isn't *all*. There's other stuff.'

'Can't you teach me?'

'All in good time. There's no call to go showing yourself yet.'

'Showing myself? Who to?'

Granny's eyes darted towards the shadows in the corners of the room.

'Never you mind.'

Then even the last lingering tails of snow had gone and the spring gales roared around the mountains. The air in the forest began to smell of leaf mould and turpentine. A few early flowers braved the night frosts, and the bees started to fly.

'Now bees,' said Granny Weatherwax, 'is real magic.'

She carefully lifted the lid of the first hive.

'Your bees,' she went on, 'is your mead, your wax, your bee gum, your honey. A wonderful thing is your bee. Ruled by a queen, too,' she added, with a touch of approval.

'Don't they sting you?' said Esk, standing back a little. Bees boiled out of the comb and overflowed the rough wooden sides of the box.

'Hardly ever,' said Granny. 'You wanted magic. Watch.'

She put a hand into the struggling mass of insects and made a shrill faint piping noise at the back of her throat. There was a movement in the mass, and a large bee, longer and fatter than the others, crawled on to her hand. A few workers followed it, stroking it and generally ministering to it.

'How did you do that?' said Esk.

'Ah,' said Granny. 'Wouldn't you like to know?'

'Yes. I would. That's why I asked, Granny,' said Esk, severely.

'Do you think I used magic?'

Esk looked down at the queen bee. She looked up at the witch.

'No,' she said, 'I think you just know a lot about bees.'

Granny grinned.

'Exactly correct. That's one form of magic, of course.'

'What, just knowing things?'

'Knowing things that other people *don't know*,' said Granny. She carefully dropped the queen back among her subjects and closed the lid of the hive.

'And I think it's time you learned a few secrets,' she added.

At last, thought Esk.

'But first, we must pay our respects to the Hive,' said Granny. She managed to sound the capital H.

Without thinking, Esk bobbed a curtsey.

Granny's hand clipped the back of her head.

'Bow, I told you,' she said, without rancour. 'Witches bow.' She demonstrated.

'But *why*?' complained Esk.

'Because witches have got to be different, and that's part of the secret,' said Granny.

They sat on a bleached bench in front of the rimward wall of the cottage. In front of them the Herbs were already a foot high, a sinister collection of pale green leaves.

'Right,' said Granny, settling herself down. 'You know the hat in the hall by the door? Go and fetch it.'

Esk obediently went inside and unhooked Granny's hat. It was tall, pointed and, of course, black.

Granny turned it over in her hands and regarded it carefully.

'Inside this hat,' she said solemnly, 'is one of the secrets of witchcraft. If you cannot tell me what it is, then I might as well teach you no more, because once you learn the secret of the hat, there is no going back. Tell me what you know about the hat.'

'Can I hold it?'

'Be my guest.'

Esk peered inside the hat. There was some wire

stiffening to give it a shape, and a couple of hatpins. That was all.

There was nothing particularly strange about it, except that no one in the village had one like it. But that didn't make it magical. Esk bit her lip; she had a vision of herself being sent home in disgrace.

It didn't feel strange, and there were no hidden pockets. It was just a typical witch's hat. Granny always wore it when she went into the village, but in the forest she just wore a leather hood.

She tried to recall the bits of lessons that Granny grudgingly doled out. It isn't what you know, it's what other people don't know. Magic can be something right in the wrong place, or something wrong in the right place. It can be—

Granny *always* wore it to the village. And the big black cloak, which certainly wasn't magical, because for most of the winter it had been a goat blanket and Granny washed it in the spring.

Esk began to feel the shape of the answer and she didn't like it much. It was like a lot of Granny's answers. Just a word trick. She just said things you knew all the time, but in a different way so they sounded important.

'I think I know,' she said at last.

'Out with it, then.'

'It's in sort of two parts.'

'Well?'

'It's a witch's hat because you wear it. But you're a witch because you wear the hat. Um.'

'So—' prompted Granny.

'So people see you coming in the hat and the cloak and they know you're a witch and that's why your magic works?' said Esk.

'That's right,' said Granny. 'It's called headology.' She tapped her silver hair, which was drawn into a tight bun that could crack rocks.

'But it's not real!' Esk protested. 'That's not magic, it's – it's—'

'Listen,' said Granny. 'If you give someone a bottle of red jollop for their wind it may work, right, but if you want it to work for sure then you let their mind *make* it work for them. Tell 'em it's moonbeams bottled in fairy wine or something. Mumble over it a bit. It's the same with cursing.'

'Cursing?' said Esk, weakly.

'Aye, cursing, my girl, and no need to look so shocked! You'll curse, when the need comes. When you're alone, and there's no help to hand, and—'

She hesitated and, uncomfortably aware of Esk's questioning eyes, finished lamely: '—and people aren't showing respect. Make it loud, make it complicated, make it long, and make it up if you have to, but it'll work all right. Next day, when they hit their thumb or they fall off a ladder or their dog drops dead, they'll remember you. They'll behave better next time.'

'But it still doesn't seem like magic,' said Esk, scuffing the dust with her feet.

'I saved a man's life once,' said Granny. 'Special medicine, twice a day. Boiled water with a bit of berry juice in it. Told him I'd bought it from the dwarves.

That's the biggest part of doct'rin, really. Most people'll get over most things if they put their minds to it, you just have to give them an interest.'

She patted Esk's hand as nicely as possible. 'You're a bit young for this,' she said, 'but as you grow older you'll find most people don't set foot outside their own heads much. You too,' she added gnomically.

'I don't understand.'

'I'd be very surprised if you did,' said Granny briskly, 'but you can tell me five herbs suitable for dry coughs.'

Spring began to unfold in earnest. Granny started taking Esk on long walks that took all day, to hidden ponds or high on to the mountain scree to collect rare plants. Esk enjoyed that, high on the hills where the sun beat down strongly but the air was nevertheless freezing cold. Plants grew thickly and hugged the ground. From some of the highest peaks she could see all the way to the Rim Ocean that ran around the edge of the world; in the other direction the Ramtops marched into the distance, wrapped in eternal winter. They went all the way to the Hub of the world where, it was generally agreed, the gods lived on a ten-mile high mountain of rock and ice.

'Gods are all right,' said Granny, as they ate their lunch and looked at the view. 'You don't bother gods, and gods don't come bothering you.'

'Do you know many gods?'

'I've seen the thundergods a few times,' said Granny, 'and Hoki, of course.'

'Hoki?'

Granny chewed a crustless sandwich. 'Oh, he's a nature god,' she said. 'Sometimes he manifests himself as an oak tree, or half a man and half a goat, but mainly I see him in his aspect as a bloody nuisance. You only find him in the deep woods, of course. He plays the flute. Very badly, if you must know.'

Esk lay on her stomach and looked out across the lands below while a few hardy, self-employed bumblebees patrolled the thyme clusters. The sun was warm on her back but, up here, there were still drifts of snow on the hubside of rocks.

'Tell me about the lands down there,' she said lazily.

Granny peered disapprovingly at ten thousand miles of landscape.

'They're just other places,' she said. 'Just like here, only different.'

'Are there cities and things?'

'I dare say.'

'Haven't you ever been to look?'

Granny sat back, gingerly arranging her skirt to expose several inches of respectable flannelette to the sun, and let the heat caress her old bones.

'No,' she said. 'There's quite enough troubles around here without going to look for them in forn parts.'

'I dreamed of a city once,' said Esk. 'It had hundreds of people in it, and there was this building with big gates, and they were magical gates—'

A sound like tearing cloth came from behind her. Granny had fallen asleep.

'Granny!'

'Mhnf?'

Esk thought for a moment. 'Are you having a good time?' she said artfully.

'Mnph.'

'You said you'd show me some real magic, all in good time,' said Esk, 'and this *is* a good time.'

'Mnph.'

Granny Weatherwax opened her eyes and looked straight up at the sky; it was darker up here, more purple than blue. She thought: why not? She's a quick learner. She knows more herblore than I do. At her age old Gammer Tumult had me Borrowing and Shifting and Sending all the hours of the day. Maybe I'm being too cautious.

'Just a bit?' pleaded Esk.

Granny turned it over in her mind. She couldn't think of any more excuses. I'm surely going to regret this, she told herself, displaying considerable foresight.

'All right,' she said shortly.

'Real magic?' said Esk. 'Not more herbs or headology?'

'Real magic, as you call it, yes.'

'A spell?'

'No. A Borrowing.'

Esk's face was a picture of expectation. She looked more alive, it seemed to Granny, than she had ever been before.

Granny looked over the valleys stretching out before them until she found what she was after. A grey eagle was circling lazily over a distant blue-hazed patch of forest. Its mind was currently at ease. It would do nicely.

She called it gently, and it began to circle towards them.

'The first thing to remember about Borrowing is that you must be comfortable and somewhere safe,' she said, smoothing out the grass behind her. 'Bed's best.'

'But what *is* Borrowing?'

'Lie down and hold my hand. Do you see the eagle up there?'

Esk squinted into the dark, hot sky.

There were . . . *two doll figures on the grass below as she pivoted on the wind* . . .

She could feel the whip and wire of the air through her feathers. Because the eagle was not hunting, but simply enjoying the feel of the sun on its wings, the land below was a mere unimportant shape. But the air, the air was a complex, changing three-dimensional *thing*, an interlocked pattern of spirals and curves that stretched away into the distance, a switchback of currents built around thermal pillars. She . . .

. . . felt a gentle pressure restraining her.

'The next thing to remember,' said Granny's voice, very close, 'is not to upset the owner. If you let it know you're there it'll either fight you or panic, and you won't stand a chance either way. It's had a lifetime of being an eagle, and you haven't.'

Esk said nothing.

'You're not frightened, are you?' said Granny.

'It can take you that way the first time, and—'

'I'm not frightened,' said Esk, and 'How do I control it?'

'You don't. Not yet. Anyway, controlling a truly wild creature isn't easily learned. You have to – sort of *suggest* to it that it might feel inclined to do things. With a tame animal, of course, it's all different. But you can't make any creature do anything that is totally against its nature. Now try and find the eagle's mind.'

Esk could sense Granny as a diffuse silver cloud at the back of her own mind. After some searching she found the eagle. She almost missed it. Its mind was small, sharp and purple, like an arrowhead. It was concentrating entirely on flying, and took no notice of her.

'Good,' said Granny approvingly. 'We're not going to go far. If you want to make it turn, you must—'

'Yes, yes,' said Esk. She flexed her fingers, wherever they were, and the bird leaned against the air and turned.

'Very good,' said Granny, taken aback. 'How did you do that?'

'I – don't know. It just seemed obvious.'

'Hmph.' Granny gently tested the tiny eagle mind. It was still totally oblivious of its passengers. She was genuinely impressed, a very rare occurrence.

They floated over the mountain, while Esk excitedly explored the eagle's senses. Granny's voice droned through her consciousness, giving instructions and guidance and warnings. She listened with half an ear. It sounded far too complicated. Why couldn't she take over the eagle's mind? It wouldn't hurt it.

She could see how to do it, it was just a knack, like snapping your fingers – which in fact she had never managed to achieve – and then she'd be able to experience flying for real, not at second hand.

Then she could—

'Don't,' said Granny calmly. 'No good will come of it.'

'What?'

'Do you really think you're the first, my girl? Do you think we haven't all thought what a fine thing it would be, to take on another body and tread the wind or breathe the water? And do you really think it would be as easy as that?'

Esk glowered at her.

'No need to look like that,' said Granny. 'You'll thank me one day. Don't you start playing around before you know what you're about, eh? Before you get up to tricks you've got to learn what to do if things go wrong. Don't try to walk before you can run.'

'I can *feel* how to do it, Granny.'

'That's as maybe. It's harder than it seems, is Borrowing, although I'll grant you've got a knack. That's enough for today, bring us in over ourselves and I'll show you how to Return.'

The eagle beat the air over the two recumbent forms and Esk saw, in her mind's eye, two channels open for them. Granny's mindshape vanished.

Now—

Granny had been wrong. The eagle mind barely

fought, and didn't have time to panic. Esk held it wrapped in her own mind. It writhed for an instant, and then melted into her.

Granny opened her eyes in time to see the bird give a hoarse cry of triumph, curve down low over the grass-grown scree, and skim away down the mountainside. For a moment it was a vanishing dot and then it had gone, leaving only another echoing shriek.

Granny looked down at Esk's silent form. The girl was light enough, but it was a long way home and the afternoon was dwindling.

'Drat,' she said, with no particular emphasis. She stood up, brushed herself down and, with a grunt of effort, hauled Esk's inert body over her shoulder.

High in the crystal sunset air above the mountains the eagle-Esk sought more height, drunk with the sheer vitality of flight.

On the way home Granny met a hungry bear. Granny's back was giving her gyp, and she was in no mood to be growled at. She muttered a few words under her breath and the bear, to its brief amazement, walked heavily into a tree and didn't regain consciousness for several hours.

When she reached the cottage Granny put Esk's body to bed and drew up the fire. She brought the goats in and milked them, and finished the chores of the evening.

She made sure all the windows were open and,

when it began to grow dark, lit a lantern and put it on the windowsill.

Granny Weatherwax didn't sleep more than a few hours a night, as a rule, and woke again at midnight. The room hadn't changed, although the lantern had its own little solar system of very stupid moths.

When she woke again at dawn the candle had long burned down and Esk was still sleeping the shallow, unwakeable sleep of the Borrower.

When she took the goats out to their paddock she looked intently at the sky.

Noon came, and gradually the light drained out of another day. She paced the floor of the kitchen aimlessly. Occasionally she would throw herself into frantic bouts of housework; ancient crusts were unceremoniously dug out of the cracks in the flagstones, and the fireback was scraped free of the winter's soot and blackleaded to within an inch of its life. A nest of mice in the back of the dresser were kindly but firmly ejected into the goatshed.

Sunset came.

The light of the Discworld was old and slow and heavy. From the cottage door Granny watched as it drained off the mountains, flowing in golden rivers through the forest. Here and there it pooled in hollows until it faded and vanished.

She drummed her fingers sharply on the doorpost, humming a small and bitter little tune.

Dawn came, and the cottage was empty except for Esk's body, silent and unmoving on the bed.

*   *   *

But as the golden light flowed slowly across the Discworld like the first freshing of the tide over mud-flats the eagle circled higher into the dome of heaven, beating the air down with slow and powerful wingbeats.

The whole of the world was spread out beneath Esk – all the continents, all the islands, all the rivers and especially the great ring of the Rim Ocean.

There was nothing else up here, not even sound.

Esk gloried in the feel of it, willing her flagging muscles into greater effort. But something was wrong. Her thoughts seemed to be chasing around beyond her control, and disappearing. Pain and exhilaration and weariness poured into her mind, but it was as if other things were spilling out at the same time. Memories dwindled away on the wind. As fast as she could latch on to a thought it evaporated, leaving nothing behind.

She was losing chunks of herself, and she couldn't remember what she was losing. She panicked, burrowing back to the things she was sure of . . .

I am Esk, and I have stolen the body of an eagle and *the feel of wind in feathers, the hunger, the search of the not-sky below* . . .

She tried again. I am Esk and *seeking the windpath, the pain of muscle, the cut of the air, the cold of it* . . .

I am Esk *high over air-damp-wet-white, above everything, the sky is thin* . . .

I am *I am.*

* * *

71

Granny was in the garden, among the beehives, the early morning wind whipping at her skirts. She went from hive to hive, tapping on their roofs. Then, in the thickets of borage and beebalm that she had planted around them, she stood with her arms outstretched in front of her and sang something in tones so high that no normal person could have heard them.

But a roar went up from the hives, and then the air was suddenly thick with the heavy, big-eyed, deep-voiced shapes of drone bees. They circled over her head, adding their own bass humming to her chant.

Then they were gone, soaring into the growing light over the clearing and streaming away over the trees.

It is well known – at least, it is well known to witches – that all colonies of bees are, as it were, just one part of the creature called the Swarm, in the same way that individual bees are component cells of the hivemind. Granny didn't mingle her thoughts with the bees very often, partly because insect minds were strange, alien things that tasted of tin, but mostly because she suspected that the Swarm was a good deal more intelligent than she was.

She knew that the drones would soon reach the wild bee colonies in the deep forest, and within hours every corner of the mountain meadows would be under very close scrutiny indeed. All she could do was wait.

At noon the drones returned, and Granny read in the sharp acid thoughts of the hivemind that there was no sign of Esk.

She went back into the cool of the cottage and sat down in the rocking chair, staring at the doorway.

She knew what the next step was. She hated the very idea of it. But she fetched a short ladder, climbed up creakily on to the roof, and pulled the staff from its hiding place in the thatch.

It was icy cold. It steamed.

'Above the snowline, then,' said Granny.

She climbed down, and rammed the staff into a flower-bed. She glared at it. She had a nasty feeling that it was glaring back.

'Don't think you've won, because you haven't,' she snapped. 'It's just that I haven't got the time to mess around. You must know where she is. I command you to take me to her!'

The staff regarded her woodenly.

'By—' Granny paused, her invocations were a little rusty, '—by stock and stone I order it!'

Activity, movement, liveliness – all these words would be completely inaccurate descriptions of the staff's response.

Granny scratched her chin. She remembered the little lesson all children get taught: what's the magic word?

'Please?' she suggested.

The staff trembled, rose a little way out of the ground, and turned in the air so that it hung invitingly at waist height.

Granny had heard that broomsticks were once again very much the fashion among younger witches, but she didn't hold with it. There was no way a body could look respectable while hurtling through the air aboard a household implement. Besides, it looked decidedly draughty.

But this was no time for respectability. Pausing only to snatch her hat from its hook behind the door she scrambled up on to the staff and perched as best she could, sidesaddle of course, and with her skirts firmly gripped between her knees.

'Right,' she said. 'Now wha-aaaaaaaaa—'

Across the forest animals broke and scattered as the shadow passed overhead, crying and cursing. Granny clung on with whitened knuckles, her thin legs kicking wildly as, high above the treetops, she learned important lessons about centres of gravity and air turbulence. The staff shot onwards, heedless of her yells.

By the time it had come out over the upland meadows she had come to terms with it somewhat, which meant that she could just about hang on with knees and hands provided she didn't mind being upside down. Her hat, at least, was useful, being aerodynamically shaped.

The staff plunged between black cliffs and along high bare valleys where, it was said, rivers of ice had once flowed in the days of the Ice Giants. The air became thin and sharp in the throat.

They came to an abrupt halt over a snowdrift. Granny fell off, and lay panting in the snow while she tried to remember why she was going through all this.

There was a bundle of feathers under an overhang a few feet away. As Granny approached it a head rose jerkily, and the eagle glared at her with fierce, frightened eyes. It tried to fly, and toppled over. When she reached out to touch it, it took a neat triangle of flesh out of her hand.

'I see,' said Granny quietly, to no one in particular. She looked around, and found a boulder of about the right size. She disappeared behind it for a few seconds, for the sake of respectability, and reappeared with a petticoat in her hand. The bird thrashed around, ruining several weeks of meticulous petit-point embroidery, but she managed to bundle it up and hold it so that she could avoid its sporadic lunges.

Granny turned to the staff, which was now upright in the snowdrift.

'I shall walk back,' she told it coldly.

It turned out that they were in a spur valley over-looking a drop of several hundred feet on to sharp black rocks.

'Very well, then,' she conceded, 'but you're to fly slowly, d'you understand? And no going high.'

In fact, because she was slightly more experienced and perhaps because the staff was taking more care, too, the ride back was almost sedate. Granny was almost persuaded that, given time, she could come to merely dislike flying, instead of loathing it. What it needed was some way of stopping yourself from having to look at the ground.

The eagle sprawled on the rag rug in front of the empty hearth. It had drunk some water, over which

Granny had mumbled a few of the charms she normally said to impress patients, but you never knew, there might be some power in them, and it had also gulped a few strips of raw meat.

What it had not done was display the least sign of intelligence.

She wondered whether she had the right bird. She risked another pecking and stared hard into its evil orange eyes, and tried to convince herself that way down in their depths, almost beyond sight, was a strange little flicker.

She probed around inside its head. The eagle mind was still there right enough, vivid and sharp, but there was something else. Mind, of course, has no colour, but nevertheless the strands of the eagle's mind seemed to be purple. Around them and tangled among them were faint strands of silver.

Esk had learned too late that mind shapes body, that Borrowing is one thing but that the dream of truly taking on another form had its built-in penalty.

Granny sat and rocked. She was at a loss, she knew that. Unravelling the tangled minds was beyond her power, beyond any power in the Ramtops, beyond even—

There was no sound, but maybe there was a change in the texture of the air. She looked up at the staff, which had been suffered to come back into the cottage.

'No,' she said firmly.

Then she thought: whose benefit did I say that for? Mine? There's power there, but it's not my kind of power.

There isn't any other kind around, though. And even now I may be too late.

I might never have been early enough.

She reached out again into the bird's head to calm its fears and dispel its panic. It allowed her to pick it up and sat awkwardly on her wrist, its talons gripping tight enough to draw blood.

Granny took the staff and made her way upstairs, to where Esk lay on the narrow bed in the low bedroom with its ancient contoured ceiling.

She made the bird perch on the bedrail and turned her attention to the staff. Once more the carvings shifted under her glare, never quite revealing their true form.

Granny was no stranger to the uses of power, but she knew she relied on gentle pressure subtly to steer the tide of things. She didn't put it like that, of course – she would have said that there was always a lever if you knew where to look. The power in the staff was harsh, fierce, the raw stuff of magic distilled out of the forces that powered the universe itself.

There would be a price. And Granny knew enough about wizardry to be certain that it would be a high one. But if you were worried about the price, then why were you in the shop?

She cleared her throat, and wondered what the hell she was supposed to do next. Perhaps if she—

The power hit her like a half-brick. She could feel it take her and lift her so that she was amazed to look down and see her feet still firmly on the floorboards. She tried to take a step forward and magical discharges crackled in the air around her. She reached out to steady herself against the wall and the ancient wooden beam under her hand stirred and started to sprout leaves. A cyclone of magic swirled around the room, picking up dust and briefly giving it some very disturbing shapes, the jug and basin on the washstand, with the particularly fetching rosebud pattern, broke into fragments. Under the bed the third member of the traditional china trio turned into something horrible and slunk away.

Granny opened her mouth to swear and thought better of it when her words blossomed out into rainbow-edged clouds.

She looked down at Esk and the eagle, which seemed oblivious to all this, and tried to concentrate. She let herself slide inside its head and again she could see the strands of mind, the silver threads bound so closely around the purple that they took on the same shape. But now she could see where the strands ended, and where a judicious tug or push would begin to unravel them. It was so obvious she heard herself laugh, and the sound curved away in shades of orange and red and vanished into the ceiling.

Time passed. Even with the power throbbing through her head it was a painfully hard task, like threading a needle by moonlight, but eventually she had a handful of silver. In the slow, heavy world in which she now appeared to be she took the hank and threw it slowly towards Esk. It became a cloud, swirled like a whirlpool, and vanished.

She was aware of a shrill chittering noise, and

shadows on the edge of sight. Well, it happened to everyone sooner or later. They had come, drawn as always by a discharge of magic. You just had to learn to ignore them.

Granny woke with bright sunlight skewering into her eyes. She was slumped against the door, and her whole body felt as though it had toothache.

She reached out blindly with one hand, found the edge of the washstand, and pulled herself into a sitting position. She was not really surprised to see that the jug and basin looked just the same as they had always done; in fact sheer curiosity overcame her aches and she gave a quick glance under the bed to check that, yes, things were as normal.

The eagle was still hunched on the bedpost. In the bed Esk was asleep, and Granny saw that it was a true sleep and not the stillness of a vacant body.

All she had to do now was hope that Esk wouldn't wake up with an irresistible urge to pounce on rabbits.

She carried the unresisting bird downstairs and let it free outside the back door. It flew heavily up into the nearest tree, where it settled to rest. It had a feeling it ought to have a grudge against somebody, but for the life of it, it couldn't remember why.

Esk opened her eyes and stared for a long time at the ceiling. Over the months she had grown familiar with every lump and crack of the plaster, which created a fantastic upside-down landscape that she had peopled with a private and complex civilization.

Her mind thronged with dreams. She pulled an arm out from under the sheets and stared at it, wondering why it wasn't covered with feathers. It was all very puzzling.

She pushed the covers back, swung her legs to the edge of the bed, *spread her wings into the rush of the wind and glided out into the world* . . .

The thump on the bedroom floor brought Granny scurrying up the stairs, to take her in her arms and hold her tight as the terror hit her. She rocked back and forth on her heels, making meaningless soothing noises.

Esk looked up at her through a mask of horror.

'I could feel myself vanishing!'

'Yes, yes. Better now,' murmured Granny.

'You don't understand! I couldn't even remember my name!' Esk shrieked.

'But you can remember now.'

Esk hesitated, checking. 'Yes,' she said, 'Yes, of course. Now.'

'So no harm done.'

'But—'

Granny sighed. 'You have learned something,' she said, and thought it safe to insert a touch of sternness into her voice. 'They say a little knowledge is a dangerous thing, but it is not one half so bad as a lot of ignorance.'

'But what *happened?*'

'You thought that Borrowing wasn't enough. You thought it would be a fine thing to steal another's body. But you must know that a body is like – like a jelly mould. It sets a shape on its contents, d'you see? You can't have a girl's mind in an eagle's body. Not for long, at any rate.'

'I *became* an eagle?'

'Yes.'

'Not *me* at all?'

Granny thought for a while. She always had to pause when conversations with Esk led her beyond the reaches of a decent person's vocabulary.

'No,' she said at last, 'not in the way you mean. Just an eagle with maybe some strange dreams sometimes. Like when you dream you're flying, perhaps it would remember walking and talking.'

'Urgh.'

'But it's all over now,' said Granny, treating her to a thin smile. 'You're your true self again and the eagle has got its mind back. It's sitting in the big beech by the privy; I should like you to put out some food for it.'

Esk sat back on her heels, staring at a point past Granny's head.

'There were some strange things,' she said conversationally. Granny spun around.

'I meant, in a sort of dream I saw things,' said Esk. The old woman's shock was so visible that she hesitated, frightened that she had said something wrong.

'What kind of things?' said Granny flatly.

'Sort of big creatures, all sorts of shapes. Just sitting around.'

'Was it dark? I mean, these Things, were they in the dark?'

'There were stars, I think. Granny?'

Granny Weatherwax was staring at the wall.

'Granny?' Esk repeated.

'Mmph? Yes? Oh.' Granny shook herself. 'Yes. I see. Now I would like you to go downstairs and get the bacon that is in the pantry and put it out for the bird, do you understand? It would be a good idea to thank it, too. You never know.'

When Esk returned Granny was buttering bread. She pulled her stool up to the table, but the old woman waved the breadknife at her.

'First things first. Stand up. Face me.'

Esk did so, puzzled. Granny stuck the knife in the breadboard and shook her head.

'Drat it,' she said to the world at large. 'I don't know what way they have of it, there should be some kind of ceremony if I know wizards, they always have to complicate things . . .'

'What do you mean?'

Granny seemed to ignore her, but crossed to the dark corner by the dresser.

'Probably you should have one foot in a bucket of cold porridge and one glove on and all that kind of stuff,' she went on. 'I didn't want to do this, but They're forcing my hand.'

'What are you talking about, Granny?'

The old witch yanked the staff out of its shadow

and waved it vaguely at Esk.

'Here. It's yours. Take it. I just hope this is the right thing to do.'

In fact the presentation of a staff to an apprentice wizard is usually a very impressive ceremony, especially if the staff has been inherited from an elder mage; by ancient lore there is a long and frightening ordeal involving masks and hoods and swords and fearful oaths about people's tongues being cut out and their entrails torn by wild birds and their ashes scattered to the eight winds and so on. After some hours of this sort of thing the apprentice can be admitted to the brother-hood of the Wise and Enlightened.

There is also a long speech. By sheer coincidence Granny got the essence of it in a nutshell.

Esk took the staff and peered at it.

'It's very nice,' she said uncertainly. 'The carvings are pretty. What's it for?'

'Sit down now. And listen properly for once. On the day you were born . . .'

'. . . and that's the shape of it.'

Esk looked hard at the staff, then at Granny.

'I've got to be a wizard?'

'Yes. No. I don't know.'

'That isn't really an answer, Granny,' Esk said reproachfully. 'Am I or amp't I?'

'Women can't be wizards,' said Granny bluntly. 'It's agin nature. You might as well have a female blacksmith.'

'Actually I've watched dad at work and I don't see why—'

'Look,' said Granny hurriedly, 'you can't have a female wizard any more than you can have a male witch, because—'

'I've heard of male witches,' said Esk meekly.

'Warlocks!'

'I think so.'

'I mean there's no male witches, only silly men,' said Granny hotly. 'If men were witches, they'd be wizards. It's all down to—' she tapped her head '—headology. How your mind works. Men's minds work different from ours, see. Their magic's all numbers and angles and edges and what the stars are doing, as if that really mattered. It's all power. It's all—' Granny paused, and dredged up her favourite word to describe all she despised in wizardry, '—jommetry.'

'That's all right, then,' said Esk, relieved. 'I'll stay here and learn witchery.'

'Ah,' said Granny gloomily, 'that's all very well for you to say. I don't think it will be as easy as that.'

'But *you* said that men can be wizards and women can be witches and it can't be the other way around.'

'That's right.'

'Well, then,' said Esk triumphantly, 'it's all solved, isn't it? I can't help but be a witch.'

Granny pointed to the staff. Esk shrugged.

'It's just an old stick.'

Granny shook her head. Esk blinked.

'No?'

'No.'

'And I can't be a witch?'

'I don't know what you can be. Hold the staff.'

'What?'

'Hold the staff. Now, I've laid the fire in the grate. Light it.'

'The tinderbox is—' Esk began.

'You once told me there were better ways of lighting fires. Show me.'

Granny stood up. In the dimness of the kitchen she seemed to grow until she filled it with shifting, ragged shadows, shot with menace. Her eyes glared down at Esk.

'Show me,' she commanded, and her voice had ice in it.

'But—' said Esk desperately, clutching the heavy staff to her and knocking her stool over in her haste to back away.

'*Show me.*'

With a scream Esk spun around. Fire flared from her fingertips and arced across the room. The kindling exploded with a force that hurled the furniture around the room and a ball of fierce green light spluttered on the hearth.

Changing patterns sped across it as it spun sizzling on the stones, which cracked and then flowed. The iron fireback resisted bravely for a few seconds before melting like wax; it made a final appearance as a red smear across the fireball and then vanished. A moment later the kettle went the same way.

Just when it seemed that the chimney would follow

them the ancient hearthstone gave up, and with a final splutter the fireball sank from view.

The occasional crackle or puff of steam signalled its passage through the earth. Apart from that there was silence, the loud hissing silence that comes after an ear-splattering noise, and after the actinic glare the room seemed pitch dark.

Eventually Granny crawled out from behind the table and crept as closely as she dared to the hole, which was still surrounded by a crust of lava. She jerked back as another cloud of superheated steam mushroomed up.

'They say there's dwarf mines under the Ramtops,' she said inconsequentially. 'My, but them little buggers is in for a surprise.'

She prodded the little puddle of cooling iron where the kettle had been, and added, 'Shame about the fire-back. It had owls on it, you know.'

She patted her singed hair gingerly with a shaking hand. 'I think this calls for a nice cup of, a nice cup of cold water.'

Esk sat looking in wonder at her hand.

'That was real magic,' she said at last. 'And I did it.'

'*One* type of real magic,' corrected Granny. 'Don't forget that. And you don't want to do that all the time, neither. If it's in you, you've got to learn to control it.'

'Can you teach me?'

'Me? No!'

'How can I learn if no one will teach me?'

'You've got to go where they can. Wizard school.'

'But you said—'

Granny paused in the act of filling a jug from the water bucket.

'Yes, yes,' she snapped. 'Never mind what I said, or common sense or anything. Sometimes you just have to go the way things take you, and I reckon you're going to wizard school one way or the other.'

Esk considered this.

'You mean it's my destiny?' she said at last.

Granny shrugged. 'Something like that. Probably. Who knows?'

That night, long after Esk had been sent to bed, Granny put on her hat, lit a fresh candle, cleared the table, and pulled a small wooden box from its secret hiding place in the dresser. It contained a bottle of ink, an elderly quill pen, and a few sheets of paper.

Granny was not entirely happy when faced with the world of letters. Her eyes protruded, her tongue stuck out, small beads of sweat formed on her forehead, but the pen scratched its way across the page to the accompaniment of the occasional quiet 'drat' or 'bugger the thing'.

The letter read as follows, although this version lacks the candle-wax, blots, crossings-out and damp patches of the original.

To ther Hed Wizzard, Unsene Universety, Greatings, I hop you ar well, I am sending to you won Escarrina Smith, shee hath thee maekings of wizzardery but whot may be ferther dun wyth hyr I knowe not shee is a gode worker and clene about hyr person allso skilled in diuerse arts of thee howse, I will send Monies wyth hyr May you liv longe and ende youre days in pese, And oblije, Esmerelder Weatherwaxe (Mss) Wytch.

Granny held it up to the candlelight and considered it critically. It was a good letter. She had got 'diuerse' out of the *Almanack*, which she read every night. It was always predicting 'diuerse plagues' and 'diuerse ill-fortune'. Granny wasn't entirely sure what it meant, but it was a damn good word all the same.

She sealed it with candle-wax and put it on the dresser. She could leave it for the carrier to take when she went into the village tomorrow, to see about a new kettle.

Next morning Granny took some pains over her dress, selecting a black dress with a frog and bat motif, a big velvet cloak, or at least a cloak made of the sort of stuff velvet looks like after thirty years of heavy wear, and the pointed hat of office which was crucified with hatpins.

Their first call was to the stonemason, to order a replacement hearthstone. Then they called on the smith.

It was a long and stormy meeting. Esk wandered out into the orchard and climbed up to her old place in the apple tree while from the house came her father's shouts, her mother's wails and long silent pauses which meant that Granny Weatherwax was speaking softly in what Esk thought of as her 'just so' voice. The old woman had a flat, measured way of speaking sometimes. It was the kind of voice the Creator had probably used. Whether there was magic in it, or just headology, it ruled out any possibility of argument. It made it clear that whatever it was talking about was exactly how things should be.

The breeze shook the tree gently. Esk sat on a branch idly swinging her legs.

She thought about wizards. They didn't often come to Bad Ass, but there were a fair number of stories about them. They were wise, she recalled, and usually very old and they did powerful, complex and mysterious magics and almost all of them had beards. They were also, without exception, men.

She was on firmer ground with witches, because she'd trailed off with Granny to visit a couple of villages' witches further along the hills, and anyway witches figured largely in Ramtop folklore. Witches were cunning, she recalled, and usually very old, or at least they tried to look old, and they did slightly suspicious, homely and organic magics and some of them had beards. They were also, without exception, women.

There was some fundamental problem in all that which she couldn't quite resolve. Why wouldn't . . .

Cern and Gulta hurtled down the path and came to a pushing, shoving halt under the tree. They peered up at their sister with a mixture of fascination and scorn. Witches and wizards were objects of awe, but sisters weren't. Somehow, knowing your own sister was learning to be a witch sort of devalued the whole profession.

'You can't really do spells,' said Cern. 'Can you?'

'Course you can't,' said Gulta. 'What's this stick?'

Esk had left the staff leaning against the tree. Cern prodded it cautiously.

'I don't want you to touch it,' said Esk hurriedly. 'Please. It's mine.'

Cern normally had all the sensitivity of a ball-bearing, but his hand stopped in mid-prod, much to his surprise.

'I didn't want to anyway,' he muttered to hide his confusion. 'It's only an old stick.'

'Is it true you can do spells?' asked Gulta. 'We heard Granny say you could.'

'We listened at the door,' added Cern.

'*You* said I couldn't,' said Esk, airily.

'Well, can you or can't you?' said Gulta, his face reddening.

'Perhaps.'

'You can't!'

Esk looked down at his face. She loved her brothers, when she reminded herself to, in a dutiful sort of way, although she generally remembered them as a collection of loud noises in trousers. But there was something awfully pig-like and unpleasant about the way Gulta was staring up at her, as though she had personally insulted him.

She felt her body start to tingle, and the world suddenly seemed very sharp and clear.

'I can,' she said.

Gulta looked from her to the staff, and his eyes narrowed. He kicked it viciously.

'Old stick!'

He looked, she thought, exactly like a small angry pig.

Cern's screams brought Granny and his parents first to the back door and then running down the cinder path.

Esk was perched in the fork of the apple tree, an expression of dreamy contemplation on her face. Cern was hiding behind the tree, his face a mere rim around a red, tonsil-vibrating bawl.

Gulta was sitting rather bewildered in a pile of clothing that no longer fitted him, wrinkling his snout.

Granny strode up to the tree until her hooked nose was level with Esk's.

'Turning people into pigs is *not allowed*,' she hissed. 'Even brothers.'

'I didn't do it, it just happened. Anyway, you must admit it's a better shape for him,' said Esk evenly.

'What's going on?' said Smith. 'Where's Gulta? What's this pig doing here?'

'This pig,' said Granny Weatherwax, 'is your son.'

There was a sigh from Esk's mother as she collapsed gently backwards, but Smith was slightly less unprepared. He looked sharply from Gulta, who had managed to untangle himself from his clothing and was now rooting enthusiastically among the early windfalls, to his only daughter.

'She did this?'

'Yes. Or it was done through her,' said Granny, looking suspiciously at the staff.

'Oh.' Smith looked at his sixth son. He had to admit that the shape suited him. He reached out without looking and fetched the screaming Cern a thump on the back of his head.

'Can you turn him back again?' he asked. Granny spun around and glared the question at Esk, who shrugged.

'He didn't believe I could do magic,' she said calmly.

'Yes, well, I think you've made the point,' said Granny. 'And now you will turn him back, madam. This instant. Do you hear?'

'Don't want to. He was rude.'

'I *see.*'

Esk glared down defiantly. Granny glared up sternly. Their wills clanged like cymbals and the air between them thickened. But Granny had spent a life-time bending recalcitrant creatures to her bidding and, while Esk was a surprisingly strong opponent, it was obvious that she would give in before the end of the paragraph.

'Oh, all right,' she whined. 'I don't know why any-one would bother turning him into a pig when he was doing such a good job of it all by himself.'

She didn't know where the magic had come from, but she mentally faced that way and made a suggestion. Gulta reappeared, naked, with an apple in his mouth.

'Awts aughtning?' he said.

Granny spun around on Smith.

'Now will you believe me?' she snapped. 'Do you really think she's supposed to settle down here and forget all about magic? Can you imagine her poor husband if she marries?'

'But you always said it was impossible for women to be wizards,' said Smith. He was actually rather impressed. Granny Weatherwax had never been known to turn anyone into *anything*.

'Never mind that now,' said Granny, calming down a bit. 'She needs training. She needs to know how to control. For pity's sake put some clothes on that child.'

'Gulta, get dressed and stop grizzling,' said his father, and turned back to Granny.

'You said there was some sort of teaching place?' he hazarded.

'The Unseen University, yes. It's for training wizards.'

'And you know where it is?'

'Yes,' lied Granny, whose grasp of geography was slightly worse than her knowledge of sub-atomic physics.

Smith looked from her to his daughter, who was sulking.

'And they'll make a wizard of her?' he said.

Granny sighed.

'I don't know what they'll make of her,' she said.

And so it was that, a week later, Granny locked the cottage door and hung the key on its nail in the privy.

The goats had been sent to stay with a sister witch further along the hills, who had also promised to keep an Eye on the cottage. Bad Ass would just have to manage without a witch for a while.

Granny was vaguely aware that you didn't find the Unseen University unless it wanted you to, and the only place to start looking was the town of Ohulan Cutash, a sprawl of a hundred or so houses about fifteen miles away. It was where you went to once or twice a year if you were a really cosmopolitan Bad Assian: Granny had only been once before in her entire life and hadn't approved of it at all. It had smelt all wrong, she'd got lost, and she distrusted city folk with their flashy ways.

They got a lift on the cart that came out periodically with metal for the smithy. It was gritty, but better than walking, especially since Granny had packed their few possessions in a large sack. She sat on it for safety.

Esk sat cradling the staff and watching the woods go by. When they were several miles outside the village she said, 'I thought you told me plants were different in forn parts.'

'So they are.'

'These trees look just the same.'

Granny regarded them disdainfully.

'Nothing like as good,' she said.

In fact she was already feeling slightly panicky. Her promise to accompany Esk to Unseen University had been made without thinking, and Granny, who picked up what little she knew of the rest of the Disc from rumour and the pages of her *Almanack*, was convinced that they were heading into earthquakes, tidal waves, plagues and massacres, many of them diuerse or even worse. But she was determined to see it through. A witch relied too much on words ever to go back on them.

She was wearing serviceable black, and concealed about her person were a number of hatpins and a breadknife. She had hidden their small store of money, grudgingly advanced by Smith, in the mysterious strata of her underwear. Her skirt pockets jingled with lucky charms, and a freshly-forged horse-shoe, always a potent preventative in time of trouble, weighed down her handbag. She felt about as ready as she ever would be to face the world.

The track wound down between the mountains. For once the sky was clear, the high Ramtops standing out crisp and white like the brides of the sky (with their trousseaux stuffed with thunderstorms) and the many little streams that bordered or crossed the path flowed sluggishly through strands of meadow-sweet and go-faster-root.

By lunchtime they reached the suburb of Ohulan (it was too small to have more than one, which was just an inn and a handful of cottages belonging to people who couldn't stand the pressures of urban life) and a few minutes later the cart deposited them in the town's main, indeed its only, square.

It turned out to be market day.

Granny Weatherwax stood uncertainly on the cobbles, holding tightly to Esk's shoulder as the crowd swirled around them. She had heard that lewd things could happen to country women who were freshly arrived in big cities, and she gripped her handbag until her knuckles whitened. If any male stranger had happened to so much as nod at her it would have gone very hard indeed for him.

Esk's eyes were sparkling. The square was a jigsaw of noise and colour and smell. On one side of it were the temples of the Disc's more demanding deities, and weird perfumes drifted out to join with the reeks of commerce in a complex rag rug of fragrances. There were stalls filled with enticing curiosities that she itched to investigate.

Granny let the both of them drift with the crowd. The stalls were puzzling her as well. She peered among them, although never for one minute relaxing her vigilance against pickpockets, earthquakes and traffickers in the erotic, until she spied something vaguely familiar.

There was a small covered stall, black draped and musty, that had been wedged into a narrow space between two houses. Inconspicuous though it was, it nevertheless seemed to be doing a very busy trade. Its customers were mainly women, of all ages, although she did notice a few men. They all had one thing in common, though. No-one approached it directly. They all sort of strolled almost past it, then suddenly ducked under its shady canopy. A moment later and they would be back again, hand just darting away from bag or pocket, competing for the world's Most Nonchalant Walk title so effectively that a watcher might actually doubt what he or she had just seen.

It was quite amazing that a stall so many people didn't know was there should be quite so popular.

'What's in there?' said Esk. 'What's everyone buying?'

'Medicines,' said Granny firmly.

'There must be a lot of very sick people in towns,' said Esk gravely.

Inside, the stall was a mass of velvet shadows and the herbal scent was thick enough to bottle. Granny poked a few bundles of dry leaves with an expert finger. Esk pulled away from her and tried to read the scrawled labels on the bottles in front of her. She was expert at most of Granny's preparations, but she didn't recognize anything here. The names were quite amusing, like Tiger Oil, Maiden's Prayer and Husband's Helper, and one or two of the stoppers smelled like Granny's scullery after she had done some of her secret distillations.

A shape moved in the stall's dim recesses and a brown wrinkled hand slid lightly on to hers.

'Can I assist you, missy?' said a cracked voice, in tones of syrup of figs. 'Is it your fortune you want telling, or is it your future you want changing, maybe?'

'She's with me,' snapped Granny, spinning around, 'and your eyes are betraying you, Hilta Goatfounder, if you can't tell her age.'

The shape in front of Esk bent forward.

'Esme Weatherwax?' it asked.

'The very same,' said Granny. 'Still selling thunder drops and penny wishes, Hilta? How goes it?'

'All the better for seeing you,' said the shape. 'What brings you down from the mountains, Esme? And this child – your assistant, perhaps?'

'What's it you're selling, please?' asked Esk. The shape laughed.

'Oh, things to stop things that shouldn't be and help things that should, love,' it said. 'Let me just close up, my dears, and I will be right with you.'

The shape bustled past Esk in a nasal kaleidoscope of fragrances and buttoned up the curtains at the front of the stall. Then the drapes at the back were thrown up, letting in the afternoon sunlight.

'Can't stand the dark and fug myself,' said Hilta Goatfounder, 'but the customers expect it. You know how it is.'

'Yes,' Esk nodded sagely. 'Headology.'

Hilta, a small fat woman wearing an enormous hat with fruit on it, glanced from her to Granny and grinned.

'That's the way of it,' she agreed. 'Will you take some tea?'

They sat on bales of unknown herbs in the private corner made by the stall between the angled walls of the houses, and drank something fragrant and green out of surprisingly delicate cups. Unlike Granny, who dressed like a very respectable raven, Hilta Goatfounder was all lace and shawls and colours and earrings and so many bangles that a mere movement of her arms sounded like a percussion section falling off a cliff. But Esk could see the likeness.

It was hard to describe. You couldn't imagine them curtseying to anyone.

'So,' said Granny, 'how goes the life?'

The other witch shrugged, causing the drummers to lose their grip again, just when they had nearly climbed back up.

'Like the hurried lover, it comes and goe—' she began, and stopped at Granny's meaningful glance at Esk.

'Not bad, not bad,' she amended hurriedly. 'The council have tried to run me out once or twice, you know, but they all have wives and somehow it never quite happens. They say I'm not the right sort, but I say there'd be many a family in this town a good deal bigger and poorer if it wasn't for Madame Goatfounder's Pennyroyal Preventives. I know who comes into my shop, I do. I remember who buys buckeroo drops and ShoNuff Ointment, I do. Life isn't bad. And how is it up in your village with the funny name?'

'Bad Ass,' said Esk helpfully. She picked a small clay pot off the counter and sniffed at its contents.

'It is well enough,' conceded Granny. 'The hand-maidens of nature are ever in demand.'

Esk sniffed again at the powder, which seemed to be pennyroyal with a base she couldn't quite identify, and carefully replaced the lid. While the two women exchanged gossip in a kind of feminine code, full of eye contact and unspoken adjectives, she examined the other exotic potions on display. Or rather, not on display. In some strange way they appeared to be arfully half-hidden, as if Hilta wasn't entirely keen to sell.

'I don't recognize any of these,' she said, half to herself. 'What do they give to people?'

'Freedom,' said Hilta, who had good hearing. She turned back to Granny. 'How much have you taught her?'

'Not *that* much,' said Granny. 'There's power there, but what kind I'm not sure. Wizard power, it might be.'

Hilta turned around very slowly and looked Esk up and down.

'Ah,' she said. 'That explains the staff. I wondered what the bees were talking about. Well, well. Give me your hand, child.'

Esk held out her hand. Hilta's fingers were so heavy with rings it was like dipping into a sack of walnuts.

Granny sat upright, radiating disapproval, as Hilta began to inspect Esk's palm.

'I really don't think that is necessary,' she said sternly. 'Not between us.'

'*You* do it, Granny,' said Esk, 'in the village. I've seen you. And teacups. And cards.'

Granny shifted uneasily. 'Yes, well,' she said. 'It's all according. You just hold their hand and people do their own fortune-telling. But there's no need to go around *believing* it, we'd all be in trouble if we went around *believing* everything.'

'The Powers That Be have many strange qualities, and puzzling and varied are the ways in which they make their desires known in this circle of firelight we call the physical world,' said Hilta solemnly. She winked at Esk.

'Well, really,' snapped Granny.

'No, straight up,' said Hilta. 'It's true.

'Hmph.'

'I see you going upon a long journey,' said Hilta.

'Will I meet a tall dark stranger?' said Esk, examining her palm. 'Granny always says that to women, she says—'

'No,' said Hilta, while Granny snorted. 'But it will be a very strange journey. You'll go a long way while staying in the same place. And the direction will be a strange one. It will be an exploration.'

'You can tell all that from my hand?'

'Well, mainly I'm just guessing,' said Hilta, sitting back and reaching for the teapot (the lead drummer, who had climbed halfway back, fell on to the toiling cymbalists). She looked carefully at Esk and added, 'A female wizard, eh?'

'Granny is taking me to Unseen University,' said Esk.

Hilta raised her eyebrows. 'Do you know where it is?'

Granny frowned. 'Not in so many words,' she admitted. 'I was hoping you could give me more explicit directions, you being more familiar with bricks and things.'

'They say it has many doors, but the ones in this world are in the city of Ankh-Morpork,' said Hilta. Granny looked blank. 'On the Circle Sea,' Hilta added.

Granny's look of polite enquiry persisted. 'Five hundred miles away,' said Hilta.

'Oh,' said Granny.

She stood up and brushed an imaginary speck of dust off her dress.

'We'd better be going, then,' she added.

Hilta laughed. Esk quite liked the sound. Granny never laughed, she merely let the corners of her mouth turn up, but Hilta laughed like someone who had thought hard about Life and had seen the joke.

'Start tomorrow, anyway,' she said. 'I've got room at home, you can stay with me, and tomorrow you'll have the light.'

'We wouldn't want to presume,' said Granny.

'Nonsense. Why not have a look around while I pack up the stall?'

Ohulan was the market town for a wide sprawling countryside and the market day didn't end at sunset. Instead, torches flared at every booth and stall and light blared forth from the open doorways of the inns. Even the temples put out coloured lamps to attract nocturnal worshippers.

Hilta moved through the crowd like a slim snake through dry grass, her entire stall and stock reduced to a surprisingly small bundle on her back, and her jewellery rattling like a sackful of flamenco dancers. Granny stumped along behind her, her feet aching from the unaccustomed prodding of the cobbles.

And Esk got lost.

It took some effort, but she managed it. It involved ducking between two stalls and then scurrying down a side alley. Granny had warned her at length about the unspeakable things that lurked in cities, which showed that the old woman was lacking in a complete understanding of headology, since Esk was now determined to see one or two of them for herself.

In fact, since Ohulan was quite barbaric and uncivilized the only things that went on after dark to any degree were a little thievery, some amateurish trading in the courts of lust, and drinking until you fell over or started singing or both.

According to the standard poetic instructions one should move through a fair like the white swan at evening moves o'er the bay, but because of certain practical difficulties Esk settled for moving through the crowds like a small dodgem car, bumping from body to body with the tip of the staff waving a yard above her head. It caused some heads to turn, and not only because it had hit them; wizards occasionally passed through the town and it was the first time anyone had seen one four feet tall with long hair.

Anyone watching closely would have noticed strange things happening as she passed by.

There was, for example, the man with three upturned cups who was inviting a small crowd to explore with him the exciting world of chance and probability as it related to the position of a small dried pea. He was vaguely aware of a small figure watching him solemnly for a few moments, and then a sackful of peas cascaded out of every cup he picked up. Within seconds he was knee-deep in legumes. He was a lot deeper in trouble – he suddenly owed everyone a lot of money.

There was a small and wretched monkey that for years had shuffled vaguely at the end of a chain while its owner played something dreadful on a pipe-organ. It suddenly turned, narrowed its little red eyes, bit its keeper sharply in the leg, snapped its chain and had it away over the rooftops with the night's takings in a tin cup. History is silent about what they were spent on.

A boxful of marzipan ducks on a nearby stall came to life and whirred past the stallholder to land, quacking happily, in the river (where, by dawn, they had all melted: that's natural selection for you).

The stall itself sidled off down an alley and was never seen again.

Esk, in fact, moved through the fair more like an arsonist moves through a hayfield or a neutron bounces through a reactor, poets notwithstanding, and the hypothetical watcher could have detected her random passage by tracing the outbreaks of hysteria and violence. But, like all good catalysts, she wasn't actually involved in the processes she initiated, and by the time all the non-hypothetical potential watchers took their eyes off them she had been buffeted somewhere else.

She was also beginning to tire. While Granny Weatherwax approved of night on general principles, she certainly didn't hold with promiscuous candle-light – if she had any reading to do after dark she generally persuaded the owl to come and sit on the back of her chair, and read through its eyes. So Esk expected to go to bed around sunset, and that was long past.

There was a doorway ahead of her that looked friendly. Cheerful sounds were sliding out on the yellow light, and pooling on the cobbles. With the staff still radiating random magic like a demon lighthouse she headed for it, weary but determined.

The landlord of the Fiddler's Riddle considered himself to be a man of the world, and this was right, because he was too stupid to be really cruel, and too lazy to be really mean and although his body had been around quite a lot his mind had never gone further than the inside of his own head.

He wasn't used to being addressed by sticks. Especially when they spoke in a small piping voice, and asked for goat's milk.

Cautiously, aware that everyone in the inn was looking at him and grinning, he pulled himself across the bar top until he could see down. Esk stared up at him. Look 'em right in the eye, Granny had always said: focus your power on 'em, stare 'em out, no one can outstare a witch, 'cept a goat, of course.

The landlord, whose name was Skiller, found himself looking directly down at a small child who seemed to be squinting.

'What?' he said.

'Milk,' said the child, still focusing furiously. 'You get it out of goats. You know?'

Skiller sold only beer, which his customers claimed

he got out of cats. No self-respecting goat would have endured the smell in the Fiddler's Riddle.

'We haven't got any,' he said. He looked hard at the staff and his eyebrows met conspiratorially over his nose.

'You could have a look,' said Esk.

Skiller eased himself back across the bar, partly to avoid the gaze, which was causing his eyes to water in sympathy, and partly because a horrible suspicion was congealing in his mind.

Even second-rate barmen tend to resonate with the beer they serve, and the vibrations, coming from the big barrels behind him no longer had the twang of hop and head. They were broadcasting an altogether more lactic note.

He turned a tap experimentally, and watched a thin stream of milk curdle in the drip bucket.

The staff still poked up over the edge of the counter, like a periscope. He could swear that it was staring at him too.

'Don't waste it,' said a voice. 'You'll be grateful for it one day.'

It was the same tone of voice Granny used when Esk was less than enthusiastic about a plateful of nourishing sallet greens, boiled yellow until the last few vitamins gave in, but to Skiller's hypersensitive ears it wasn't an injunction but a prediction. He shivered. He didn't know where he would have to be to make him grateful for a drink of ancient beer and curdled milk. He'd rather be dead first.

Perhaps he *would* be dead first.

He very carefully wiped a nearly clean mug with his thumb and filled it from the tap. He was aware that a large number of his guests were quietly leaving. No-one liked magic, especially in the hands of a woman. You never could tell what they might take it into their heads to do next.

'Your milk,' he said, adding, 'Miss.'

'I've got some money,' Esk said. Granny had always told her: always be ready to pay and you won't have to, people always like you to feel good about them, it's all headology.

'No, wouldn't dream of it,' said Skiller hastily. He leaned over the bar. 'If you could see, er, your way clear to turning the rest back, though? Not much call for milk in these parts.'

He sidled along a little way. Esk had leaned the staff against the bar while she drank her milk, and it was making him uncomfortable.

Esk looked at him over a moustache of cream.

'I didn't turn it into milk, I just knew it would be milk because I wanted milk,' she said. 'What did you think it was?'

'Er. Beer.'

Esk thought about this. She vaguely remembered trying beer once, and it had tasted sort of second-hand. But she could recall something which everyone in Bad Ass reckoned was much better than beer. It was one of Granny's most guarded recipes. It was good for you, because there was only fruit in it, plus lots of freezing and boiling and careful testing of little drops with a lighted flame.

Granny would put a very small spoonful in her milk if it was a really cold night. It had to be a wooden spoon, on account of what it did to metal.

She concentrated. She could picture the taste in her mind, and with the little skills that she was beginning to accept but couldn't understand she found she could take the taste apart into little coloured shapes . . .

Skiller's thin wife came out of their back room to see why it had all gone so quiet, and he waved her into shocked silence as Esk stood swaying very slightly with her eyes closed and her lips moving.

. . . little shapes that you didn't need went back into the great pool of shapes, and then you found the extra ones you needed and put them together, and then there was a sort of hook thing which meant that they would turn anything suitable into something just like them, and then . . .

Skiller turned very carefully and regarded the barrel behind him. The smell of the room had changed, he could feel the pure gold sweating gently out of that ancient woodwork.

With some care he took a small glass from his store under the counter and let a few splashes of the dark golden liquid escape from the tap. He looked at it thoughtfully in the lamplight, turned the glass around methodically, sniffed it a few times and tossed its contents back in one swallow.

His face remained unchanged, although his eyes went moist and his throat wobbled somewhat. His wife and Esk watched him as a thin beading of sweat broke out on his forehead. Ten seconds passed, and he was obviously out to break some heroic record. There may have been steam curling out of his ears, but that could have been a rumour. His fingers drummed a strange tattoo on the bartop.

At last he swallowed, appeared to reach a decision, turned solemnly to Esk, and said, 'Hwarl, ish gnish saaaaghs ishghs oorgsh?'

His brow wrinkled as he ran the sentence past his mind again and made a second attempt.

'Aargh argh shaah gok?'

He gave up.

'Bharrgsh nargh!'

His wife snorted and took the glass out of his unprotesting hand. She sniffed it. She looked at the barrels, all ten of them. She met his unsteady eye. In a private paradise for two they soundlessly calculated the selling price of six hundred gallons of triple-distilled white mountain peach brandy and ran out of numbers.

Mrs Skiller was quicker on the uptake than her husband. She bent down and smiled at Esk, who was too tired to squint back. It wasn't a particularly good smile, because Mrs Skiller didn't get much practice.

'How did you get here, little girl?' she said, in a voice that suggested gingerbread cottages and the slamming of big stove doors.

'I got lost from Granny.'

'And where's Granny now, dear?' Clang went the oven doors again; it was going to be a tough night for all wanderers in metaphorical forests.

'Just somewhere, I expect.'

'Would you like to go to sleep in a big feather bed, all nice and warm?'

Esk looked at her gratefully, even while vaguely realizing that the woman had a face just like an eager ferret, and nodded.

You're right. It's going to take more than a passing wood-chopper to sort *this* out.

Granny, meanwhile, was two streets away. She was also, by the standards of other people, lost. She would not see it like that. She knew where she was, it was just that everywhere else didn't.

It has already been mentioned that it is much harder to detect a human mind than, say, the mind of a fox. The human mind, seeing this as some kind of a slur, wants to know why. This is why.

Animal minds are simple, and therefore sharp. Animals never spend time dividing experience into little bits and speculating about all the bits they've missed. The whole panoply of the universe has been neatly expressed to them as things to (a) mate with, (b) eat, (c) run away from, and (d) rocks. This frees the mind from unnecessary thoughts and gives it a cutting edge where it matters. Your normal animal, in fact, never tries to walk and chew gum at the same time.

The average human, on the other hand, thinks about all sorts of things, around the clock, on all sorts of levels, with interruptions from dozens of biological calendars and timepieces. There's thoughts about to be said, and private thoughts, and real thoughts, and thoughts about thoughts, and a whole gamut of sub-conscious thoughts. To a telepath the human head is a din. It is a railway terminus with all the Tannoys talking at once. It is a complete FM waveband – and some of those stations aren't reputable, they're out-lawed pirates on forbidden seas who play late-night records with limbic lyrics.

Granny, trying to locate Esk by mind magic alone, was trying to find a straw in a haystack.

She was not succeeding, but enough blips of sense reached her through the heterodyne wails of a thousand brains all thinking at once to convince her that the world was, indeed, as silly as she had always believed it was.

She met Hilta at the corner of the street. She was carrying her broomstick, the better to conduct an aerial search (with great stealth, however; the men of Ohulan were right behind Stay Long Ointment but drew the line at flying women). She was distraught.

'Not so much as a hint of her,' said Granny.

'Have you been down to the river? She might have fallen in!'

'Then she'd have just fallen out again. Anyway, she can swim. I think she's hiding, drat her.'

'What are we going to do?'

Granny gave her a withering look. 'Hilta Goatfounder, I'm ashamed of you, acting like a cowin. Do I look worried?'

Hilta peered at her.

'You do. A bit. Your lips have gone all thin.'

'I'm just angry, that's all.'

'Gypsies always come here for the fair, they might have taken her.'

Granny was prepared to believe anything about city folk but here she was on firmer ground.

'Then they're a lot dafter than I'd give them credit for,' she snapped. 'Look, she's got the staff.'

'What good would that do?' said Hilta, who was close to tears.

'I don't think you've understood anything I've told you', said Granny severely. 'All we need to do is go back to your place and wait.'

'What for?'

'The screams or the bangs or the fireballs or whatever,' Granny said vaguely.

'That's heartless!'

'Oh, I expect they've got it coming to them. Come on, you go on ahead and put the kettle on.'

Hilta gave her a mystified look, then climbed on her broom and rose slowly and erratically into the shadows among the chimneys. If broomsticks were cars, this one would be a split-window Morris Minor.

Granny watched her go, then stumped along the wet streets after her. She was determined that they wouldn't get her up in one of those things.

Esk lay in the big, fluffy and slightly damp sheets of the spare bed in the attic room of the Riddle. She was tired, but couldn't sleep. The bed was too chilly, for one thing. She wondered uneasily if she dared try to warm it up, but thought better of it. She couldn't seem to get the hang of fire spells, no matter how carefully she experimented. They either didn't work at all or worked only too well. The woods around the cottage were becoming treacherous with the holes left by disappearing fire-balls; at least, if the wizardry thing didn't work then Granny said she'd have a fine future as a privy builder or well sinker.

She turned over and tried to ignore the bed's faint smell of mushrooms. Then she reached out in the darkness until her hand found the staff, propped against the bedhead. Mrs Skiller had been quite insistent about taking it downstairs, but Esk had hung on like grim death. It was the only thing in the world she was absolutely certain belonged to her.

The varnished surface with its strange carvings felt oddly comforting. Esk went to sleep, and dreamed bangles, and strange packages, and mountains. And distant stars above the mountains, and a cold desert where strange creatures lurched across the dry sand and stared at her through insect eyes . . .

There was a creak on the stairs. Then another. Then a silence, the sort of choking, furry silence made by someone standing as still as possible.

The door swung open. Skiller made a blacker shadow against the candlelight on the stairs, and there was a faintly whispered conversation before he tip-toed as silently as he could towards the bedhead. The staff slipped sideways as his first cautious grope dislodged it, but he caught it quickly and let his breath out very slowly.

So he hardly had enough left to scream with when the staff *moved* in his hands. He felt the scaliness, the coil and muscle of it . . .

Esk sat bolt upright in time to see Skiller roll backwards down the steep stairladder, still flailing desperately at something quite invisible that coiled around his arms. There was another scream from below as he landed on his wife.

The staff clattered to the floor and lay surrounded by a faint octarine glow.

Esk got out of bed and padded across the floor. There was a terrible cursing; it sounded unhealthy. She peered around the door and looked down on the face of Mrs Skiller.

'Give me that staff!'

Esk reached down behind her and gripped the polished wood. 'No,' she said. 'It's mine.'

'It's not the right sort of thing for little girls,' snapped the barman's wife.

'It belongs to me,' said Esk, and quietly closed the door. She listened for a moment to the muttering from below and tried to think of what to do next. Turning the couple into something would probably only cause a fuss and, anyway, she wasn't quite certain how to do it.

The fact was the magic only really worked when she wasn't thinking about it. Her mind seemed to get in the way.

She padded across the room and pushed open the

tiny window. The strange night-time smells of civilization drifted in – the damp smell of streets, the fragrance of garden flowers, the distant hint of an overloaded privy. There were wet tiles outside.

As Skiller started back up the stairs she pushed the staff out on to the roof and crawled after it, steadying herself on the carvings above the window. The roof dipped down to an outhouse and she managed to stay at least vaguely upright as she half-slid, half-scrambled down the uneven tiles. A six-foot drop on to a stack of old barrels, a quick scramble down the slippery wood, and she was trotting easily across the inn yard.

As she kicked up the street mists she could hear the sounds of argument coming from the Riddle.

Skiller rushed past his wife and laid a hand on the tap of the nearest barrel. He paused, and then wrenched it open.

The smell of peach brandy filled the room, sharp as knives. He shut off the flow and relaxed.

'Afraid it would turn into something nasty?' asked his wife. He nodded.

'If you hadn't been so clumsy—' she began.

'I tell you it bit me!'

'You could have been a wizard and we wouldn't have to bother with all this. Have you got no *ambition*?'

Skiller shook his head. 'I reckon it takes more than a staff to make a wizard,' he said. 'Anyway, I heard where it said wizards aren't allowed to get married, they're not even allowed to—' he hesitated.

'To what? Allowed to what?'

Skiller writhed. 'Well. You know. Thing.'

'I'm sure I don't know what you're talking about,' said Mrs Skiller briskly.

'No, I suppose not.'

He followed her reluctantly out of the darkened bar-room. It seemed to him that perhaps wizards didn't have such a bad life, at that.

He was proved right when the following morning revealed that the ten barrels of peach brandy had, indeed, turned into something nasty.

Esk wandered aimlessly through the grey streets until she reached Ohulan's tiny river docks. Broad flat-bottomed barges bobbed gently against the wharves, and one or two of them curled wisps of smoke from friendly stovepipes. Esk clambered easily on to the nearest, and used the staff to lever up the oilcloth that covered most of it.

A warm smell, a mixture of lanolin and midden, drifted up. The barge was laden with wool.

It's silly to go to sleep on an unknown barge, not knowing what strange cliffs may be drifting past when you awake, not knowing that bargees traditionally get an early start (setting out before the sun is barely up), not knowing what new horizons might greet one on the morrow . . .

You know that. Esk didn't.

* * *

Esk awoke to the sound of someone whistling. She lay quite still, reeling the evening's events across her mind until she remembered why she was here, and then rolled over very carefully and raised the oilcloth a fraction.

Here she was, then. But 'here' had moved.

'This is what they call sailing, then,' she said, watching the far bank glide past. 'It doesn't seem very special.'

It didn't occur to her to start worrying. For the first eight years of her life the world had been a particularly boring place and now that it was becoming interesting Esk wasn't about to act ungrateful.

The distant whistler was joined by a barking dog. Esk lay back in the wool and reached out until she found the animal's mind, and Borrowed it gently. From its inefficient and disorganized brain she learned that there were at least four people on this barge, and many more on the others that were strung out in line with it on the river. Some of them seemed to be children.

She let the animal go and looked out at the scenery again for a long time – the barge was passing between high orange cliffs now, banded with so many colours of rock it looked as though some hungry god had made the all-time record club sandwich – and tried to avoid the next thought. But it persisted, arriving in her mind like the unexpected limbo dancer under the lavatory door of Life. Sooner or later she would have to go out. It wasn't her stomach that was pressing the point, but her bladder brooked no delay.

Perhaps if she—

The oilcloth over her head was pulled aside swiftly and a big bearded head beamed down at her.

'Well, well,' it said. 'What have we here, then? A stowaway, yesno?'

Esk gave it a stare. 'Yes,' she said. There seemed no sense in denying it. 'Could you help me out please?'

'Aren't you afraid I shall throw you to the – the pike?' said the head. It noticed her perplexed look. 'Big freshwater fish,' it added helpfully. 'Fast. Lot of teeth. Pike.'

The thought hadn't occurred to her at all. 'No,' she said truthfully. 'Why? Will you?'

'No. Not really. There's no need to be frightened.'

'I'm not.'

'Oh.' A brown arm appeared, attached to the head by the normal arrangements, and helped her out of her nest in the fleeces.

Esk stood on the deck of the barge and looked around. The sky was bluer than a biscuit barrel, fitting neatly over a broad valley through which the river ran as sluggishly as a planning inquiry.

Behind her the Ramtops still acted as a hitching rail for clouds, but they no longer dominated as they had done for as long as Esk had known them. Distance had eroded them.

'Where's this?' she said, sniffing the new smells of swamp and sedge.

'The Upper Valley of the River Ankh,' said her captor. 'What do you think of it?'

Esk looked up and down the river. It was already much wider than it had been at Ohulan.

'I don't know. There's certainly a lot of it. Is this your ship?'

'Boat,' he corrected. He was taller than her father, although not quite so old, and dressed like a gypsy. Most of his teeth had turned gold, but Esk decided it wasn't the time to ask why. He had the kind of real deep tan that rich people spend ages trying to achieve with expensive holidays and bits of tinfoil, when really all you need to do to obtain one is work your arse off in the open air every day. His brow crinkled.

'Yes, it's mine,' he said, determined to regain the initiative. 'And what are you doing on it, I would like to know? Running away from home, yesno? If you were a boy I'd say are you going to seek your fortune?'

'Can't girls seek their fortune?'

'I think they're supposed to seek a boy with a fortune,' said the man, and gave a 200-carat grin. He extended a brown hand, heavy with rings. 'Come and have some breakfast.'

'I'd actually like to use your privy,' she said. His mouth dropped open.

'This is a barge, yesno?'

'Yes?'

'That means there's only the river.' He patted her hand. 'Don't worry,' he added. 'It's quite used to it.'

Granny stood on the wharf, her boot tap-tap-tapping on the wood. The little man who was the nearest thing

Ohulan had to a dockmaster was being treated to the full force of one of her stares, and was visibly wilting. Her expression wasn't perhaps as vicious as thumbscrews, but it did seem to suggest that thumbscrews were a real possibility.

'They left before dawn, you say,' she said.

'Yes-ss,' he said. 'Er. I didn't know they weren't supposed to.'

'Did you see a little girl on board?' Tap-tap went her boot.

'Um. No. I'm sorry.' He brightened. 'They were Zoons,' he said. 'If the child was with them she won't come to harm. You can always trust a Zoon, they say. Very keen on family life.'

Granny turned to Hilta, who was fluttering like a bewildered butterfly, and raised her eyebrows.

'Oh, yes,' Hilta trilled. 'The Zoons have a very good name.'

'Mmph,' said Granny. She turned on her heel and stumped back towards the centre of the town. The dockmaster sagged as though a coathanger had just been removed from his shirt.

Hilta's lodgings were over a herbalist's and behind a tannery, and offered splendid views of the rooftops of Ohulan. She liked it because it offered privacy, always appreciated by, as she put it, 'my more discerning clients who prefer to make their very special purchases in an atmosphere of calm where discretion is forever the watchword.'

Granny Weatherwax looked around the sitting room with barely-concealed scorn. There were

altogether too many tassels, bead curtains, astrological charts and black cats in the place. Granny
couldn't abide cats. She sniffed.

'Is that the tannery?' she said accusingly.

'Incense,' said Hilta. She rallied bravely in the face
of Granny's scorn. 'The customers appreciate it,' she
said. 'It puts them in the right frame of mind. You
know how it is.'

'I would have thought one could carry out a
perfectly respectable business, Hilta, without resort-
ing to *parlour* tricks,' said Granny, sitting down and
beginning the long and tricky business of removing
her hatpins.

'It's different in towns,' said Hilta. 'One has to move
with the times.'

'I'm sure I don't know why. Is the kettle on?'
Granny reached across the table and took the velvet
cover off Hilta's crystal ball, a sphere of quartz as big
as her head.

'Never could get the hang of this damn silicon stuff,'
she said. 'A bowl of water with a drop of ink in it was
good enough when I was a girl. Let's see, now . . .'

She peered into the dancing heart of the ball, trying
to use it to focus her mind on the whereabouts of Esk.
A crystal was a tricky thing to use at the best of times,
and usually staring into it meant that the one thing
the future could be guaranteed to hold was a severe
migraine. Granny distrusted them, considering
them to smack of wizardry; for two pins, it always
seemed to her, the wretched thing would suck your
mind out like a whelk from a shell.

'Damn thing's all sparkly,' she said, huffing on it and wiping it with her sleeve. Hilta peered over her shoulder.

'That's not sparkle, that means something,' she said slowly.

'What?'

'I'm not sure. Can I try? It's used to me.' Hilta pushed a cat off the other chair and leaned forward to peer into the glass depths.

'Mnph. Feel free,' said Granny, 'but you won't find—'

'Wait. Something's coming through.'

'Looks all sparkly from here,' Granny insisted. 'Little silver lights all floating around, like in them little snowstorms-in-a-bottle toys. Quite pretty, really.'

'Yes, but look beyond the flakes . . .'

Granny looked.

This was what she saw.

The viewpoint was very high up and a wide swathe of country lay below her, blue with distance, through which a broad river wriggled like a drunken snake. There were silver lights floating in the foreground but they were, in a manner of speaking, just a few flakes in the great storm of lights that turned in a great lazy spiral, like a geriatric tornado with a bad attack of snow, and funnelled down, down to the hazy land-scape. By screwing up her eyes Granny could just make out some dots on the river.

Occasionally some sort of lighting would sparkle briefly inside the gently turning funnel of motes.

Granny blinked and looked up. The room seemed very dark.

'Odd sort of weather,' she said, because she couldn't really think of anything better. Even with her eyes shut the glittering motes still danced across her vision.

'I don't think it's weather,' said Hilta. 'I don't actually think people can see it, but the crystal shows it. I think it's magic, condensing out of the air.'

'Into the staff?'

'Yes. That's what a wizard's staff does. It sort of distils magic.'

Granny risked another glance at the crystal.

'Into Esk,' she said, carefully.

'Yes.'

'There looks like quite a lot of it.'

'Yes.'

Not for the first time, Granny wished she knew more about how wizards worked their magic. She had a vision of Esk filling up with magic, until every tissue and pore was bloated with the stuff. Then it would start leaking – slowly at first, arcing to ground in little bursts, but then building up to a great discharge of occult potentiality. It could do all kinds of damage.

'Drat,' she said. 'I never did like that staff.'

'At least she's heading towards the University place,' said Hilta. 'They'll know what to do.'

'That's as may be. How far down river do you reckon they are?'

'Twenty miles or so. Those barges only go at walking pace. The Zoons aren't in any hurry.'

'Right.' Granny stood up, her jaw set defiantly. She reached for her hat and picked up her sack of possessions.

'Reckon I can walk faster than a barge,' she said. 'The river's all bendy but I can go in straight lines.'

'You're going to *walk* after her?' said Hilta, aghast. 'But there's forests and wild animals!'

'Good, I could do with getting back to civilization. She needs me. That staff is taking over. I said it would, but did anyone listen?'

'Did they?' said Hilta, still trying to work out what Granny meant by getting back to civilization.

'No,' said Granny coldly.

His name was Amschat B'hal Zoon. He lived on the raft with his three wives and three children. He was a Liar.

What always annoyed the enemies of the Zoon tribe was not simply their honesty, which was infuriatingly absolute, but their total directness of approach. The Zoons had never heard about a euphemism, and wouldn't understand what to do with it if they had one, except that they would certainly have called it 'a nice way of saying something nasty'.

Their rigid adherence to the truth was apparently on them by a god, as is usually the case, to have a genetic base. The average Zoon tell a lie than breathe underwater and, concept was enough to upset them

124

considerably; telling a Lie meant no less than totally altering the universe.

This was something of a drawback to a trading race and so, over the millennia, the elders of the Zoon studied this strange power that everyone else had in such abundance and decided that they should possess it too.

Young men who showed faint signs of having such a talent were encouraged, on special ceremonial occasions, to bend the Truth ever further on a competitive basis. The first recorded Zoon proto-lie was: 'Actually, my grandfather is quite tall,' but eventually they got the hang of it and the office of tribal Liar was instituted.

It must be understood that while the majority of Zoon cannot lie they have great respect for any Zoon who can say that the world is other than it is, and the Liar holds a position of considerable eminence. He represents his tribe in all his dealings with the outside world, which the average Zoon long ago gave up trying to understand. Zoon tribes are very proud of their Liars.

Other races get very annoyed about all this. They feel that the Zoon ought to have adopted more suitable titles, like 'diplomat' or 'public relations officer'. They feel they are poking fun at the whole thing.

'Is all that true?' said Esk suspiciously, looking around the barge's crowded cabin.

'No,' said Amschat firmly. His junior wife, who was cooking porridge over a tiny ornate stove, giggled. His three children watched Esk solemnly over the edge of the table.

'Don't you ever tell the truth?'

'Do you?' Amschat grinned his goldmine grin, but his eyes were not smiling. 'Why do I find you on my fleeces? Amschat is no kidnapper. There will be people at home who will worry, yesno?'

'I expect Granny will come looking for me,' said Esk, 'but I don't think she will worry much. Just be angry, I expect. Anyway, I'm going to Ankh-Morpork. You can put me off the ship—'

'—boat—'

'—if you like. I don't mind about the pike.'

'I can't do that,' said Amschat.

'Was that a lie?'

'No! There is wild country around us, robbers and – things.'

Esk nodded brightly. 'That's settled, then,' she said. 'I don't mind sleeping in the fleeces. And I can pay my way. I can do—' She hesitated; her unfinished sentence hung like a little curl of crystal in the air while discretion made a successful bid for control of her tongue. '—helpful things,' she finished lamely.

She was aware that Amschat was looking slightly sideways at his senior wife, who was sewing by the stove. By Zoon tradition she wore nothing but black. Granny would have thoroughly approved.

'What sort of helpful things?' he asked. 'Washing and sweeping, yesno?'

'If you like,' said Esk, 'or distillation using the bifold

or triple alembic, the making of varnishes, glazes, creams, zuum-chats and punes, the rendering of waxes, the manufacture of candles, the proper selection of seeds, roots and cuttings, and most preparations from the Eighty Marvellous Herbs; I can spin, card, rett, flallow and weave on the hand, frame, harp and Noble looms and I can knit if people start the wool on for me, I can read soil and rock, do carpentry up to the three-way mortise and tenon, predict weather by means of beastsign and skyreck, make increase in bees, brew five types of mead, make dyes and mordants and pigments, including a fast blue, I can do most types of whitesmithing, mend boots, cure and fashion most leathers, and if you have any goats I can look after them. I like goats.'

Amschat looked at her thoughtfully. She felt she was expected to continue.

'Granny never likes to see people sitting around doing nothing,' she offered. 'She always says a girl who is good with her hands will never want for a living,' she added, by way of further explanation.

'Or a husband, I expect,' nodded Amschat, weakly.

'Actually, Granny had a lot to say about that—'

'I bet she did,' said Amschat. He looked at the senior wife, who nodded almost imperceptibly.

'Very well,' he said. 'If you can make yourself useful you can stay. And can you play a musical instrument?'

Esk returned his steady gaze, not batting an eyelid. 'Probably.'

* * *

127

And so Esk, with the minimum of difficulty and only a little regret, left the Ramtops and their weather and joined the Zoons on their great trading journey down the Ankh.

There were at least thirty barges with at least one sprawling Zoon family on each, and no two vessels appeared to be carrying the same cargo; most of them were strung together, and the Zoons simply hauled on the cable and stepped on to the next deck if they fancied a bit of socializing.

Esk set up home in the fleeces. It was warm, smelled slightly of Granny's cottage and, much more important, meant that she was undisturbed.

She was getting a bit worried about magic.

It was definitely getting out of control. She wasn't doing magic, it was just happening around her. And she sensed that people probably wouldn't be too happy if they knew.

It meant that if she washed up she had to clatter and splash at length to conceal the fact that the dishes were cleaning themselves. If she did some darning she had to do it on some private part of the deck to conceal the fact that the edges of the hole ravelled themselves together as if . . . as if by magic. Then she woke up on the second day of her voyage to find that several of the fleeces around the spot where she had hidden the staff had combed, carded and spun themselves into neat skeins during the night.

She put all thoughts of lighting fires out of her head.

There were compensations, though. Every sluggish

turn of the great brown river brought new scenes. There were dark stretches hemmed in with deep forest, through which the barges travelled in the dead centre of the river with the men armed and the women below – except for Esk, who sat listening with interest to the snortings and sneezings that followed them through the bushes on the banks. There were stretches of farmland. There were several towns much larger than Ohulan. There were even some mountains, although they were old and flat and not young and frisky like her mountains. Not that she was homesick, exactly, but sometimes she felt like a boat herself, drifting on the edge of an infinite rope but always attached to an anchor.

The barges stopped at some of the towns. By tradition only the men went ashore, and only Amschat, wearing his ceremonial Lying hat, spoke to non-Zoons. Esk usually went with him. He tried hinting that she should obey the unwritten rules of Zoon life and stay afloat, but a hint was to Esk what a mosquito bite was to the average rhino because she was already learning that if you ignore the rules people will, half the time, quietly rewrite them so that they don't apply to you.

Anyway, it seemed to Amschat that when Esk was with him he always got a very good price. There was something about a small child squinting determinedly at them from behind his legs that made even market-hardened merchants hastily conclude their business.

In fact, it began to worry him. When a market broker in the walled town of Zemphis offered him a

bag of ultramarines in exchange for a hundred fleeces
a voice from the level of his pockets said: 'They're not
ultramarines.'

'Listen to the child!' said the broker, grinning.
Amschat solemnly held one of the stones to his eye.

'I am listening,' he said, 'and they do indeed look
like ultramarines. They have the glit and shimmy.'

Esk shook her head. 'They're just spircles,' she said.
She said it without thinking, and regretted it immediately as both men turned to stare at her.

Amschat turned the stone over in his palm. Putting
the chameleon spircle stones into a box with some
real gems so that they appeared to change their hue
was a traditional trick, but these had the true inner
blue fire. He looked up sharply at the broker. Amschat
had been finely trained in the art of the Lie. He
recognized the subtle signs, now that he came to think
about it.

'There seems to be a doubt,' he said, 'but 'tis easily
resolved, we need only take them to the assayer in
Pine Street because the world knows that spircles will
dissolve in hypactic fluid, yesno?'

The broker hesitated. Amschat had changed
position slightly, and the set of his muscles suggested
that any sudden movement on the broker's part
would see him flat in the dust. And that damn child
was squinting at him as though she could see through
to the back of his mind. His nerve broke.

'I regret this unfortunate dispute,' he said. 'I had
accepted the stones as ultramarines in good faith but
rather than cause disharmony between us I will ask

you to accept them as – as a gift, and for the fleeces may I offer this roseatte of the first sorting?'

He took a small red stone from a tiny velvet pouch. Amschat hardly looked at it but, without taking his eyes off the man, passed it down to Esk. She nodded.

When the merchant had hurried off Amschat took Esk's hand and half-dragged her to the assayer's stall, which was little more than a niche in the wall. The old man took the smallest of the blue stones, listened to Amschat's hurried explanation, poured out a saucerful of hypactic fluid and dropped the stone in. It frothed into nothingness.

'Very interesting,' he said. He took another stone in a tweezer and examined it under a glass.

'They are indeed spircles, but remarkably fine specimens in their own right,' he concluded. 'They are by no means worthless, and I for example would be prepared to offer you – is there something wrong with the little girl's eyes?'

Amschat nudged Esk, who stopped trying out another Look.

'—I would offer you, shall we say, two *zats* of silver?'

'Shall we say five?' said Amschat pleasantly.

'And I would like to keep one of the stones,' said Esk. The old man threw up his hands.

'But they are mere curios!' he said. 'Of value only to a collector!'

'A collector may yet sell them to an unsuspecting purchaser as finest roseattes or ultramarines,' said Amschat, 'especially if he was the only assayer in town.'

The assayer grumbled a bit at this, but at last they settled on three *zats* and one of the spircles on a thin silver chain for Esk.

When they were out of earshot Amschat handed her the tiny silver coins and said: 'These are yours. You have earned them. But—' he hunkered down so that his eyes were on a level with hers, '—you must tell me how you knew the stones were false.'

He looked worried, but Esk sensed that he wouldn't really like the truth. Magic made people uncomfortable. He wouldn't like it if she said simply: spircles are spircles and ultramarines are ultramarines, and though you may think they look the same that is because most people don't use their eyes in the right way. Nothing can entirely disguise its true nature.

Instead she said: 'The dwarves mine spircles near the village where I was born, and you soon learn to see how they bend light in a funny way.'

Amschat looked into her eyes for some time. Then he shrugged.

'Okay,' he said. 'Fine. Well, I have some further business here. Why don't you buy yourself some new clothes, or something? I'd warn you against unscrupulous traders but, somehow, I don't know, I don't think you will have any trouble.'

Esk nodded. Amschat strode off through the market place. At the first corner he turned, looked at her thoughtfully, and then disappeared among the crowds.

Well, that's the end of sailing, Esk told herself. He's not quite sure but he's going to be watching me now and before I know what's happening the staff will be taken away and there'll be all sorts of trouble. Why does everyone get so upset about magic?

She gave a philosophical sigh and set about exploring the possibilities of the town.

There was the question of the staff, though. Esk had rammed it deep among the fleeces, which were not going to be unloaded yet. If she went back for it people would start asking questions, and she didn't know the answers.

She found a convenient alleyway and scuttled down it until a deep doorway gave her the privacy she required.

If going back was out of the question then only one thing remained. She held out a hand and closed her eyes.

She knew exactly what she wanted to do – it lay in front of her eyes. The staff mustn't come flying through the air, wrecking the barge and drawing attention to itself. All she wanted, she told herself, was for there to be a slight change in the way the world was organized. It shouldn't be a world where the staff was in the fleeces, it should be a world where it was in her hand. A tiny change, an infinitesimal alteration to the Way Things Were.

If Esk had been properly trained in wizardry she would have known that this was impossible. All wizards knew how to move things about, starting with protons and working upwards, but the important thing about moving something from A to Z, according to basic physics, was that at some point it should pass through the rest of the alphabet. The only way one could cause something to vanish at A and appear at Z would be to shuffle the whole of Reality sideways. The problems this would cause didn't bear thinking about.

Esk, of course, had not been trained, and it is well known that a vital ingredient of success is not knowing that what you're attempting can't be done. A person ignorant of the possibility of failure can be a half-brick in the path of the bicycle of history.

As Esk tried to work out how to move the staff the ripples spread out in the magical ether, changing the Discworld in thousands of tiny ways. Most went entirely unnoticed. Perhaps a few grains of sand lay on their beaches in a slightly different position, or the occasional leaf hung on its tree in a marginally different way. But then the wavefront of probability struck the edge of Reality and rebounded like the slosh off the side of the pond which, meeting the laggard ripples coming the other way, caused small but important whirlpools in the very fabric of existence. You can have whirlpools in the fabric of existence, because it is a very strange fabric.

Esk was completely ignorant of all this, of course, but was quite satisfied when the staff dropped out of thin air into her hand.

It felt warm.

She looked at it for some time. She felt that she ought to do something about it; it was too big, too distinctive, too inconvenient. It attracted attention.

'If I'm taking you to Ankh-Morpork,' she said thoughtfully, 'you've got to go in disguise.'

A few late flickers of magic played around the staff, and then it went dark.

Eventually Esk solved the immediate problem by finding a stall in the main Zemphis market place that sold broomsticks, buying the largest, carrying it back to her doorway, removing the handle and ramming the staff deep into the birch twigs. It didn't seem right to treat a noble object in this way, and she silently apologized to it.

It made a difference, anyway. No-one looked twice at a small girl carrying a broom.

She bought a spice pasty to eat while exploring (the stall-holder carelessly shortchanged her, and only realized later that he had inexplicably handed over two silver pieces; also, rats mysteriously got in and ate all his stock during the night, and his grandmother was struck by lightning).

The town was smaller than Ohulan, and very different because it lay on the junction of three trade routes quite apart from the river itself. It was built around one enormous square which was a cross between a permanent exotic traffic jam and a tent village. Camels kicked mules, mules kicked horses, horses kicked camels and they all kicked humans; there was a riot of colours, a din of noise, a nasal orchestration of smells and the steady, heady sound of hundreds of people working hard at making money.

One reason for the bustle was that over large parts of the continent other people preferred to make money without working at all, and since the Disc had yet to develop a music recording industry they were forced to fall back on older, more traditional forms of banditry.

Strangely enough these often involved considerable effort. Rolling heavy rocks to the top of cliffs for a decent ambush, cutting down trees to block the road, and digging a pit lined with spikes while still keeping a wicked edge on a dagger probably involved a much greater expenditure of thought and muscle than more socially-acceptable professions but, nevertheless, there were still people misguided enough to endure all this, plus long nights in uncomfortable surroundings, merely to get their hands on perfectly ordinary large boxes of jewels.

So a town like Zemphis was the place where caravans split, mingled and came together again, as dozens of merchants and travellers banded together for protection against the socially disadvantaged on the trails ahead. Esk, wandering unregarded amidst the bustle, learned all this by the simple method of finding someone who looked important and tugging on the hem of his coat.

This particular man was counting bales of tobacco and would have succeeded but for the interruption.

'What?'

'I said, what's happening here?'

The man meant to say: 'Push off and bother someone else.' He meant to give her a light cuff about the head. So he was astonished to find himself bending down and talking seriously to a small, grubby-faced child holding a large broomstick (which also, it seemed to him later, was in some indefinable way *paying attention*).

He explained about the caravans. The child nodded.

'People all get together to travel?'

'Precisely.'

'Where to?'

'All sorts of places. Sto Lat, Pseudopolis . . . Ankh-Morpork, of course . . .'

'But the river goes there,' said Esk, reasonably. 'Barges. The Zoons.'

'Ah, yes,' said the merchant, 'but they charge high prices and they can't carry everything and, anyway, no one trusts them much.'

'But they're very honest!'

'Huh, yes,' he said. 'But you know what they say: never trust an honest man.' He smiled knowingly.

'Who says that?'

'They do. You know. People,' he said, a certain uneasiness entering his voice.

'Oh,' said Esk. She thought about it. 'They must be very silly,' she said primly. 'Thank you, anyway.'

He watched her wander off and got back to his counting. A moment later there was another tug at his coat.

'Fiftysevenfiftysevenfiftysevenwell?' he said, trying not to lose his place.

'Sorry to bother you again,' said Esk, 'but those bale things . . .'

'What about them fiftysevenfiftysevenfiftyseven?'

'Well, are they supposed to have little white worm things in them?'

'Fiftysev – *what*?' The merchant lowered his slate and stared at Esk. 'What little worms?'

'Wriggly ones. White,' added Esk, helpfully. 'All sort of burrowing about in the middle of the bales.'

'You mean tobacco threadworm?' He looked wild-eyed at the stack of bales being unloaded by, now he came to think about it, a vendor with the nervous look of a midnight sprite who wants to get away before you find out what fairy gold turns into in the morning. 'But he told me these had been well stored and – how do you know, anyway?'

The child had disappeared among the crowds. The merchant looked hard at the spot where she had been. He looked hard at the vendor, who was grinning nervously. He looked hard at the sky. Then took his sampling knife out of his pocket, stared at it for a moment, appeared to reach a decision, and sidled towards the nearest bale.

Esk, meanwhile, had by random eavesdropping found the caravan being assembled for Ankh-Morpork. The trail boss was sitting at a table made up of a plank across two barrels.

He was busy.

He was talking to a wizard.

Seasoned travellers know that a party setting out to cross possibly hostile country should have a fair number of swords in it but should definitely have a wizard in case there is any need for magic arts and, even if these do not become necessary, for lighting fires. A wizard of the third rank or above does not expect to pay for the privilege of joining the party.

Rather, he expects to be paid. Delicate negotiations were even now coming to a conclusion.

'Fair enough, Master Treatle, but what of the young man?' said the trail boss, one Adab Gander, an impressive figure in a trollhide jerkin, rakishly floppy hat and a leather kilt. 'He's no wizard, I can see.'

'He is in training,' said Treatle – a tall skinny wizard whose robes declared him to be a mage of the Ancient and Truly Original Brothers of the Silver Star, one of the eight orders of wizardry.

'Then no wizard he,' said Gander. 'I know the rules, and you're not a wizard unless you've got a staff. And he hasn't.'

'Even now he travels to the Unseen University for that small detail,' said Treatle loftily. Wizards parted with money slightly less readily than tigers parted with their teeth.

Gander looked at the lad in question. He had met a good many wizards in his time and considered himself a good judge and he had to admit that this boy looked like good wizard material. In other words, he was thin, gangling, pale from reading disturbing books in unhealthy rooms, and had watery eyes like two lightly-poached eggs. It crossed Gander's mind that one must speculate in order to accumulate.

All he needs to get right to the top, he thought, is a bit of a handicap. Wizards are martyrs to things like asthma and flat feet, it somehow seems to give them their drive.

'What's your name, lad?' he said, as kindly as possible.

'Sssssssssssssss,' said the boy. His Adam's apple bobbed like a captive balloon. He turned to his companion, full of mute appeal.

'Simon,' said Treatle.

'—imon,' agreed Simon, thankfully.

'Can you cast fireballs or whirling spells, such as might be hurled against an enemy?'

Simon looked sideways at Treatle.

'Nnnnnnnnnn,' he ventured.

'My young friend follows higher magic than the mere hurling of sorceries,' said the wizard.

'—o,' said Simon.

Gander nodded.

'Well,' he said, 'maybe you will indeed be a wizard, lad. Maybe when you have your fine staff you'll consent to travel with me one time, yes? I will make an investment in you, yes?'

'Y—'

'Just nod,' said Gander, who was not naturally a cruel man.

Simon nodded gratefully. Treatle and Gander exchanged nods and then the wizard strode off, with his apprentice trailing behind under a weight of baggage.

Gander looked down at the list in front of him and carefully crossed out 'wizard'.

A small shadow fell across the page. He glanced up and gave an involuntary start.

'Well?' he said coldly.

'I want to go to Ankh-Morpork,' said Esk, 'please. I've got some money.'

'Go home to your mother, child.'

'No, really. I want to seek my fortune.'

Gander sighed. 'Why are you holding that broomstick?' he said.

Esk looked at it as though she had never seen it before.

'Everything's got to be somewhere,' she said.

'Just go home, my girl,' said Gander. 'I'm not taking any runaways to Ankh-Morpork. Strange things can happen to little girls in big cities.'

Esk brightened. 'What sort of strange things?'

'Look, I said go home, right? Now!'

He picked up his chalk and went on ticking off items on his slate, trying to ignore the steady gaze that seemed to be boring through the top of his head.

'I can be helpful,' said Esk, quietly.

Gander threw down the chalk and scratched his chin irritably.

'How old are you?' he said.

'Nine.'

'Well, Miss nine-years-old, I've got two hundred animals and a hundred people that want to go to Ankh, and half of them hate the other half, and I've not got enough people who can fight, and they say the roads are pretty bad and the bandits are getting really cheeky up in the Paps and the trolls are demanding a bigger bridge toll this year and there's weevils in the supplies and I keep getting these headaches and where, in all this, do I need you?'

'Oh,' said Esk. She looked around the crowded square. 'Which one of these roads goes to Ankh, then?'

'The one over there, with the gate.'

'Thank you,' she said gravely. 'Goodbye. I hope you don't have any more trouble and your head gets better.'

'Right,' said Gander uncertainly. He drummed his fingers on the tabletop as he watched Esk walk away in the direction of the Ankh road. A long, winding road. A road haunted by thieves and gnolls. A road that wheezed through high mountain passes and crawled, panting, over deserts.

'Oh bugger,' he said, under his breath. 'Hey! You.'

Granny Weatherwax was in trouble.

First of all, she decided, she should never have allowed Hilta to talk her into borrowing her broomstick. It was elderly, erratic, would fly only at night and even then couldn't manage a speed much above a trot.

Its lifting spells had worn so thin that it wouldn't even begin to operate until it was already moving at a fair lick. It was, in fact, the only broomstick ever to need bump-starting.

And it was while Granny Weatherwax, sweating and cursing, was running along a forest path holding the damn thing at shoulder height for the tenth time that she had found the bear trap.

The second problem was that a bear had found it first. In fact this hadn't been too much of a problem because Granny, already in a bad temper, hit it right between the eyes with the broomstick and it was now sitting as far away from her as it was possible to get in a pit, and trying to think happy thoughts.

It was not a very comfortable night and the morning wasn't much better for the party of hunters who, around dawn, peered over the edge of the pit.

'About time, too,' said Granny. 'Get me out.'

The startled heads withdrew and Granny could hear a hasty whispered conversation. They had seen the hat and broomstick.

Finally a bearded head reappeared, rather reluctantly, as if the body it was attached to was being pushed forward.

'Um,' it began, 'look, mother—'

'I'm not a mother,' snapped Granny. 'I'm certainly not your mother, if you ever had mothers, which I doubt. If I was your mother I'd have run away before you were born.'

'It's only a figure of speech,' said the head reproachfully.

'It's a damned insult is what it is!'

There was another whispered conversation.

'If I don't get out,' said Granny in ringing tones, 'there will be Trouble. Do you see my hat, eh? Do you see it?'

The head reappeared.

'That's the whole point, isn't it?' it said. 'I mean, what will there be if we let you out? It seems less risky all round if we just sort of fill the pit in. Nothing personal, you understand.'

Granny realized what it was that was bothering her about the head.

'Are you kneeling down?' she said accusingly. 'You're not, are you! You're dwarves!'

Whisper, whisper.

'Well, what about it?' asked the head defiantly. 'Nothing wrong with that, is there? What have you got against dwarves?'

'Do you know how to repair broomsticks?'

'Magic broomsticks?'

'Yes!'

Whisper, whisper.

'What if we do?'

'Well, we could come to some arrangement . . .'

The dwarf halls rang to the sound of hammers, although mainly for effect. Dwarves found it hard to think without the sound of hammers, which they found soothing, so well-off dwarves in the clerical professions paid goblins to hit small ceremonial anvils, just to maintain the correct dwarvish image.

The broomstick lay between two trestles. Granny Weatherwax sat on a rock outcrop while a dwarf half her height, wearing an apron that was a mass of pockets, walked around the broom and occasionally poked it.

Eventually he kicked the bristles and gave a long intake of breath, a sort of reverse whistle, which is the secret sign of craftsmen across the universe and means that something expensive is about to happen.

'Weellll,' he said. 'I could get the apprentices in to look at this, I could. It's an education in itself.

And you say it actually managed to get airborne?'

'It flew like a bird,' said Granny.

The dwarf lit a pipe. 'I should very much like to see that bird,' he said reflectively. 'I should imagine it's quite something to watch, a bird like that.'

'Yes, but can you repair it?' said Granny. 'I'm in a hurry.'

The dwarf sat down, slowly and deliberately.

'As for *repair*,' he said, 'well, I don't know about *repair*. Rebuild, maybe. Of course, it's hard to get the bristles these days even if you can find people to do the proper binding, and the spells need—'

'I don't want it rebuilt, I just want it to work properly,' said Granny.

'It's an early model, you see,' the dwarf plugged on. 'Very tricky, those early models. You can't get the wood—'

He was picked up bodily until his eyes were level with Granny's. Dwarves, being magical in themselves as it were, are quite resistant to magic but her expression looked as though she was trying to weld his eyeballs to the back of his skull.

'Just repair it,' she hissed. 'Please?'

'What, make a bodge job?' said the dwarf, his pipe clattering to the floor.

'Yes.'

'Patch it up, you mean? Betray my training by doing half a job?'

'Yes,' said Granny. Her pupils were two little black holes.

'Oh,' said the dwarf. 'Right, then.'

* * *

Gander the trail boss was a worried man.

They were three mornings out from Zemphis, making good time, and were climbing now towards the rocky pass through the mountains known as the Paps of Scilla (there were eight of them; Gander often wondered who Scilla had been, and whether he would have liked her).

A party of gnolls had crept up on them during the night. The nasty creatures, a variety of stone goblin, had slit the throat of a guard and must have been poised to slaughter the entire party. Only . . .

Only no one knew quite what had happened next. The screams had woken them up, and by the time people had puffed up the fires and Treatle the wizard had cast a blue radiance over the campsite the surviving gnolls were distant, spidery shadows, running as if the legions of Hell were after them.

Judging by what had happened to their colleagues, they were probably right. Bits of gnolls hung from the nearby rocks, giving them a sort of jolly, festive air. Gander wasn't particularly sorry about that – gnolls liked to capture travellers and practise hospitality of the red-hot-knife-and-bludgeon kind – but he was nervous of being in the same area as Something that went through a dozen wiry and wickedly armed gnolls like a spoon through a lightly-boiled egg but left no tracks.

In fact the ground was swept clean.

It had been a very long night, and the morning

didn't seem to be an improvement. The only person more than half-awake was Esk, who had slept through the whole thing under one of the wagons and had complained only of odd dreams.

Still, it was a relief to get away from that macabre sight. Gander considered that gnolls didn't look any better inside than out. He hated their guts.

Esk sat on Treatle's wagon, talking to Simon who was steering inexpertly while the wizard caught up with some sleep behind them.

Simon did everything inexpertly. He was really good at it. He was one of those tall lads apparently made out of knees, thumbs and elbows. Watching him walk was a strain, you kept waiting for the strings to snap, and when he talked the spasm of agony on his face if he spotted an S or W looming ahead in the sentence made people instinctively say them for him. It was worth it for the grateful look which spread across his acned face like sunrise on the moon.

At the moment his eyes were streaming with hayfever.

'Did you want to be a wizard when you were a little boy?'

Simon shook his head. 'I just www—'

'—wanted—'

'—tto find out how things www—'

'—worked?—'

'Yes. Then someone in my village told the University and Mmaster T-Treatle was sent to bring me. I shall be a www—'

'—wizard—'

147

'—one day. Master Treatle says I have an exceptional grasp of th-theory.' Simon's damp eyes misted over and an expression almost of bliss drifted across his ravaged face.

'He t-tells me they've got thousands of b-books in the library at Unseen University,' he said, in the voice of a man in love. 'More b-books than anyone could read in a lifetime.'

'I'm not sure I like books,' said Esk conversationally. 'How can paper know things? My granny says books are only good if the paper is thin.'

'No, that's not right,' said Simon urgently. 'Books are full of www—' he gulped air and gave her a pleading look.

'—words?—' said Esk, after a moment's thought.

'—yes, and they can change th-things. Th-that's wuwuw, that wuwuw – whha-whha—'

'—what—'

'—I must f-find. I know it's th-there, somewhere in all the old books. They ssss—'

'—say—'

'there's no new spells but I know that it's there somewhere, hiding, the wwwwwuwu—'

'—words—'

'yes, that no wiwiwi—'

'—Wizard?—' said Esk, her face a frown of concentration.

'Yes, has ever found.' His eyes closed and he smiled a beatific smile and added, 'The Words that Will change the World.'

'What?'

'Eh?' said Simon, opening his eyes in time to stop the oxen wandering off the track.

'You said all those wubbleyous!'

'I did?'

'I heard you! Try again.'

Simon took a deep breath. 'The worworwor – the wuwuw—' he said. 'The wowowoo—' he continued.

'It's no good, it's gone,' he said. 'It happens sometimes, if I don't think about it. Master Treatle says I'm allergic to something.'

'Allergic to double-yous?'

'No, sisssisi—'

'—silly—' said Esk, generously.

'—there's sososo—'

'—something—'

'—in the air, p-pollen maybe, or g-grass dust. Master Treatle has tried to find the cause of it but no magic seems to h-help it.'

They were passing through a narrow pass of orange rock. Simon looked at it disconsolately.

'My granny taught me some hayfever cures,' Esk said. 'We could try those.'

Simon shook his head. It looked touch and go whether it would fall off.

'Tried everything,' he said. 'Fine wwiwwi – magician I'd make, eh, can't even sss – utter the wowo – name.

'I could see where that would be a problem,' said Esk. She watched the scenery for a while, marshalling a train of thought.

'Is it, er, possible for a woman to be, you know, a wizard?' she said eventually.

Simon stared at her. She gave him a defiant look.

His throat strained. He was trying to find a sentence that didn't start with a W. In the end he was forced to make concessions.

'A curious idea,' he said. He thought some more, and started to laugh until Esk's expression warned him.

'Rather funny, really,' he added, but the laughter in his face faded and was replaced by a puzzled look. 'Never really t-thought about it, before.'

'Well? Can they?' You could have shaved with Esk's voice.

'Of course they can't. It is self-evident, child. Simon, return to your studies.'

Treatle pushed aside the curtain that led into the back of the wagon and climbed out on to the seat board.

The look of mild panic took up its familiar place on Simon's face. He gave Esk a pleading glance as Treatle took the reins from his hands, but she ignored him.

'Why not? What's so self-evident?'

Treatle turned and looked down at her. He hadn't really paid much attention before, she was simply just another figure around the campfires.

He was the Vice-Chancellor of Unseen University, and quite used to seeing vague scurrying figures getting on with essential but unimportant jobs like serving his meals and dusting his rooms. He was stupid, yes, in the particular way that very clever people can be stupid, and maybe he had all the tact of an avalanche and was as self-centred as a tornado, but it would never have occurred to him that children were important enough to be unkind to.

From long white hair to curly boots, Treatle was a wizard's wizard. He had the appropriate long bushy eyebrows, spangled robe and patriarchal beard that was only slightly spoiled by the yellow nicotine stains (wizards are celibate but, nevertheless, enjoy a good cigar).

'It will all become clear to you when you grow up,' he said. 'It's an amusing idea, of course, a nice play on words. A female wizard! You might as well invent a male witch!'

'Warlocks,' said Esk.

'Pardon me?'

'My granny says men can't be witches,' said Esk. 'She says if men tried to be witches they'd be wizards.'

'She sounds a very wise woman,' said Treatle.

'She says women should stick to what they're good at,' Esk went on.

'Very sensible of her.'

'She says if women were as good as men they'd be a lot better!'

Treatle laughed.

'She's a witch,' said Esk, and added in her mind: there, what do you think of that, Mr so-called clever-wizard?

'My dear good young lady, am I supposed to be shocked? I happen to have a great respect for witches.'

Esk frowned. He wasn't supposed to say that.

'You have?'

'Yes indeed. I happen to believe that witchcraft

is a fine career, for a woman. A very noble calling.'

'You do? I mean, it is?'

'Oh yes. Very useful in rural districts for, for people who are – having babies, and so forth. However, witches are not wizards. Witchcraft is Nature's way of allowing women access to the magical fluxes, but you must remember it is not *high* magic.'

'I see. Not high magic,' said Esk grimly.

'Oh, no. Witchcraft is very suitable for helping people through life, of course, but—'

'I expect women aren't really sensible enough to be wizards,' said Esk. 'I expect that's it, really.'

'I have nothing but the highest respect for women,' said Treatle, who hadn't noticed the fresh edge to Esk's tone. 'They are without parallel when, when—'

'For having babies and so forth?'

'There is that, yes,' the wizard conceded generously. 'But they can be a little unsettling at times. A little too excitable. High magic requires great clarity of thought, you see, and women's talents do not lie in that direction. Their brains tend to overheat. I am sorry to say there is only one door into wizardry and that is the main gate at Unseen University and no woman has ever passed through it.'

'Tell me,' said Esk, 'what good is high magic, exactly?'

Treatle smiled at her.

'High magic, my child,' he said, 'can give us everything we want.'

'Oh.'

'So put all this wizard nonsense out of your head,

all right?' Treatle gave her a benevolent smile. 'What is your name, child?'

'Eskarina.'

'And why do you go to Ankh, my dear?'

'I thought I might seek my fortune,' muttered Esk, 'but I think perhaps girls don't have fortunes to seek. Are you sure wizards give people what they want?'

'Of course. That is what high magic is for.'

'I see.'

The whole caravan was travelling only a little faster than walking pace. Esk jumped down, pulled the staff from its temporary hiding place among the bags and pails on the side of the wagon, and ran back along the line of carts and animals. Through her tears she caught a glimpse of Simon peering from the back of the wagon, an open book in his hands. He gave her a puzzled smile and started to say something, but she ran on and veered off the track.

Scrubby whinbrushes scratched her legs as she scrambled up a clay bank and then she was running free across a barren plateau, hemmed in by the orange cliffs.

She didn't stop until she was good and lost but the anger still burned brightly. She had been angry before, but never like this, normally anger was like the red flame you got when the forge was first lit, all glow and sparks, but this anger was different – it had the bellows behind it, and had narrowed to the tiny blue-white flame that cuts iron.

It made her body tingle. She had to do something about it or burst.

Why was it that when she heard Granny ramble on about witchcraft she longed for the cutting magic of wizardry, but whenever she heard Treatle speak in his high-pitched voice she would fight to the death for witchcraft? She'd be both, or none at all. And the more they intended to stop her, the more she wanted it.

She'd be a witch and a wizard *too*. And she would *show* them.

Esk sat down under a low-spreading juniper bush at the foot of a steep, sheer cliff, her mind seething with plans and anger. She could sense doors being slammed before she had barely begun to open them. Treatle was right; they wouldn't let her inside the University. Having a staff wasn't enough to be a wizard, there had to be training too, and no one was going to train her.

The midday sun beat down off the cliff and the air around Esk began to smell of bees and gin. She lay back, looking at the near-purple dome of the sky through the leaves and, eventually, she fell asleep.

One side-effect of using magic is that one tends to have realistic and disturbing dreams. There is a reason for this, but even thinking about it is enough to give a wizard nightmares.

The fact is that the minds of wizards can give thoughts a shape. Witches normally work with what actually exists in the world, but a wizard can, if he's good enough, put flesh on his imagination. This wouldn't cause any trouble if it wasn't for the fact that the little circle of candlelight loosely called 'the universe of time and space' is adrift in something much more unpleasant and unpredictable. Strange Things circle and grunt outside the flimsy stockades of normality; there are weird hootings and howlings in the deep crevices at the edge of Time. There are things so horrible that even the dark is afraid of them.

Most people don't know this and this is just as well because the world could not really operate if everyone stayed in bed with the blankets over their head, which is what would happen if people knew what horrors lay a shadow's width away.

The problem is people interested in magic and mysticism spend a lot of time loitering on the very edge of the light, as it were, which gets them noticed by the creatures from the Dungeon Dimensions who then try to use them in their indefatigable efforts to break into this particular Reality.

Most people can resist this, but the relentless probing by the Things is never stronger than when the subject is asleep.

Bel-Shamharoth, C'hulagen, the Insider – the hideous old dark gods of the Necrotelicomnicon, the book known to certain mad adepts by its true name of *Liber Paginarum Fulvarum*, are always ready to steal into a slumbering mind. The nightmares are often colourful and always unpleasant.

Esk had got used to them ever since that first dream after her first Borrowing, and familiarity had almost replaced terror. When she found herself sitting on a glittering, dusty plain under unexplained stars she knew it was time for another one.

'Drat,' she said. 'All right, come on then. Bring on the monsters. I just hope it isn't the one with his winkle on his face.'

But this time it seemed that the nightmare had changed. Esk looked around and saw, rearing up behind her, a tall black castle. Its turrets disappeared among the stars. Lights and fireworks and interesting music cascaded from its upper battlements. The huge double doors stood invitingly open. There seemed to be quite an amusing party going on in there.

She stood up, brushed the silver sand off her dress, and set off for the gates.

She had almost reached them when they slammed. They didn't appear to move; it was simply that in one instant they were lounging ajar, and the next they were tight shut with a clang that shook the horizons.

Esk reached out and touched them. They were black, and so cold that ice was beginning to form on them.

There was a movement behind her. She turned around and saw the staff, without its broomstick disguise, standing upright in the sand. Little worms of light crept around its polished wood and crept around the carvings no one could ever quite identify.

She picked it up and smashed it against the doors. There was a shower of octarine sparks, but the black metal was unscathed.

Esk's eyes narrowed. She held the staff at arm's length and concentrated until a thin line of fire leapt from the wood and burst against the gate. The ice flashed into steam but the darkness – she was sure

156

now that it wasn't metal – absorbed the power without so much as glowing. She doubled the energy, letting the staff put all its stored magic into a beam that was now so bright that she had to shut her eyes (and could still see it as a brilliant line in her mind).

Then it winked out.

After a few seconds Esk ran forward and touched the doors gingerly. The coldness nearly froze her fingers off.

And from the battlements above she could hear the sound of sniggering. Laughter wouldn't have been so bad, especially an impressive demonic laugh with lots of echo, but this was just – sniggering.

It went on for a long time. It was one of the most unpleasant sounds Esk had ever heard.

She woke up shivering. It was long after midnight and the stars looked damp and chilly; the air was full of the busy silence of the night, which is created by hundreds of small furry things treading very carefully in the hope of finding dinner while avoiding being the main course.

A crescent moon was setting and a thin grey glow towards the Rim of the world suggested that, against all probability, another day was on the cards.

Someone had wrapped Esk in a blanket.

'I know you're awake,' said the voice of Granny Weatherwax. 'You could make yourself useful and light a fire. There's damn all wood in these parts.'

Esk sat up, and clutched at the juniper bush. She felt light enough to float away.

'Fire?' she muttered.

'Yes. You know. Pointing the finger and whoosh,' said Granny sourly. She was sitting on a rock, trying to find a position that didn't upset her arthritis.

'I – I don't think I can.'

'You tell me?' said Granny cryptically.

The old witch leaned forward and put her hand on Esk's forehead; it was like being caressed by a sock full of warm dice.

'You're running a bit of a temperature,' she added. 'Too much hot sun and cold ground. That's forn parts for you.'

Esk let herself slump forward until her head lay in Granny's lap, with its familiar smells of camphor, mixed herbs and a trace of goat. Granny patted her in what she hoped was a soothing way.

After a while Esk said, in a low voice, 'They're not going to allow me into the University. A wizard told me, and I dreamed about it, and it was one of those true dreams. You know, like you told me, a maty-thing.'

'Metterfor,' said Granny calmly.

'One of them.'

'Did you think it would be easy?' asked Granny. 'Did you think you'd walk into their gates waving your staff? Here I am, I want to be a wizard, thank you very much?'

'He told me there's no women allowed in the University!'

'He's wrong.'

'No, I could tell he was telling the truth. You know, Granny, you can tell how—'

'Foolish child. All you could tell was that he thought he was telling the truth. The world isn't always as people see it.'

'I don't understand,' said Esk.

'You'll learn,' said Granny. 'Now tell me. This dream. They wouldn't let you into their university, right?'

'Yes, and they laughed!'

'And then you tried to burn down the doors?'

Esk turned her head in Granny's lap and opened a suspicious eye.

'How did you know?'

Granny smiled, but as a lizard would smile.

'I was miles away,' she said. 'I was bending my mind towards you, and suddenly you seemed to be everywhere. You shone out like a beacon, so you did. As for the fire – look around.'

In the halflight of dawn the plateau was a mass of baked clay. In front of Esk the cliff was glassy and must have flowed like tar under the onslaught; there were great gashes across it which had dripped molten rock and slag. When Esk listened she could hear the faint 'pink, pink' of cooling rock.

'Oh,' she said, 'did I do that?'

'So it would appear,' said Granny.

'But I was asleep! I was only dreaming!'

'It's the magic, said Granny. 'It's trying to find a way out. The witch magic and the wizard magic are, I don't know, sort of feeding off each other. I think.'

Esk bit her lip.

'What can I do?' she asked. 'I dream of all sorts of things!'

'Well, for a start we're going straight to the University,' decided Granny. 'They must be used to apprentices not being able to control magic and having hot dreams, else the place would have burned down years ago.'

She glanced towards the Rim, and then down at the broomstick beside her.

We will pass over the running up and down, the tightening of the broomstick's bindings, the muttered curses against dwarves, the brief moments of hope as the magic flickered fitfully, the horrible black feelings as it died, the tightening of the bindings again, the running again, the sudden catching of the spell, the scrambling aboard, the yelling, the take-off . . .

Esk clung to Granny with one hand and held her staff in the other as they, frankly, pottered along a few hundred feet above the ground. A few birds flew alongside them, interested in this new flying tree.

'Bugger off!' screamed Granny, taking off her hat and flapping it.

'We're not going very fast, Granny,' said Esk meekly.

'We're going quite fast enough for me!'

Esk looked around. Behind them the Rim was a blaze of gold, barred with cloud.

'I think we ought to go lower, Granny,' she said urgently. 'You said the broomstick won't fly in sunlight.' She glanced down at the landscape below them. It looked sharp and inhospitable. It also looked expectant.

'I know what I'm doing, Miss,' snapped Granny, gripping the broomstick hard and trying to make herself as light as possible.

It has already been revealed that light on the Discworld travels slowly, the result of its passage through the Disc's vast and ancient magical field.

So dawn isn't the sudden affair that it is on other worlds. The new day doesn't erupt, it sort of sloshes gently across the sleeping landscape in the same way that the tide sneaks in across the beach, melting the sandcastles of the night. It tends to flow around mountains. If the trees are close together it comes out of woods cut to ribbons and sliced with shadows.

An observer on some suitable high point, let's say for the sake of argument a wisp of cirro-stratus on the edge of space, would remark on how lovingly the light spreads across the land, how it leaps forward on the plains and slows down when it encounters high ground, how beautifully it . . .

Actually, there are some kinds of observers who, faced with all this beauty, will whine that you can't have heavy light and certainly wouldn't be able to see it, even if you could. To which one can only reply, so how come you're standing on a cloud?

So much for cynicism. But down on the Disc itself the broomstick barrelled forward on the cusp of dawn, dropping ever backward in the shadow of night.

'Granny!'

Day burst upon them. Ahead of the broomstick the rocks seemed to flash into flame as the light washed over them. Granny felt the stick lurch and stared with horrified fascination at the little scudding shadow below them. It was getting closer.

'What will happen when we hit the ground?'

'That depends if I can find some soft rocks,' said Granny in a preoccupied voice.

'The broomstick's going to crash! Can't we do anything?'

'Well, I suppose we could get off.'

'Granny,' said Esk, in the exasperated and remarkably adult voice children use to berate their wayward elders. 'I don't think you quite understand. I don't want to hit the ground. It's never done anything to me.'

Granny was trying to think of a suitable spell and regretting that headology didn't work on rocks, and had she detected the diamond edge to Esk's tone perhaps she wouldn't have said: 'Tell the broomstick that, then.'

And they would indeed have crashed. But she remembered in time to grab her hat and brace herself. The broomstick gave a shudder, tilted—

—and the landscape blurred.

It was really quite a short trip but one that Granny knew she would always remember, generally around three o'clock in the morning after eating rich food. She would remember the rainbow colours that hummed in the rushing air, the horrible heavy feeling, the impression that something very big and heavy was sitting on the universe.

She would remember Esk's laughter. She would remember, despite her best efforts, the way the ground sped below them, whole mountain ranges flashing past with nasty zipping noises.

Most of all, she would remember *catching up* with the night.

It appeared ahead of her, a ragged line of darkness running ahead of the remorseless morning. She stared in horrified fascination as the line became a blot, a stain, a whole continent of blackness that raced towards them.

For an instant they were poised on the crest of the dawn as it broke in silent thunder on the land. No surfer ever rode such a wave, but the broomstick broke through the broil of light and shot smoothly through into the coolness beyond.

Granny let herself breathe out.

Darkness took some of the terror out of the flight. It also meant that if Esk lost interest the broomstick ought to be able to fly under its own rather rusty magic.

'.' Granny said, and cleared her bone-dry throat for a second try. 'Esk?'

'This is fun, isn't it? I wonder how I make it happen?'

'Yes, fun,' said Granny weakly. 'But can I fly the

stick, please? I don't want us to go over the Edge. Please?'

'Is it true that there's a giant waterfall all around the Edge of the world, and you can look down and see stars?' said Esk.

'Yes. Can we slow down now?'

'I'd like to see it.'

'No! I mean, no, not now.'

The broomstick slowed. The rainbow bubble around it vanished with an audible pop. Without a jolt, without so much as a shudder, Granny found herself flying at a respectable speed again.

Granny had built a solid reputation on always knowing the answer to everything. Getting her to admit ignorance, even to herself, was an astonishing achievement. But the worm of curiosity was chewing at the apple of her mind.

'How,' she said at last, 'did you do that?'

There was a thoughtful silence behind her. Then Esk said: 'I don't know. I just needed it, and it was in my head. Like when you remember something you've forgotten.'

'Yes, but *how*?'

'I – I don't know. I just had a picture of how I wanted things to be, and, and I, sort of – went into the picture.'

Granny stared into the night. She had never heard of magic like that, but it sounded awfully powerful and probably lethal. Went into the picture! Of course, all magic changed the world in some way, wizards thought there was no other use for it – they didn't truck with the idea of leaving the world as it was and changing the people – but this sounded more literal. It needed thinking about. On the ground.

For the first time in her life Granny wondered whether there might be something important in all these books people were setting such store by these days, although she was opposed to books on strict moral grounds, since she had heard that many of them were written by dead people and therefore it stood to reason reading them would be as bad as necromancy. Among the many things in the infinitely varied universe with which Granny did not hold was talking to dead people, who by all accounts had enough troubles of their own.

But not, she was inclined to feel, as many as her. She looked down bemusedly at the dark ground and wondered vaguely why the stars were below her.

For a cardiac moment she wondered if they had indeed flown over the Edge, and then she realized that the thousands of little pinpoints below her were too yellow, and flickered. Besides, whoever heard of stars arranged in such a neat pattern?

'It's very pretty,' said Esk. 'Is it a city?'

Granny scanned the ground wildly. If it was a city, then it was too big. But now she had time to think about it, it certainly smelled like a lot of people.

The air around them reeked of incense and grain and spices and beer, but mainly of the sort of smell that was caused by a high water-table, thousands of people, and a robust approach to drainage.

She mentally shook herself. The day was hard on

their heels. She looked for an area where the torches were dim and widely spaced, reasoning that this would mean a poor district and poor people did not object to witches, and gently pointed the broom handle downwards.

She managed to get within five feet of the ground before dawn arrived for the second time.

The gates were indeed big and black and looked as if they were made out of solid darkness.

Granny and Esk stood among the crowds that thronged the square outside the University and stared up at them. Finally Esk said: 'I can't see how people get in.'

'Magic, I expect,' said Granny sourly. 'That's wizards for you. Anyone else would have bought a doorknocker.'

She waved her broomstick in the direction of the tall doors.

'You've got to say some hocuspocus word to get in, I shouldn't wonder,' she added.

They had been in Ankh-Morpork for three days and Granny was beginning to enjoy herself, much to her surprise. She had found them lodgings in The Shades, an ancient part of the city whose inhabitants were largely nocturnal and never enquired about one another's business because curiosity not only killed the cat but threw it in the river with weights tied to its feet. The lodgings were on the top floor next to the well-guarded premises of a respectable dealer in stolen property because, as Granny had heard, good fences make good neighbours.

The Shades, in brief, were an abode of discredited gods and unlicensed thieves, ladies of the night and pedlars in exotic goods, alchemists of the mind and strolling mummers; in short, all the grease on civilization's axle.

And yet, despite the fact that these people tend to appreciate the soft magics, there was a remarkable shortage of witches. Within hours the news of Granny's arrival had seeped through the quarter and a stream of people crept, sidled or strutted towards her door, seeking potions and charms and news of the future and various personal and specialized services that witches traditionally provide for those whose lives are a little clouded or full of stormy weather.

She was at first annoyed, and then embarrassed, and then flattered; her clients had money, which was useful, but they also paid in respect, and that was a rock-hard currency.

In short, Granny was even wondering about the possibility of acquiring slightly larger premises with a bit of garden and sending for her goats. The smell might be a problem, but the goats would just have to put up with it.

They had visited the sights of Ankh-Morpork, its crowded docks, its many bridges, its souks, its casbahs, its streets lined with nothing but temples. Granny had counted the temples with a thoughtful look in her eyes; gods were always demanding that their followers acted other than according to their true natures, and the human fallout this caused made plenty of work for witches.

The terrors of civilization had so far failed to materialize, although a cutpurse had tried to make off with Granny's handbag. To the amazement of passers-by Granny called him back, and back he came, fighting his feet which had totally ceased to obey him. No-one quite saw what happened to her eyes when she stared into his face or heard the words she whispered in his cowering ear, but he gave her back all her money plus quite a lot of money belonging to other people, and before she let him go had promised to have a shave, stand up straight, and be a better person for the rest of his life. By nighfall Granny's description was circulated to all the chapter houses of the Guild of Thieves, Cutpurses, Housebreakers and Allied Trades*, with strict instructions to avoid her at all costs. Thieves, being largely creatures of the night themselves, know trouble when it stares them in the face.

---

* A very respectable body which in fact represented the major law enforcement agency in the city. The reason for this is as follows: the Guild was given an annual quota which represented a socially acceptable level of thefts, muggings and assassinations, and in return saw to it in very definite and final ways that unofficial crime was not only rapidly stamped out but knifed, garrotted, dismembered and left around the city in an assortment of paper bags as well. This was held to be a cheap and enlightened arrangement, except by those malcontents who *were* actually mugged or assassinated and refused to see it as their social duty, and it enabled the city's thieves to plan a decent career structure, entrance examinations and codes of conduct similar to those adopted by the city's other professions – which, the gap not being very wide in any case, they rapidly came to resemble.

Granny had also written two more letters to the University. There had been no reply.

'I liked the forest best,' said Esk.

'I dunno,' said Granny. 'This is a bit like the forest, really. Anyway, people certainly appreciate a witch here.'

'They're very friendly,' Esk conceded. 'You know the house down the street, where that fat lady lives with all those young ladies you said were her relatives?'

'Mrs Palm,' said Granny cautiously. 'Very respectable lady.'

'People come to visit them *all night long*. I watched. I'm surprised they get any sleep.'

'Um,' said Granny.

'It must be a trial for the poor woman with all those daughters to feed, too. I think people could be more considerate.'

'Well now,' said Granny, 'I'm not sure that—'

She was rescued by the arrival at the gates of the University of a large, brightly painted wagon. Its driver reined in the oxen a few feet from Granny and said: 'Excuse me, my good woman, but would you be so kind as to move, please?'

Granny stepped aside, affronted by this display of downright politeness and particularly upset at being thought of as anyone's good woman, and the driver saw Esk.

It was Treatle. He grinned like a worried snake.

'I say. It's the young lady who thinks women should be wizards, isn't it?'

'Yes,' said Esk, ignoring a sharp kick on the ankle from Granny.

'What fun. Come to join us, have you?'

'Yes,' said Esk, and then because something about Treatle's manner seemed to demand it, she added, 'sir. Only we can't get in.'

'We?' said Treatle, and then glanced at Granny. 'Oh, yes, of course. This would be your aunt?'

'My granny. Only not really my granny, just sort of everyone's granny.'

Granny gave a stiff nod.

'Well, we cannot have this,' said Treatle, in a voice as hearty as a plum pudding. 'My word, no. Our first lady wizard left on the doorstep? That would be a disgrace. May I accompany you?'

Granny grasped Esk firmly by the shoulder.

'If it's all the same to you—' she began. But Esk twisted out of her grip and ran towards the cart.

'You can really take me in?' she said, her eyes shining.

'Of course. I am sure the heads of the orders will be most gratified to meet you. Most astonished and astounded,' he said, and gave a little laugh.

'Eskarina Smith—' said Granny, and then stopped. She looked at Treatle.

'I don't know what is in your mind, Mr Wizard, but I don't like it,' she said. 'Esk, you know where we live. Be a fool if you must, but you might at least be your *own* fool.'

She turned on her heel and strode off across the square.

'What a remarkable woman,' said Treatle, vaguely. 'I see you still have your broomstick. Capital.'

He let go of the reins for a moment and made a complicated sign in the air with both hands.

The big doors swung back, revealing a wide court-yard surrounded by lawns. Behind them was a great rambling building, or buildings: it was hard to tell, because it didn't look so much as if it had been designed as that a lot of buttresses, arches, towers, bridges, domes, cupolas and so forth had huddled together for warmth.

'Is that it?' said Esk. 'It looks sort of – melted.'

'Yes, that's it,' said Treatle. 'Alma mater, gaudy armours eagle tour and so on. Of course, it's a lot bigger inside than out, like an iceberg or so I'm given to understand, I've never seen the things. Unseen University, only of course a lot of it is unseen. Just go in the back and fetch Simon, will you?'

Esk pushed aside the heavy curtains and peered into the back of the wagon. Simon was lying on a pile of rugs, reading a very large book and making notes on scraps of paper.

He looked up, and gave her a worried smile.

'Is that you?' he said.

'Yes,' said Esk, with conviction.

'We thought you'd left us. Everyone thought you were riding with everyone else and then wwwwhen we stopped—'

'I sort of caught up. I think Mr Treatle wants you to come and look at the University.'

'We're here?' he said, and gave her an odd look: '*You're* here?'

'Yes.'

'How?'

'Mr Treatle invited me in, he said everyone would be astounded to meet me.' Uncertainty flashed a fin in the depths of her eyes. 'Was he right?'

Simon looked down at his book, and dabbed at his running eyes with a red handkerchief.

'He has t-these little f-fancies,' he muttered, 'bbbut he's not a bad person.'

Bewildered, Esk looked down at the yellowed pages open in front of the boy. They were full of complicated red and black symbols which in some inexplicable way were as potent and unpleasant as a ticking parcel, but which nevertheless drew the eye in the same way that a really bad accident does. One felt that one would like to know their purpose, while at the same time suspecting that if you found out you would really prefer not to have done.

Simon saw her expression and hastily shut the book.

'Just some magic,' he mumbled. 'Something I'm wwwww—'

'—working—' said Esk, automatically.

'Thank you. On.'

'It must be quite interesting, reading books,' said Esk.

'Sort of. Can't you read, Esk?'

The astonishment in his voice stung her.

'I expect so,' she said defiantly. 'I've never tried.'

Esk wouldn't have known what a collective noun was if it had spat in her eye, but she knew there was a herd of goats and a coven of witches. She didn't know what you called a lot of wizards. An order of wizards? A conspiracy? A circle?

Whatever it was, it filled the University. Wizards strolled among the cloisters and sat on benches under the trees. Young wizards scuttled along pathways as bells rang, with their arms full of books or – in the case of senior students – with their books flapping through the air after them. The air had the greasy feel of magic and tasted of tin.

Esk walked along between Treatle and Simon and drank it all in. It wasn't just that there was magic in the air, but it was tamed and working, like a millrace. It was power, but it was harnessed.

Simon was as excited as she was, but it showed only because his eyes watered more and his stutter got worse. He kept stopping to point out the various colleges and research buildings.

One was quite low and brooding, with high narrow windows.

'T-that's the l-l-library,' said Simon, his voice bursting with wonder and respect. 'Can I have a l-l-look?'

'Plenty of time for that later,' said Treatle. Simon gave the building a wistful look.

'All the b-books of magic ever written,' he whispered.

'Why are the windows barred?' said Esk.

Simon swallowed. 'Um, b-because b-books of m-magic aren't like other b-books, they lead a—'

'That's enough,' snapped Treatle. He looked

down at Esk as if he had just noticed her, and frowned.

'Why are you here?'

'You invited me in,' said Esk.

'Me? Oh, yes. Of course. Sorry, mind wandering. The young lady who wants to be a wizard. Let us see, shall we?'

He led the way up a broad flight of steps to an impressive pair of doors. At least, they were designed to be impressive. The designer had invested deeply in heavy locks, curly hinges, brass studs and an intricately-carved archway to make it absolutely clear to anyone entering that they were not very important people at all.

He was a wizard. He had forgotten the door-knocker.

Treatle rapped on the door with his staff. It hesitated for a while, and then slowly slid back its bolts and swung open.

The hall was full of wizards and boys. And boys' parents.

There are two ways of getting into Unseen University (in fact there are three, but at this time wizards hadn't realized it).

The first is to achieve some great work of magic, such as the recovery of an ancient and powerful relic or the invention of a totally new spell, but in these times it was seldom done. In the past there had been great wizards capable of forming whole new spells from the chaotic raw magic of the world, wizards from whom as it were all the spells of wizardry had flowed, but those days had gone; there were no more sourcerers.

So the more typical method was to be sponsored by a senior and respected wizard, after a suitable period of apprenticeship.

Competition was stiff for a University place and the honour and privileges an Unseen degree could bring. Many of the boys milling around the hall, and launching minor spells at each other, would fail and have to spend their lives as lowly *magicians*, mere magical technologists with defiant beards and leather patches on their elbows who congregated in small jealous groups at parties.

Not for them the coveted pointy hat with optional astrological symbols, or the impressive robes, or the staff of authority. But at least they could look down on *conjurers*, who tended to be jolly and fat and inclined to drop their aitches and drink beer and go around with sad thin women in spangly tights and really infuriate magicians by not realizing how lowly they were and kept telling them jokes. Lowliest of all – apart from witches, of course – were thaumaturgists, who never got any schooling at all. A thaumaturgist could just about be trusted to wash out an alembic. Many spells required things like mould from a corpse dead of crushing, or the semen of a living tiger, or the root of a plant that gave an ultrasonic scream when it was uprooted. Who was sent to get them? Right.

It is a common error to refer to the lower magical ranks as hedge wizards. In fact hedge wizardry is a very honoured and specialized form of magic that attracts silent, thoughtful men of the druidical persuasion and topiaric inclinations. If you invited a hedge wizard to a party he would spend half the evening talking to your potted plant. And he would spend the other half listening.

Esk noticed that there were some women in the hall, because even young wizards had mothers and sisters. Whole families had turned up to bid the favoured sons farewell. There was a considerable blowing of noses, wiping of tears and the clink of coins as proud fathers tucked a little spending money into their offspring's hands.

Very senior wizards were perambulating among the crowds, talking to the sponsoring wizards and examining the prospective students.

Several of them pushed through the throng to meet Treatle, moving like gold-trimmed galleons under full sail. They bowed gravely to him and looked approvingly at Simon.

'This is young Simon, is it?' said the fattest of them, beaming at the boy. 'We've heard great reports of you, young man. Eh? What?'

'Simon, bow to Archchancellor Cutangle, Archmage of the Wizards of the Silver Star,' said Treatle. Simon bowed apprehensively.

Cutangle looked at him benevolently. 'We've heard great things about you, my boy,' he said. 'All this mountain air must be good for the brain, eh?'

He laughed. The wizards around him laughed. Treatle laughed. Which Esk thought was rather funny, because there wasn't anything particularly amusing happening.

'I ddddon't know, ssss—'

'From what we hear it must be the only thing you don't know, lad!' said Cutangle, his jowls waggling. There was another carefully timed bout of laughter.

Cutangle patted Simon on the shoulder.

'This is the scholarship boy,' he said. 'Quite astounding results, never seen better. Self-taught, too. Astonishing, what? Isn't that so, Treatle?'

'Superb, Archchancellor.'

Cutangle looked around at the watching wizards.

'Perhaps you could give us a sample,' he said. 'A little demonstration, perhaps?'

Simon looked at him in animal panic.

'A-actually I'm not very g-g-g—'

'Now, now,' said Cutangle, in what he probably really did think was an encouraging tone of voice. 'Do not be afraid. Take your time. When you are ready.'

Simon licked his dry lips and gave Treatle a look of mute appeal.

'Um,' he said, 'y-you s-s-s-s—.' He stopped and swallowed hard. 'The f-f-f-f—'

His eyes bulged. The tears streamed from his eyes, and his shoulders heaved.

Treatle patted him reassuringly on the back.

'Hayfever,' he explained. 'Don't seem to be able to cure it. Tried everything.'

Simon swallowed, and nodded. He waved Treatle away with his long white hands and closed his eyes.

For a few seconds nothing happened. He stood

with his lips moving soundlessly, and then silence spread out from him like candlelight. Ripples of noiselessness washed across the crowds in the hall, striking the walls with all the force of a blown kiss and then curling back in waves. People watched their companions mouthing silently and then went red with effort when their own laughter was as audible as a gnat's squeak.

Tiny motes of light winked into existence around his head. They whirled and spiralled in a complex three-dimensional dance, and then formed a shape.

In fact it seemed to Esk that the shape had been there all the time, waiting for her eyes to see it, in the same way that a perfectly innocent cloud can suddenly become, without changing in any way, a whale or a ship or a face.

The shape around Simon's head was the world.

That was quite clear, although the glitter and rush of the little lights blurred some of the detail. But there was Great A'Tuin the sky turtle, with the four Elephants on its back, and on them the Disc itself. There was the sparkle of the great waterfall around the edge of the world, and there at the very hub a tiny needle of rock that was the great mountain Cori Celesti, where the gods lived.

The image expanded and homed in on the Circle Sea and then on Ankh itself, the little lights flowing away from Simon and winking out of existence a few feet from his head. Now they showed the city from the air, rushing towards the watchers. There was the

University itself, growing larger. There was the Great Hall—

—there were the people, watching silent and open-mouthed, and Simon himself, outlined in specks of silver light. And a tiny sparkling image in the air around him, and *that* image contained an image and another and another—

There was a feeling that the universe had been turned inside out in all dimensions at once. It was a bloated, swollen sensation. It sounded as though the whole world had said 'gloop'.

The walls faded. So did the floor. The paintings of former great mages, all scrolls and beards and slightly constipated frowns, vanished. The tiles underfoot, a rather nice black and white pattern, evaporated – to be replaced by fine sand, grey as moonlight and cold as ice. Strange and unexpected stars glittered over-head; on the horizon were low hills, eroded not by wind or rain in this weatherless place but by the soft sandpaper of Time itself.

No-one else seemed to have noticed. No-one else, in fact, seemed alive. Esk was surrounded by people as still and silent as statues.

And they weren't alone. There were other – Things – behind them, and more were appearing all the time. They had no shape, or rather they seemed to be taking their shapes at random from a variety of creatures; they gave the impression that they had heard about arms and legs and jaws and claws and organs but didn't really know how they all fitted together. Or didn't care. Or were so hungry they hadn't bothered to find out.

They made a sound like a swarm of flies.

They were the creatures out of her dreams, come to feed on magic. She knew they weren't interested in her now, except in the nature of an after-dinner mint. Their whole concentration was focused on Simon, who was totally unaware of their presence.

Esk kicked him smartly on the ankle.

The cold desert vanished. The real world rushed back. Simon opened his eyes, smiled faintly, and gently fell backwards into Esk's arms.

A buzz went up from the wizards, and several of them started to clap. No-one seemed to have noticed anything odd, apart from the silver lights.

Cutangle shook himself, and raised a hand to quell the crowd.

'Quite – astonishing,' he said to Treatle. 'You say he worked it out all by himself?'

'Indeed, lord.'

'No-one helped him at all?'

'There was no one to help him,' said Treatle. 'He was just wandering from village to village, doing small spells. But only if people paid him in books or paper.'

Cutangle nodded. 'It was no illusion,' he said, 'yet he didn't use his hands. What was he saying to himself? Do you know?'

'He says it's just words to make his mind work properly,' said Treatle, and shrugged. 'I can't understand half of what he says and that's a fact. He says he's having to invent words because there aren't any for the things he's doing.'

Cutangle glanced sideways at his fellow mages. They nodded.

'It will be an honour to admit him to the University,' he said. 'Perhaps you would tell him so when he wakes up.'

He felt a tugging at his robe, and looked down.

'Excuse me,' said Esk.

'Hallo, young lady,' said Cutangle, in a sugarmouse voice. 'Have you come to see your brother enter the University?'

'He's not my brother,' said Esk. There were times when the world had seemed to be full of brothers, but this wasn't one of them.

'Are you important?' she said.

Cutangle looked at his colleagues, and beamed. There were fashions in wizardry, just like anything else; sometimes wizards were thin and gaunt and talked to animals (the animals didn't listen, but it's the thought that counts) while at other times they tended towards the dark and saturnine, with little black pointed beards. Currently Aldermanic was In. Cutangle swelled with modesty.

'Quite important,' he said. 'One does one's best in the service of one's fellow man. Yes. Quite important, I would say.'

'I want to be a wizard,' said Esk.

The lesser wizards behind Cutangle stared at her as if she was a new and interesting kind of beetle. Cutangle's face went red and his eyes bulged. He looked down at Esk and seemed to be holding his breath. Then he started to laugh. It started somewhere down in his extensive stomach regions and worked its way up, echoing from rib to rib and causing minor wizard-quakes across his chest until it burst forth in a series of strangled snorts. It was quite fascinating to watch, that laugh. It had a personality all of its own.

But he stopped when he saw Esk's stare. If the laugh was a music-hall clown then Esk's determined squint was a whitewash bucket on a fast trajectory.

'A wizard?' he said. '*You* want to be a wizard?'

'Yes,' said Esk, pushing the dazed Simon into Treatle's reluctant arms. 'I'm the eighth son of an eighth son. I mean daughter.'

The wizards around her were looking at one another and whispering. Esk tried to ignore them.

'What did she say?'

'Is she serious?'

'I always think children are so delightful at that age, don't you?'

'You're the eighth son of an eighth daughter?' said Cutangle. 'Really?'

'The other way around, only not exactly,' said Esk, defiantly.

Cutangle dabbed his eyes with a handkerchief.

'This is quite fascinating,' he said. 'I don't think I've ever heard of something quite like this before. Eh?'

He looked around at his growing audience. The people at the back couldn't see Esk and were craning to check if some interesting magic was going on. Cutangle was at a loss.

'Well, now,' he said. 'You want to be a wizard?'

'I keep telling everyone but no one seems to listen,' said Esk.

'How old are you, little girl?'

'Nine.'

'And you want to be a wizard when you grow up.'

'I want to be a wizard *now*,' said Esk firmly. 'This *is* the right place, isn't it?'

Cutangle looked at Treatle and winked.

'I saw that,' said Esk.

'I don't think there's ever been a lady wizard before,' said Cutangle. 'I rather think it might be against the lore. Wouldn't you rather be a witch? I understand it's a fine career for girls.'

A minor wizard behind him started to laugh. Esk gave him a look.

'Being a witch is quite good,' she conceded. 'But I think wizards have more fun. What do you think?'

'I think you are a very singular little girl,' said Cutangle.

'What does that mean?'

'It means there's only one of you,' said Treatle.

'That's right,' said Esk, 'and I still want to be a wizard.'

Words failed Cutangle. 'Well, you can't,' he said. 'The very idea!'

He drew himself up to his full width and turned away. Something tugged at his robe.

'Why not?' said a voice.

He turned.

'Because,' he said, slowly and deliberately, 'because . . . the whole idea is completely laughable, that's why.

And it's absolutely against the lore!'

'But I can do wizard magic!' said Esk, the faintest suggestion of a tremble in her voice.

Cutangle bent down until his face was level with hers.

'No you can't,' he hissed. 'Because you are not a wizard. Women aren't wizards, do I make myself clear?'

'Watch,' said Esk.

She extended her right hand with the fingers spread and sighted along it until she spotted the statue of Malich the Wise, the founder of the University. Instinctively the wizards between her and it edged out of the way, and then felt rather silly.

'I mean it,' she said.

'Go away, little girl,' said Cutangle.

'Right,' said Esk. She squinted hard at the statue and concentrated . . .

The great doors of Unseen University are made of octiron, a metal so unstable that it can only exist in a universe saturated with raw magic. They are impregnable to all force save magic: no fire, no battering ram, no army can breach them.

Which is why most ordinary visitors to the University use the back door, which is made of perfectly normal wood and doesn't go around terrorizing people, or even stand still terrorizing people. It had a proper knocker and everything.

Granny examined the doorposts carefully and gave

a grunt of satisfaction when she spotted what she was looking for. She hadn't doubted that it *would* be there, cunningly concealed by the natural grain of the wood.

She grasped the knocker, which was shaped like a dragon's head, and rapped smartly, three times. After a while the door was opened by a young woman with her mouth full of clothes-pegs.

'Ot oo oo ont?' she enquired.

Granny bowed, giving the girl a chance to take in the pointy black hat with the batwing hatpins. It had an impressive effect: she blushed and, peering out into the quiet alley-way, hurriedly motioned Granny inside.

There was a big mossy courtyard on the other side of the wall, crisscrossed with washing lines. Granny had the chance to become one of the very few women to learn what it really is that wizards wear under their robes, but modestly averted her eyes and followed the girl across the flagstones and down a wide flight of steps.

They led into a long, high tunnel lined with archways and, currently, full of steam. Granny caught sight of long lines of washtubs in the big rooms off to the sides; the air had the warm fat smell of ironing. A gaggle of girls carrying washbaskets pushed past her and hurried up the steps – then stopped, halfway up, and turned slowly to look at her.

Granny set her shoulders back and tried to look as mysterious as possible.

Her guide, who still hadn't got rid of her clothes-pegs, led her down a side-passage into a room that was a maze of shelves piled with laundry. In the very centre of the maze, sitting at a table, was a very fat woman with a ginger wig. She had been writing in a very large laundry book – it was still open in front of her – but was currently inspecting a large stained vest.

'Have you tried bleaching?' she asked.

'Yes, m'm,' said the maid beside her.

'What about tincture of myrryt?'

'Yes, m'm. It just turned it blue, m'm.'

'Well, it's a new one on me,' said the laundry woman. 'And Ay've seen brimstone and soot and dragon blood and demon blood and Aye don't know what else.' She turned the vest over and read the nametape carefully sewn inside. 'Hmm. Granpone the White. He's going to be Granpone the Grey if he doesn't take better care of his laundry. Aye tell you, girl, a white magician is just a black magician with a good housekeeper. Take it—'

She caught sight of Granny, and stopped.

'Ee ocked hat hee oor,' said Granny's guide, dropping a hurried curtsey. 'Oo ed hat—'

'Yes, yes, thank you, Ksandra, you may go,' said the fat woman. She stood up and beamed at Granny, and with an almost perceptible click wound her voice up several social classes.

'Pray hexcuse us,' she said. 'You find us hall at sixes and sevens, it being washing day and heverything. His this a courtesy call or may I make so bold as to ask—' she lowered her voice – 'his there a message from the Hother Sade?'

Granny looked blank, but only a fraction of a second. The witchmarks on the doorpost had said that the housekeeper welcomed witches and was particularly anxious for news of her four husbands; she was also in random pursuit of a fifth, hence the ginger wig and, if Granny's ears weren't deceiving her, the creak of enough whalebone to infuriate an entire ecology movement. Gullible and foolish, the signs had said. Granny withheld judgement, because city witches didn't seem that bright themselves.

The housekeeper must have mistaken her expression.

'Don't be afraid,' she said. 'May staff have distinct instructions to welcome witches, although of course *they upstairs* don't approve. No doubt you would like a cup of tea and something to eat?'

Granny bowed solemnly.

'And Aye will see if we can't find a nice bundle of old clothes for you, too,' the housekeeper beamed.

'Old clothes? Oh. Yes. Thank you, m'm.'

The housekeeper swept forward with a sound like an elderly tea clipper in a gale, and beckoned Granny to follow her.

'Aye'll have the tea brought to my flat. Tea with a lot of tea-leaves.'

Granny stumped along after her. Old clothes? Did this fat woman really mean it? The nerve! Of course, if they were good quality . . .

There seemed to be a whole world under the University. It was a maze of cellars, coldrooms, still-rooms, kitchens and sculleries, and every inhabitant was either carrying something, pumping something, pushing something or just standing around and shouting. Granny caught glimpses of rooms full of ice, and others glowing with the heat from red-hot cooking stoves, wall-sized. Bakeries smelled of new bread and taprooms smelled of old beer. Everything smelled of sweat and wood-smoke.

The housekeeper led her up an old spiral staircase and unlocked the door with one of the large number of keys that hung from her belt.

The room inside was pink and frilly. There were frills on things that no one in their right mind would frill. It was like being inside candyfloss.

'Very nice,' said Granny. And, because she felt it was expected of her, 'Tasteful.' She looked around for something unfrilly to sit on, and gave up.

'Whatever am Aye thinking of?' the housekeeper trilled. 'Aye'm Mrs Whitlow but I expect you know, of course. And Aye have the honour to be addressing—?'

'Eh? Oh, Granny Weatherwax,' said Granny. The frills were getting to her. They gave pink a bad name.

'Ay'm psychic myself, of course,' said Mrs Whitlow.

Granny had nothing against fortune-telling provided it was done badly by people with no talent for it. It was a different matter if people who ought to know better did it, though. She considered that the future was a frail enough thing at best, and if people looked at it hard they changed it. Granny had some quite complex theories about space and time and why they shouldn't be tinkered with, but fortunately good fortune-tellers were rare and anyway people preferred bad fortune-tellers, who could be relied upon for the correct dose of uplift and optimism.

Granny knew all about bad fortune-telling. It was harder than the real thing. You needed a good imagination.

She couldn't help wondering if Mrs Whitlow was a born witch who somehow missed her training. She was certainly laying siege to the future. There was a crystal ball under a sort of pink frilly tea cosy, and several sets of divinatory cards, and a pink velvet bag of rune stones, and one of those little tables on wheels that no prudent witch would touch with a ten-foot broomstick, and – Granny wasn't sure on this point – either some special dried monkey turds from a llamassary or some dried llama turds from a monastery, which apparently could be thrown in such a way as to reveal the sum total of knowledge and wisdom in the universe. It was all rather sad.

'Or there's the tea-leaves, of course,' said Mrs Whitlow, indicating the big brown pot on the table between them. 'Aye know witches often prefer them, but they always seem so, well, *common* to me. No offence meant.'

There probably wasn't any offence meant, at that, thought Granny. Mrs Whitlow was giving her the sort of look generally used by puppies when they're not sure what to expect next, and are beginning to worry that it may be the rolled-up newspaper.

She picked up Mrs Whitlow's cup and had started

to peer into it when she caught the disappointed expression that floated across the housekeeper's face like a shadow across a snowfield. Then she remembered what she was doing, and turned the cup widdershins three times, made a few vague passes over it and mumbled a charm (which she normally used to cure mastitis in elderly goats, but never mind). This display of obvious magical talent seemed to cheer up Mrs Whitlow no end.

Granny wasn't normally very good at tea-leaves, but she squinted at the sugar-encrusted mess at the bottom of the cup and let her mind wander. What she really needed now was a handy rat or even a cockroach that happened to be somewhere near Esk, so that she could Borrow its mind.

What Granny actually found was that the University had a mind of its own.

It is well known that stone can think, because the whole of electronics is based on that fact, but in some universes men spend ages looking for other intelligences in the sky without once looking under their feet. That is because they've got the time-span all wrong. From stone's point of view the universe is hardly created and mountain ranges are bouncing up and down like organ-stops while continents zip backwards and forwards in general high spirits, crashing into each other from the sheer joy of momentum and getting their rocks off. It is going to be quite some time before stone notices its disfiguring little skin disease and starts to scratch, which is just as well.

The rocks from which Unseen University was built, however, have been absorbing magic for several thousand years and all that random power has had to go somewhere.

The University has, in fact, developed a personality.

Granny could sense it like a big and quite friendly animal, just waiting to roll over on its roof and have its floor scratched. It was paying no attention to her, however. It was watching Esk.

Granny found the child by following the threads of the University's attention and watched in fascination as the scenes unfolded in the Great Hall . . .

'—in there?'

The voice came from a long way away.

'Mmph?'

'Aye said, what do you see in there?' repeated Mrs Whitlow.

'Eh?'

'Aye *said*, what do—'

'Oh.' Granny reeled her mind in, quite confused. The trouble with *Borrowing* another mind was, you always felt out of place when you got back to your own body, and Granny was the first person ever to read the mind of a building. Now she was feeling big and gritty and full of passages.

'Are you all right?'

Granny nodded, and opened her windows. She extended her east and west wings and tried to concentrate on the tiny cup held in her pillars.

Fortunately Mrs Whitlow put her plaster

complexion and stony silence down to occult powers at work, while Granny found that a brief exposure to the vast silicon memory of the University had quite stimulated her imagination.

In a voice like a draughty corridor, which made the housekeeper very impressed, she wove a future full of keen young men fighting for Mrs Whitlow's ample favours. She also spoke very quickly, because what she had seen in the Great Hall made her anxious to go around to the main gates again.

'There is another thing,' she added.

'Yes? Yes?'

'I see you hiring a new servant – you do hire the servants here, don't you? Right – and this one is a young girl, very economical, very good worker, can turn her hand to anything.'

'What about her, then?' said Mrs Whitlow, already savouring Granny's surprisingly graphic descriptions of her future and drunk with curiosity.

'The spirits are a little unclear on this point,' said Granny, 'but it is very important that you hire her.'

'No problem there,' said Mrs Whitlow, 'can't keep servants here, you know, not for long. It's all the magic. It *leaks* down here, you know. Especially from the library, where they keep all them magical books. Two of the top floor maids walked out yesterday, actually, they said they were fed up going to bed not knowing what shape they would wake up in the morning. The senior wizards turn them back, you know. But it's not the same.'

'Yes, well, the spirits say this young lady won't be

any trouble as far as that is concerned,' said Granny grimly.

'If she can sweep and scrub she's welcome, Aye'm sure,' said Mrs Whitlow, looking puzzled.

'She even brings her own broom. According to the spirits, that is.'

'How very helpful. When is this young lady going to arrive?'

'Oh, soon, soon – that's what the spirits say.'

A faint suspicion clouded the housekeeper's face. 'This ain't the sort of thing spirits normally say. Where do they say that, exactly?'

'Here,' said Granny. 'Look, the little cluster of tea-leaves between the sugar and this crack here. Am I right?'

Their eyes met. Mrs Whitlow might have had her weaknesses but she was quite tough enough to rule the below-stairs world of the University. However, Granny could outstare a snake; after a few seconds the housekeeper's eyes began to water.

'Yes, Aye expect you are,' she said meekly, and fished a handkerchief from the recesses of her bosom.

'Well then,' said Granny, sitting back and replacing the teacup in its saucer.

'There are plenty of opportunities here for a young woman willing to work hard,' said Mrs Whitlow. 'Aye myself started as a maid, you know.'

'We all do,' said Granny vaguely. 'And now I must be going.' She stood up and reached for her hat.

'But—'

'Must hurry. Urgent appointment,' said Granny

over her shoulder as she hurried down the steps.

'There's a bundle of old clothes—'

Granny paused, her instincts battling for mastery.

'Any black velvet?'

'Yes, and some silk.'

Granny wasn't sure she approved of silk, she'd heard it came out of a caterpillar's bottom, but black velvet had a powerful attraction. Loyalty won.

'Put it on one side, I may call again,' she shouted, and ran down the corridor.

Cooks and scullery maids darted for cover as the old woman pounded along the slippery flagstones, leapt up the stairs to the courtyard and skidded out into the lane, her shawl flying out behind her and her boots striking sparks from the cobbles. Once out into the open she hitched up her skirts and broke into a full gallop, turning the corner into the main square in a screeching two-boot drift that left a long white scratch across the stones.

She was just in time to see Esk come running through the gates, in tears.

'The magic just wouldn't work! I could feel it there but it just wouldn't come out!'

'Perhaps you were trying too hard,' said Granny. 'Magic's like fishing. Jumping around and splashing never caught any fish, you have to bide quiet and let it happen natural.'

'And then everyone laughed at me! Someone even gave me a sweet!'

'You got some profit out of the day, then,' said Granny.

'Granny!' said Esk accusingly.

'Well, what did you expect?' she asked. 'At least they only laughed at you. Laughter don't hurt. You walked up to chief wizard and showed off in front of everyone and only got laughed at? You're doing well, you are. Have you eaten the sweet?'

Esk scowled. 'Yes.'

'What kind was it?'

'Toffee.'

'Can't abide toffee.'

'Huh,' said Esk, 'I suppose you want me to get peppermint next time?'

'Don't you sarky me, young-fellow-me-lass. Nothing wrong with peppermint. Pass me that bowl.'

Another advantage of city life, Granny had discovered, was glassware. Some of her more complicated potions required apparatus which either had to be bought from the dwarves at extortionate rates or, if ordered from the nearest human glassblower, arrived in straw and, usually, pieces. She had tried blowing her own and the effort always made her cough, which produced some very funny results. But the city's thriving alchemy profession meant that there were whole shops full of glass for the buying, and a witch could always arrange bargain prices.

She watched carefully as yellow steam surged along a twisty maze of tubing and eventually condensed as one large, sticky droplet. She caught it neatly on the end of a glass spoon and very carefully tipped it into a tiny glass phial.

Esk watched her through her tears.

'What's that?' she asked.

'It's a neveryoumind,' said Granny, sealing the phial's cork with wax.

'A medicine?'

'In a manner of speaking.' Granny pulled her writing set towards her and selected a pen. Her tongue stuck out of the corner of her mouth as she very carefully wrote out a label, with much scratching and pausing to work out the spellings.

'Who's it for?'

'Mrs Herapath, the glassblower's wife.'

Esk blew her nose. 'He's the one who doesn't blow much glass, isn't he?'

Granny looked at her over the top of the desk.

'How do you mean?'

'When she was talking to you yesterday she called him Old Mister Once A Fortnight.'

'Mmph,' said Granny. She carefully finished the sentence: 'Dylewt in won pint warter and won droppe in hys tee and be shure to wear loose clowthing allso that no vysitors exspected.'

One day, she told herself, I'm going to have to have that talk with her.

The child seemed curiously dense. She had already assisted at enough births and taken the goats to old Nanny Annaple's billy without drawing any obvious conclusions. Granny wasn't quite certain what she should do about it, but the time never seemed appropriate to bring up the subject. She wondered whether, in her heart of hearts, she was too embarrassed; she felt like a farrier who could shoe horses, cure them, rear them and judge them, but had only the sketchiest idea about how one rode them.

She pasted the label on to the phial and wrapped it carefully in plain paper.

Now.

'There is another way into the University,' she said, looking sidelong at Esk, who was making a disgruntled job of mashing herbs in a mortar. 'A witches' way.'

Esk looked up. Granny treated herself to a thin smile and started work on another label; writing labels was always the hard part of magic, as far as she was concerned.

'But I don't expect you'd be interested,' she went on. 'It's not very glamorous.'

'They laughed at me,' Esk mumbled.

'Yes. You said. So you won't be wanting to try again, then. I *quite* understand.'

There was silence broken only by the scratching of Granny's pen. Eventually Esk said: 'This way—'

'Mmph?'

'It'll get me into the University?'

'Of course,' said Granny haughtily. 'I said I'd find a way, didn't I? A very good way, too. You won't have to bother with lessons, you can go all over the place, no one will notice you – you'll be invisible really – and, well, you can really clean up. But of course, after all that laughing, you won't be interested. Will you?'

* * *

'Pray have another cup of tea, Mrs Weatherwax?' said Mrs Whitlow.

'Mistress,' said Granny.

'Pardon?'

'It's Mistress Weatherwax,' said Granny. 'Three sugars, please.'

Mrs Whitlow pushed the bowl towards her. Much as she looked forward to Granny's visits it came expensive in sugar. Sugar lumps never seemed to last long around Granny.

'Very bad for the figure,' she said. 'And the teeth, so Aye hear.'

'I never had a figure to speak of and my teeth take care of themselves,' said Granny. It was true, more's the pity. Granny suffered from robustly healthy teeth, which she considered a big drawback in a witch. She really envied Nanny Annaple, the witch over the mountain, who managed to lose all her teeth by the time she was twenty and had real crone-credibility. It meant you ate a lot of soup, but you also got a lot of respect. And then there was warts. Without any effort Nanny managed to get a face like a sockful of marbles, while Granny had tried every reputable wart-causer and failed to raise even the obligatory nose wart. Some witches had all the luck.

'Mmph?' she said, aware of Mrs Whitlow's fluting.

'Aye said,' said Mrs Whitlow, 'that young Eskarina is a real treasure. *Quate* the little find. She keeps the floors spotless, *spotless*. No task too big. Aye said to her yesterday, Aye said, that broom of yours might as well have a life of its own, and do you know what she said?'

'I couldn't even venture a guess,' said Granny, weakly.

'She said the dust was afraid of it! Can you imagine?'

'Yes,' said Granny.

Mrs Whitlow pushed her teacup towards her and gave her an embarrassed smile.

Granny sighed inwardly and squinted into the none-too-clean depths of the future. She was definitely beginning to run out of imagination.

The broom whisked down the corridor raising a great cloud of dust which, if you looked hard at it, seemed somehow to be sucked back into the broomstick. If you looked even harder you'd see that the broom handle had strange markings on it, which were not so much carved as clinging and somehow changed shape as you watched.

But no one looked.

Esk sat at one of the high deep windows and stared out over the city. She was feeling angrier than usual, so the broom attacked the dust with unusual vigour. Spiders ran desperate eight-legged dashes for safety as ancestral cobwebs disappeared into the void. In the walls mice clung to each other, legs braced against the inside of their holes. Woodworm scrabbled in the ceiling beams as they were drawn, inexorably, backwards down their tunnels.

'You can really clean up,' said Esk. 'Huh!'

There were some good points, she had to admit. The food was simple but there was plenty of it, and she had a room to herself somewhere in the roof and it was quite luxurious because here she could lie in until five a.m., which to Granny's way of thinking was practically noon. The work certainly wasn't hard. She just started sweeping until the staff realized what was expected of it, and then she could amuse herself until it was finished. If anyone came the staff would immediately lean itself nonchalantly against a wall.

But she wasn't learning any wizardry. She could wander into empty classrooms and look at the diagrams chalked on the board, and on the floor too in the more advanced classes, but the shapes were meaningless. And unpleasant.

They reminded Esk of the pictures in Simon's book. They looked alive.

She gazed out across the rooftops of Ankh-Morpork and reasoned like this: writing was only the words that people said, squeezed between layers of paper until they were fossilized (fossils were well known on the Discworld, great spiralled shells and badly-constructed creatures that were left over from the time when the Creator hadn't really decided what He wanted to make and was, as it were, just idly messing around with the Pleistocene). And the words people said were just shadows of real things. *But* some things were too big to be really trapped in words, and even the words were too powerful to be completely tamed by writing.

So it followed that some writing was actually trying to become *things*. Esk's thoughts became confused things at this point, but she was certain that the really magic words were the ones that pulsed angrily, trying to escape and become real.

They didn't look very nice.

But then she remembered the previous day.

It had been rather odd. The University classrooms were designed on the funnel principle, with tiers of seats – polished by the bottoms of the Disc's greatest mages – looking precipitously down into a central area where there was a workbench, a couple of blackboards and enough floor space for a decent-sized instructional octogram. There was a lot of dead space under the tiers and Esk had found it a quite useful observation post, peering around between the apprentice wizards' pointy boots at the instructor. It was very restful, with the droning of the lecturers drifting over her as gently as the buzzing of the slightly zonked bees in Granny's special herb garden. There never seemed to be any practical magic, it always seemed to be just words. Wizards seemed to like words.

But yesterday had been different. Esk had been sitting in the dusty gloom, trying to do even some very simple magic, when she heard the door open and boots clump across the floor. That was surprising in itself. Esk knew the timetable, and the Second Year students who normally occupied this room were down for Beginners' Dematerialization with Jeophal the Spry in the gym. (Students of magic had little use for physical exercise; the gym was a large room lined with lead and rowan wood, where neophytes could work out at High magic without seriously unbalancing the universe, although not always without seriously unbalancing themselves. Magic had no mercy on the ham-fisted. Some clumsy students were lucky enough to walk out, others were removed in bottles.)

Esk peeped between the slats. These weren't students, they were wizards. Quite high ones, to judge by their robes. And there was no mistaking the figure that climbed on to the lecturer's dais like a badly-strung puppet, bumping heavily into the lectern and absent-mindedly apologizing to it. It was Simon. No-one else had eyes like two raw eggs in warm water and a nose bright red from blowing. For Simon, the pollen count always went to infinity.

It occurred to Esk that, minus his general allergy to the whole of Creation and with a decent haircut and a few lessons in deportment, the boy could look quite handsome. It was an unusual thought, and she squirrelled it away for future consideration.

When the wizards had settled down, Simon began to talk. He read from notes, and every time he stuttered over a word the wizards, as one man, without being able to stop themselves, chorused it for him.

After a while a stick of chalk rose from the lectern and started to write on the blackboard behind him. Esk had picked up enough about wizard magic to know that this was an astounding achievement – Simon had been at the University for a couple of weeks, and most students hadn't mastered Light Levitation by the end of their second year.

The little white stub skittered and squeaked across the blackness to the accompaniment of Simon's voice. Even allowing for the stutter, he was not a very good speaker. He dropped notes. He corrected himself. He ummed and ahhed. And as far as Esk was concerned he wasn't saying anything very much. Phrases filtered down to her hiding place. 'Basic fabric of the universe' was one, and she didn't understand what that was, unless he meant denim, or maybe flannelette. 'Mutability of the possibility matrix' she couldn't guess at all.

Sometimes he seemed to be saying that nothing existed unless people thought it did, and the world was really only there at all because people kept on imagining it. But then he seemed to be saying that there were lots of worlds, all nearly the same and all sort of occupying the same place but all separated by the thickness of a shadow, so that everything that ever could happen would have somewhere to happen *in*.

(Esk could get to grips with this. She had half-suspected it ever since she cleaned out the senior wizards' lavatory, or rather while the staff got on with the job and Esk examined the urinals and, with the assistance of some half-remembered details of her brothers in the tin bath in front of the fire at home, formulated her unofficial General Theory of comparative anatomy. The senior wizards' lavatory was a magical place, with real running water and interesting tiles and, most importantly, two big silver mirrors fixed to opposite walls so that someone looking into one could see themselves repeated again and again until the image was too small to see. It was Esk's first introduction to the idea of infinity. More to the point, she had a suspicion that one of the mirror Esks, right on the edge of sight, was waving at her.)

There was something disturbing about the phrases Simon used. Half the time he seemed to be saying that the world was about as real as a soap bubble, or a dream.

The chalk shrieked its way across the board behind him. Sometimes Simon had to stop and explain symbols to the wizards, who seemed to Esk to be getting excited at some very silly sentences. Then the chalk would start again, curving across the darkness like a comet, trailing its dust behind it.

The light was fading out of the sky outside. As the room grew more gloomy the chalked words glowed and the blackboard appeared to Esk to be not so much dark as simply not there at all, but just a square hole cut out of the world.

Simon talked on, about the world being made up of tiny things whose presence could only be determined by the fact that they were not there, little spinning balls of nothingness that magic could shunt together to make stars and butterflies and diamonds. Everything was made up of emptiness.

The funny thing was, he seemed to find this fascinating.

Esk was only aware that the walls of the room grew as thin and insubstantial as smoke, as if the emptiness in them was expanding to swallow whatever it was that defined them as walls, and instead there was nothing but the familiar cold, empty, glittering plain with its distant worn hills, and the creatures that stood as still as statues, looking down.

There were a lot more of them now. They seemed for all the world to be clustering like moths around a light.

One important difference was that a moth's face, even close up, was as friendly as a bunny rabbit's compared to the things watching Simon.

Then a servant came in to light the lamps and the creatures vanished, turning into perfectly harmless shadows that lurked in the corners of the room.

At some time in the recent past someone had decided to brighten the ancient corridors of the University by painting them, having some vague notion that Learning Should Be Fun. It hadn't worked. It's a fact known throughout the universes that no matter how carefully the colours are chosen, institutional décor ends up as either vomit green, unmentionable brown, nicotine yellow or surgical appliance pink. By some little-understood process of sympathetic resonance, corridors painted in those colours *always smell slightly of boiled cabbage* – even if no cabbage is ever cooked in the vicinity.

Somewhere in the corridors a bell rang. Esk dropped lightly from her windowsill, grabbed the staff and started to sweep industriously as doors were flung open and the corridors filled with students. They streamed past her on two sides, like water around a rock. For a few minutes there was utter confusion. Then doors slammed, a few laggard feet pattered away in the distance, and Esk was by herself again.

Not for the first time, Esk wished that the staff could talk. The other servants were friendly enough, but you couldn't *talk* to them. Not about magic, anyway.

She was also coming to the conclusion that she ought to learn to read. This reading business seemed to be the key to wizard magic, which was all about words. Wizards seemed to think that names were the same as things, and that if you changed the name, you changed the thing. At least, it seemed to be something like that . . .

Reading. That meant the library. Simon had said there were thousands of books in it, and amongst all those words there were bound to be one or two she could read. Esk put the staff over her shoulder and set off resolutely for Mrs Whitlow's office.

She was nearly there when a wall said 'Psst!' When Esk stared at it it turned out to be Granny. It wasn't that Granny could make herself invisible, it was just that she had this talent for being able to fade into the foreground so that she wasn't noticed.

'How are you getting on, then?' asked Granny. 'How's the magic coming along?'

'What are you doing here, Granny?' said Esk.

'Been to tell Mrs Whitlow her fortune,' said Granny,

holding up a large bundle of old clothes with some satisfaction. Her smile faded under Esk's stern gaze.

'Well, things are different in the city,' she said. 'City people are always worried about the future, it comes from eating unnatural food. Anyway,' she added, suddenly realizing that she was whining, 'why shouldn't I tell fortunes?'

'*You* always said Hilta was playing on the foolishness of her sex,' said Esk. '*You* said that them as tell fortunes should be ashamed of themselves, and anyway, you don't need old clothes.'

'Waste not, want not,' said Granny primly. She had spent her entire life on the old-clothes standard and wasn't about to let temporary prosperity dislodge her: 'Are you getting enough to eat?'

'Yes,' said Esk. 'Granny, about this wizard magic, it's all words—'

'Always said it was,' said Granny.

'No, I mean—' Esk began, but Granny waved a hand irritably.

'Can't be bothered with this at the moment,' she said. 'I've got some big orders to fill by tonight, if it goes on like this I'm going to have to train someone up. Can't you come and see me when you get an afternoon off, or whatever it is they give you?'

'Train someone up?' said Esk, horrified. 'You mean as a witch?'

'No,' said Granny. 'I mean, perhaps.'

'But what about me?'

'Well, you're going your own way,' said Granny. 'Wherever that is.'

'Mmph,' said Esk. Granny stared at her.

'I'll be off, then,' she said at last. She turned and strode off towards the kitchen entrance. As she did so her cloak swirled out, and Esk saw that it was now lined with red. A dark, winy red, but red nevertheless. On Granny, who had never been known to wear any visible clothing that was other than a serviceable black, it was quite shocking.

'The library?' said Mrs Whitlow. 'Aye don't think anyone cleans the library!' She looked genuinely puzzled.

'Why?' said Esk. 'Doesn't it get dusty?'

'Well,' said Mrs Whitlow. She thought for a while. 'Aye suppose it must do, since you come to mention it. Aye never really thought about it.'

'You see, I've cleaned everywhere else,' said Esk, sweetly.

'Yes,' said Mrs Whitlow. 'You have, haven't you.'

'Well, then.'

'It's just that we've never – done it before,' said Mrs Whitlow, 'but for the life of me, Aye can't think why.'

'Well, then,' said Esk.

'Ook?' said the Head Librarian and backed away from Esk. But she had heard about him and had come prepared. She offered him a banana.

The orang-outang reached out slowly and then snatched it with a grin of triumph.

There may be universes where librarianship is

considered a peaceful sort of occupation, and where the risks are limited to large volumes falling off the shelves on to one's head, but the keeper of a *magic* library is no job for the unwary. Spells have power, and merely writing them down and shoving them between covers doesn't do anything to reduce it. The stuff leaks. Books tend to react with one another, creating randomized magic with a mind of its own. Books of magic are usually chained to their shelves, but not to prevent them being stolen . . .

One such accident had turned the librarian into an ape, since when he had resisted all attempts to turn him back, explaining in sign language that life as an orang-outang was considerably better than life as a human being, because all the big philosophical questions resolved themselves into wondering where the next banana was coming from. Anyway, long arms and pre-hensile feet were ideal for dealing with high shelves.

Esk gave him the whole bunch of bananas and scurried away amongst the books before he could object.

Esk had never seen more than one book at a time and so the library was, for all she knew, just like any other library. True, it was a bit odd the way the floor seemed to become the wall in the distance, and there was something strange about the way the shelves played tricks on the eyes and seemed to twist through rather more dimensions than the normal three, and it was quite surprising to look up and see shelves on the ceiling, with the occasional student wandering unconcernedly amongst them.

The truth was that the presence of so much magic distorted the space around it. Down in the stacks the very denim, or possibly flannelette, of the universe was tortured into very peculiar shapes. The millions of trapped words, unable to escape, bent reality around them.

It seemed logical to Esk that among all these books should be one that told you how to read all the others. She wasn't sure how to find it, but deep in her soul she felt it would probably have pictures of cheerful rabbits and happy kittens on the cover.

The library certainly wasn't silent. There was the occasional zip and sizzle of a magical discharge, and an octarine spark would flash from shelf to shelf. Chains clinked, faintly. And, of course, there was the faint rustle of thousands of pages in their leather-bound prisons.

Esk made sure no one was paying her any attention and pulled at the nearest volume. It sprang open in her hands, and she saw gloomily that there were the same unpleasant types of diagram that she had noticed in Simon's book. The writing was entirely unfamiliar, and she was glad about that – it would be horrible to know what all those letters, which seemed to be made up of ugly creatures doing complicated things to each other, actually meant. She forced the cover shut, even though the words seemed to be desperately pushing back. There was a drawing of a creature on the front; it looked suspiciously like one of the things from the cold desert. It certainly didn't look like a happy kitten.

'Hallo! Esk, isn't it? H-how d-did you get h-here?'

It was Simon, standing there with a book under each arm. Esk blushed.

'Granny won't tell me,' she said. 'I think it's something to do with men and women.'

Simon looked at her blankly. Then he grinned. Esk thought about the question a second time.

'I work here. I sweep up.' She waved the staff in explanation.

'In *here*?'

Esk stared at him. She felt alone, and lost, and more than a little betrayed. Everyone seemed to be busy living their own lives, except her. She would spend the rest of *her* life cleaning up after wizards. It wasn't fair, and she'd had enough.

'Actually I don't. Actually I'm learning to read so I can be a wizard.'

The boy regarded her through his damp eyes for some seconds. Then he gently took the book out of Esk's hands and read its title.

'*Demonylogie Malyfycorum of Henchanse thee Unsatysfactory*. How did you think you could learn to r-read this?'

'Um,' said Esk, 'well, you just keep trying until you can, don't you? Like milking, or knitting, or . . .' Her voice faded away.

'I don't know about that. These books can be a bit, well, aggressive. If you d-don't be careful they start reading *you*.'

'What do you mean?'

'T-they ssss—'

'—say—' said Esk, automatically.

'—that there was once a wwww—'

'—wizard—'

'—who started to r-read the *Necrotelecomnicon* and let his m-mind wwwwww—'

'—wander—'

'—and next morning they f-found all his clothes on the chair and h-his hat on t-top of them and the b-book had—'

Esk put her fingers in her ears, but not too hard in case she missed anything.

'I don't want to know about it if it's horrid.'

'—had *a lot more pages*.'

Esk took her fingers out of her ears. 'Was there anything on the pages?'

Simon nodded solemnly. 'Yes. On every sssingle one of th-them there www—'

'No,' said Esk. 'I don't even want to imagine it. I thought reading was more peaceful than that, I mean, Granny read her *Almanack* every day and nothing ever happened to her.'

'I d-dare say ordinary tame www—'

'—words—'

'—are all right,' Simon conceded, magnanimously.

'Are you absolutely certain?' said Esk.

'It's just that words can have power,' said Simon, slotting the book firmly back on its shelf, where it rattled its chains at him. 'And they do say the p-pen is mightier than the sss—'

'—sword,' said Esk. 'All right, but which would you rather be hit with?'

'Um, I d-don't think it's any use m-me t-telling you you shouldn't be in here, is it?' said the young wizard.

Esk gave this due consideration. 'No,' she said, 'I don't think it is.'

'I could send for the p-porters and have you t-taken away.'

'Yes, but you won't.'

'I just d-don't www—'

'—want—'

'—you to get hurt, you see. I r-really don't. This can b-be a ddddangerou—'

Esk caught a faint swirling in the air above his head. For a moment she saw them, the great grey shapes from the cold place. Watching. And in the calm of the library, when the weight of magic was wearing the universe particularly thin, they had decided to Act.

Around her the muted rustling of the books rose to a desperate riffling of pages. Some of the more powerful books managed to jerk out of their shelves and swung, flapping madly, from the end of their chains. A huge grimoire plunged from its eyrie on the topmost shelf – tearing itself free of its chain in the process – and flopped away like a frightened chicken, scattering its pages behind it.

A magical wind blew away Esk's headscarf and her hair streamed out behind her. She saw Simon trying to steady himself against a bookshelf as books exploded around him. The air was thick and tasted of tin. It buzzed.

'They're trying to get in!' she screamed.

Simon's tortured face turned to her. A fear-crazed

incunable hit him heavily in the small of the back and knocked him to the heaving floor before it bounced high over the shelves. Esk ducked as a flock of thesauri wheeled past, towing their shelf behind them, and scuttled on hands and knees towards him.

'That's what's making the books so frightened!' she shrieked in his ear. 'Can't you *see* them up there?'

Simon mutely shook his head. A book burst its bindings over them, showering them in pages.

Horror can steal into the mind via all the senses. There's the sound of the little meaningful chuckle in the locked dark room, the sight of half a caterpillar in your forkful of salad, the curious smell from the lodger's bedroom, the taste of slug in the cauliflower cheese. Touch doesn't normally get a look-in.

But something happened to the floor under Esk's hands. She looked down, her face a rictus of horror, because the dusty floorboards suddenly felt gritty. And dry. And very, very cold.

There was fine silver sand between her fingers.

She grabbed the staff and, sheltering her eyes against the wind, waved it at the towering figures above her. It would have been nice to report that a searing flash of pure white fire cleansed the greasy air. It failed to materialize . . .

The staff twisted like a snake in her hand and caught Simon a crack on the side of the head.

The grey Things wavered and vanished.

Reality returned, and tried to pretend that it had never left. Silence settled like thick velvet, wave after wave of it. A heavy echoing silence. A few books dropped heavily out of the air, feeling silly.

The floor under Esk's feet was undoubtedly wooden. She kicked it hard to make sure.

There was blood on the floor, and Simon lay very quietly in the centre of it. Esk stared down at him, and then up at the still air, and then at the staff. It looked smug.

She was aware of distant voices and hurrying feet.

A hand like a fine leather glove slipped gently into hers and a voice behind said 'ook,' very softly. She turned, and found herself staring down into the gentle, inner-tube face of the librarian. He put his finger to his lips in an unmistakable gesture and tugged gently at her hand.

'I've killed him!' she whispered.

The librarian shook his head, and tugged insistently.

'Ook,' he explained, 'ook.'

He dragged her reluctantly down a side alley-way in the maze of ancient shelving a few seconds before a party of senior wizards, drawn by the noise, rounded the corner.

'The books have been fighting again . . .'

'Oh, no! It'll take ages to capture all the spells again, you know they go and find places to hide . . .'

'Who's that on the floor?'

There was a pause.

'He's knocked out. A shelf caught him, by the looks of it.'

'Who is he?'

'That new lad. You know, the one they say has got a whole head full of brains?'

'If that shelf had been a bit closer we'd be able to see if they were right.'

'You two, get him along to the infirmary. The rest of you better get these books rounded up. Where's the damn librarian? He ought to know better than to let a Critical Mass build up.'

Esk glanced sideways at the orang-outang, who waggled his eyebrows at her. He pulled a dusty volume of gardening spells out of the shelves beside him, extracted a soft brown banana from the recess behind it, and ate it with the quiet relish of one who knows that whatever the problems are, they belong firmly to human beings.

She looked the other way, at the staff in her hand, and her lips went thin. She knew her grip hadn't slipped. The staff had *lunged* at Simon, with murder in its heartwood.

The boy lay on a hard bed in a narrow room, a cold towel folded across his forehead. Treatle and Cutangle watched him carefully.

'How long has it been?' said Cutangle.

Treatle shrugged. 'Three days.'

'And he hasn't come around once?'

'No.'

Cutangle sat down heavily on the edge of the bed, and pinched the bridge of his nose wearily. Simon had never looked particularly healthy, but now his face had a horrible sunken look.

'A brilliant mind, that one,' he said. 'His

explanation of the fundamental principles of magic and matter – quite astounding.'

Treatle nodded.

'The way he just absorbs knowledge,' said Cutangle: 'I've been a working wizard all my life, and somehow I never really understood magic until he explained it. So clear. So, well, *obvious*.'

'Everyone says that,' said Treatle gloomily. 'They say it's like having a hoodwink pulled off and seeing the daylight for the first time.'

'That's exactly it,' said Cutangle. 'He's sourcerer material, sure enough. You were right to bring him here.'

There was a thoughtful pause.

'Only—' said Treatle.

'Only what?' asked Cutangle.

'Only *what* was it you understood?' said Treatle. 'That's what's bothering me. I mean, can you explain it?'

'How do you mean, explain?' Cutangle looked worried.

'What he keeps talking about,' said Trestle, a hint of desperation in his voice. 'Oh, it's the genuine stuff, I know. But what exactly *is* it?'

Cutangle looked at him, his mouth open. Eventually he said, 'Oh, that's easy. Magic fills the universe, you see, and every time the universe changes, no, I mean every time magic is invoked, the universe changes, only in every direction at once, d'you see, and—' he moved his hands uncertainly, trying to recognize a spark of comprehension in

Treatle's face. 'To put it another way, any piece of matter, like an orange or the world or, or—'

'—a crocodile?' suggested Treatle.

'Yes, a crocodile, or – whatever, is basically shaped like a carrot.'

'I don't remember that bit,' said Treatle.

'I'm sure that's what he said,' said Cutangle. He was starting to sweat.

'No, I remember the bit where he seemed to suggest that if you went far enough in any direction you would see the back of your head,' Treatle insisted.

'You're sure he didn't mean someone else's head?'

Treatle thought for a bit.

'No, I'm pretty sure he said the back of your own head,' he said. 'I think he said he could prove it.'

They considered this in silence.

Finally Cutangle spoke, very slowly and carefully.

'I look at it like this,' he said. 'Before I heard him talk, I was like everyone else. You know what I mean? I was confused and uncertain about all the little details of life. But now,' he brightened up, 'while I'm still confused and uncertain it's on a much higher plane, d'you see, and at least I know I'm bewildered about the really fundamental and important facts of the universe.'

Treatle nodded. 'I hadn't looked at it like that,' he said, 'but you're absolutely right. He's really pushed back the boundaries of ignorance. There's so much about the universe we don't know.'

They both savoured the strange warm glow of

being much more ignorant than ordinary people, who were ignorant of only ordinary things.

Then Treatle said: 'I just hope he's all right. He's over the fever but he just doesn't seem to want to wake up.'

A couple of servants came in with a bowl of water and fresh towels. One of them carried a rather tatty broomstick. As they began to change the sweat-soaked sheets under the boy the two wizards left, still discussing the vast vistas of unknowingness that Simon's genius had revealed to the world.

Granny waited until their footsteps had died away and took off her headscarf.

'Damn thing,' she said. 'Esk, go and listen at the door.' She removed the towel from Simon's head and felt his temperature.

'It was very good of you to come,' said Esk. 'And you so busy with your work, and everything.'

'Mmmph.' Granny pursed her lips. She pulled up Simon's eyelids and sought his pulse. She laid an ear on his xylophone chest and listened to his heart. She sat for some time quite motionless, probing around inside his head.

She frowned.

'Is he all right?' said Esk anxiously.

Granny looked at the stone walls.

'Drat this place,' she said. 'It's no place for sick people.'

'Yes, but is he all right?'

'What?' Granny was startled out of her thoughts. 'Oh. Yes. Probably. Wherever he is.'

Esk stared at her, and then at Simon's body.

'Nobody's home,' said Granny, simply.

'What do you mean?'

'Listen to the child,' said Granny. 'You'd think I taught her nothing. I mean his mind's Wandering. He's gone Out of his Head.'

She looked at Simon's body with something verging on admiration.

'Quite surprisin', really,' she added. 'I never yet met a wizard who could Borrow.'

She turned to Esk, whose mouth was a horrified O.

'I remember when I was a girl, old Nanny Annaple went Wanderin'. Got too wrapped up with being a vixen, as I recall. Took us days to find her. And then there was you, too. I never would have found you if it wasn't for that staff thing, and – what have you done with it, girl?'

'It hit him,' Esk muttered. 'It tried to kill him. I threw it in the river.'

'Not a nice thing to do to it after it saved you,' said Granny.

'It saved me by hitting him?'

'Didn't you realize? He was callin' to – them Things.'

'That's not true!'

Granny stared into Esk's defiant eyes and the thought came to her mind: I've lost her. All that work down the privy. She couldn't be a wizard but she might have been a witch.

'Why isn't it true, Miss Clever?' she said.

'He wouldn't do something like that!' Esk was near

to tears. 'I heard him speak, he's – well, he's not evil, he's a brilliant person, he nearly understands how everything works, he's—'

'I expect he's a very nice boy,' said Granny sourly. 'I never said he was a black wizard, did I?'

'They're horrible Things!' Esk sobbed. 'He wouldn't call out to them, he wants everything that they're not, and you're a wicked old—'

The slap rang like a bell. Esk staggered back, white with shock. Granny stood with her hand upraised, trembling.

She'd struck Esk once before – the blow a baby gets to introduce it to the world and give it a rough idea of what to expect from life. But that had been the last time. In twelve months under the same roof there had been cause enough, when milk had been left to boil over or the goats had been carelessly left without water, but a sharp word or a sharper silence had done more than force ever could and left no bruises.

She grabbed Esk firmly by the shoulders and stared into her eyes.

'Listen to me,' she said urgently. 'Didn't I always say to you that if you use magic you should go through the world like a knife goes through water? Didn't I say that?'

Esk, mesmerized like a cornered rabbit, nodded.

'And you thought that was just old Granny's way, didn't you? But the fact is that if you use magic you draw attention to yourself. From Them. They watch the world all the time. Ordinary minds are just vague to them, they hardly bother with them, but a mind with magic in it shines out, you see, it's a beacon to them. It's not darkness that calls Them, it's light, light that creates the shadows!'

'But – but – why are They interested? What do They w-want?'

'Life and shape,' said Granny.

She sagged, and let go of Esk.

'They're pathetic, really,' she said. 'They've got no life or shape themselves but what they can steal. They could no more survive in this world than a fish could live in a fire, but that doesn't stop Them trying. And they're just bright enough to hate us because we're alive.'

Esk shivered. She remembered the gritty feel of the cold sand.

'What are They? I always thought they were just a sort – a sort of demon?'

'Nah. No-one really knows. They're just the Things from the Dungeon Dimensions outside the universe, that's all. Shadow creatures.'

She turned back to the prone form of Simon.

'You wouldn't have any idea where he is, would you?' she said, looking shrewdly at Esk. 'Not gone off flying with the seagulls, has he?'

Esk shook her head.

'No,' said Granny, 'I didn't think so. They've got him, haven't they.'

It wasn't a question. Esk nodded, her face a mask of misery.

'It's not your fault,' said Granny. 'His mind gave Them an opening, and when he was knocked out they took it back with them. Only . . .'

She drummed her fingers on the edge of the bed, and appeared to reach a decision.

'Who's the most important wizard around here?' she demanded.

'Um, Lord Cutangle,' said Esk. He's the Arch-chancellor. He was one of the ones who was in here.'

'The fat one, or the one like a streak of vinegar?'

Esk dragged her mind from the image of Simon on the cold desert and found herself saying: 'He's an Eighth Level wizard and a 33° mage, actually.'

'You mean he's bent?' said Granny. 'All this hanging around wizards has made you take them seriously, my girl. They all call themselves the Lord High This and the Imperial That, it's all part of the game. Even magicians do it, you'd think they'd be more sensible at least, but no, they call around saying they're the Amazing-Bonko-and-Doris. Anyway, where is this High Rumtiddlypo?'

'They'll be at dinner in the Great Hall,' said Esk. 'Can he bring Simon back, then?'

'That's the difficult part,' said Granny. 'I dare say we could all get *something* back easily enough, walking and talking just like anyone. Whether it would be Simon is quite another sack of ferrets.'

She stood up. 'Let's find this Great Hall then. No time to waste.'

'Um, women aren't allowed in,' said Esk.

Granny stopped in the doorway. Her shoulders rose. She turned around very slowly.

'*What* did you say?' she said. 'Did these old ears deceive me, and don't say they did because they didn't.'

'Sorry,' said Esk. 'Force of habit.'

'I can see you've been getting ideas below your station,' said Granny coldly. 'Go and find someone to watch over the lad, and let's see what's so great about this hall that I mustn't set foot in it.'

And thus it was that while the entire faculty of Unseen University were dining in the venerable hall the doors were flung back with a dramatic effect that was rather spoiled when one of them rebounded off a waiter and caught Granny a crack on the shin. Instead of the defiant strides she had intended to make across the chequered floor she was forced to half-hop, half-limp. But she hoped that she hopped with dignity.

Esk hurried along behind her, acutely aware of the hundreds of eyes that were turned towards them.

The roar of conversation and the clatter of cutlery faded away. A couple of chairs were knocked over. At the far end of the hall she could see the most senior wizards at their high table, which in fact bobbed a few feet off the floor. They were staring.

A medium-grade wizard – Esk recognized him as a lecturer in Applied Astrology – rushed towards them, waving his hands.

'Nononono,' he shouted. 'Wrong door. You must go away.'

'Don't mind me,' said Granny calmly, pushing past him.

'Nonono, it's against the lore, you must go away *now*. Ladies are not allowed in here!'

'I'm not a lady, I'm a witch,' said Granny. She turned to Esk. 'Is he very important?'

'I don't think so,' said Esk.

'Right.' Granny turned to the lecturer: 'Go and find me an important wizard, please. Quickly.'

Esk tapped her on the back. A couple of wizards with a rather greater presence of mind had nipped smartly out of the door behind them, and now several college porters were advancing threateningly up the hall, to the cheers and catcalls of the students. Esk had never much liked the porters, who lived a private life in their lodge, but now she felt a pang of sympathy for them.

Two of them reached out hairy hands and grabbed Granny's shoulders. Her arm disappeared behind her back and there was a brief flurry of movement that ended with the men hopping away, clutching bits of themselves and swearing.

'Hatpin,' said Granny. She grabbed Esk with her free hand and swept towards the high table, glaring at anyone who so much as looked as if they were going to get in her way. The younger students, who knew free entertainment when they saw it, stamped and cheered and banged their plates on the long tables. The high table settled on the tiles with a thump and the senior wizards hurriedly lined up behind Cutangle as he tried to summon up his reserves of dignity. His efforts didn't really work; it is very hard to look dignified with a napkin tucked into one's collar.

He raised his hands for silence, and the hall waited expectantly as Granny and Esk approached him. Granny was looking interestedly at the ancient paintings and statues of bygone mages.

'Who are them buggers?' she said out of the corner of her mouth.

'They used to be chief wizards,' whispered Esk.

'They look constipated. I never met a wizard who was regular,' said Granny.

'They're a nuisance to dust, that's all I know,' said Esk.

Cutangle stood with legs planted wide apart, arms akimbo and stomach giving an impression of a beginners' ski slope, the whole of him therefore adopting a pose usually associated with Henry VIII but with an option on Henry IX and X as well.

'*Well?*' he said. 'What is the meaning of this *outrage?*'

'Is he important?' said Granny to Esk.

'*I*, madam, am the Archchancellor! And I happen to run this University! And you, madam, are trespassing in very dangerous territory indeed! I warn you that – *stop looking at me like that!*'

Cutangle staggered backwards, his hands raised to ward off Granny's gaze. The wizards behind him scattered, turning over tables in their haste to avoid the stare.

Granny's eyes had changed.

Esk had never seen them like this before. They were perfectly silver, like little round mirrors, reflecting all they saw. Cutangle was a vanishingly small dot in their depths, his mouth open, his tiny matchstick arms waving in desperation.

The Archchancellor backed into a pillar, and the shock made him recover. He shook his head irritably, cupped a hand and sent a stream of white fire streaking towards the witch.

Without dropping her iridescent stare Granny raised a hand and deflected the flames towards the roof. There was an explosion and a shower of tile fragments.

Her eyes widened.

Cutangle vanished. Where he had been standing a huge snake coiled, poised to strike.

Granny vanished. Where she had been standing was a large wicker basket.

The snake became a giant reptile from the mists of time.

The basket became the snow wind of the Ice Giants, coating the struggling monster with ice.

The reptile became a sabre-toothed tiger, crouched to spring.

The gale became a bubbling tar pit.

The tiger managed to become an eagle, stooping.

The tar pits became a tufted hood.

Then the images began to flicker as shape replaced shape. Stroboscope shadows danced around the hall. A magical wind sprang up, thick and greasy, striking octarine sparks from beards and fingers. In the middle of it all Esk, peering through streaming eyes, could just make out the two figures of Granny and Cutangle, glossy statues in the midst of the hurtling images.

She was also aware of something else, a high-pitched sound almost beyond hearing.

She had heard it before, on the cold plain – a busy

chittering noise, a beehive noise, an anthill sound . . .

'They're coming!' she screamed above the din. 'They're coming *now*!'

She scrambled out from behind the table where she had taken refuge from the magical duel and tried to reach Granny. A gust of raw magic lifted her off her feet and bowled her into a chair.

The buzzing was louder now, so that the air roared like a three-week corpse on a summer's day. Esk made another attempt to reach Granny and recoiled when green fire roared along her arm and singed her hair.

She looked around wildly for the other wizards, but those who had fled from the effects of the magic were cowering behind overturned furniture while the occult storm raged over their heads.

Esk ran down the length of the hall and out into the dark corridor. Shadows curled around her as she hurried, sobbing, up the steps and along the buzzing corridors towards Simon's narrow room.

Something would try to enter the body, Granny had said. Something that would walk and talk like Simon, but would be something else . . .

A cluster of students were hovering anxiously outside the door. They turned pale faces towards Esk as she darted towards them, and were sufficiently shaken to draw back nervously in the face of her determined progress.

'Something's in there,' said one of them.

'We can't open the door!'

They looked at her expectantly. Then one of them said: 'You wouldn't have a pass key, by any chance?'

Esk grabbed the doorhandle and turned it. It moved slightly, but then spun back with such force it nearly took the skin off her hands. The chittering inside rose to a crescendo and there was another noise, too, like leather flapping.

'You're wizards!' she screamed. 'Bloody well wizz!'

'We haven't done telekinesis yet,' said one of them.

'I was ill when we did Firethrowing—'

'Actually, I'm not very good at Dematerialization—'

Esk went to the door, and then stopped with one foot in the air. She remembered Granny talking about how even buildings had a mind, if they were old enough. The University was very old.

She stepped carefully to one side and ran her hands over the ancient stones. It had to be done carefully, so as not to frighten it – and now she could feel the mind in the stones, slow and simple, but still mind. It pulsed around her, she could feel the little sparkles deep in the rock.

Something was hooting behind the door.

The three students watched in astonishment as Esk stood rock still with her hands and forehead pressed against the wall.

She was almost there. She could feel the weight of herself, the ponderousness of her body, the distant memories of the dawn of time when rock was molten and free. For the first time in her life she knew what it was like to have balconies.

She moved gently through the building-mind, refining her impressions, looking as fast as she dared for *this* corridor, this door.

She stretched out one arm, very carefully. The students watched as she uncurled one finger, very slowly.

The door hinges began to creak.

There was a moment of tension and then the nails sprang from the hinges and clattered into the wall behind her. The planks began to bend as the door still tried to force itself open against the strength of – whatever was holding it shut.

The wood *billowed*.

Beams of blue light lanced out into the corridor, moving and dancing as indistinct shapes shuffled through the blinding brilliance inside the room. The light was misty and actinic, the sort of light to make Steven Spielberg reach for his copyright lawyer.

Esk's hair leapt from her head so that she looked like an ambulant dandelion. Little firesnakes of magic crackled across her skin as she stepped through the doorway.

The students outside watched in horror as she disappeared into the light.

It vanished in a silent explosion.

When they eventually found enough courage to look inside the room, they saw nothing there but the sleeping body of Simon. And Esk, silent and cold on the floor, breathing very slowly. And the floor was covered with a fine layer of silver sand.

Esk floated through the mists of the world, noticing with a curious impersonal feeling the precise way in which she passed through solid matter.

There were others with her. She could hear their chittering.

Fury rose like bile. She turned and set out after the noise, fighting the seductive forces that kept telling her how nice it would be just to relax her grip on her mind and sink into a warm sea of nothingness. Being angry, that was the thing. She knew it was most important to stay really angry.

The Discworld fell away, and lay below her as it did on the day she had been an eagle. But this time the Circle Sea was below her – it certainly was circular, as if God had run out of ideas – and beyond it lay the arms of the continent, and the long chain of the Ramtops marching all the way to the Hub. There were other continents she had never heard of, and tiny island chains.

As her point of view changed, the Rim came into sight. It was night time and, since the Disc's orbiting sun was below the world, it lit up the long waterfall that girdled the Edge.

It also lit up Great A'Tuin the World Turtle. Esk had often wondered if the Turtle was really a myth. It seemed a lot of trouble to go to just to move a world. But there It was, almost as big as the Disc it carried, frosted with stardust and pocked with meteor craters.

Its head passed in front of her and she looked directly into an eye big enough to float all the fleets in the world. She had heard it said that if you could look far enough into the direction that Great A'Tuin was staring, you would see the end of the universe. Maybe it was just the set of Its beak but Great A'Tuin looked vaguely hopeful, even optimistic. Perhaps the end of everything wasn't as bad as all that.

Dreamlike, she reached out and tried to Borrow the biggest mind in the universe.

She stopped herself just in time, like a child with a toy toboggan who expected a little gentle slope and suddenly looks out on the magnificent mountains, snow-covered, stretching into the icefields of infinity. No-one would ever Borrow that mind, it would be like trying to drink all the sea. The thoughts that moved through it were as big and as slow as glaciers.

Beyond the Disc were the stars, and there was something wrong with them. They were swirling like snowflakes. Every now and again they would settle down and look as immobile as they always did, and then they'd suddenly take it into their heads to dance.

Real stars shouldn't do that, Esk decided. Which meant she wasn't looking at real stars. Which meant she wasn't exactly in a real place. But a chittering close at hand reminded her that she could almost certainly really die if she once lost track of those noises. She turned and pursued the sounds through the stellar snowstorm.

And the stars jumped, and settled, jumped, and settled . . .

As she swooped upward Esk tried to concentrate on everyday things, because if she let her mind dwell on precisely what it was she was following then she knew she would turn back, and she wasn't sure she knew the way. She tried to remember the eighteen herbs that cured ear-ache, which kept her occupied for a while because she could never recall the last four.

A star swooped past, and then was violently jerked away; it was about twenty feet across.

When she ran out of herbs she started on the diseases of goats, which took quite a long time because goats can catch a lot of things that cows can catch plus a lot of things that sheep catch plus a complete range of horrible ailments of their very own. When she had finished listing wooden udder, ear wilt and the octarine garget she tried to recall the complex code of dots and lines that they used to cut in the trees around Bad Ass, so that lost villagers could find their way home on snowy nights.

She was as far as dot dot dot dash dot dash (Hub-by-Turnwise, one mile from the village) when the universe around her vanished with a faint pop. She fell forward, hit something hard and gritty and rolled to a halt.

The grittiness was sand. Fine, dry, *cold* sand. You could tell that even if you dug down several feet it would be just as cold and just as dry.

Esk lay with her face in it for a moment, summoning the courage to look up. She could just see, a few feet away from her, the hem of someone's dress. Something's dress, she corrected herself. Unless it was a wing. It *could* be a wing, a particularly tatty and leathery one.

Her eyes followed it up until she found a face, higher than a house, outlined against the starry sky. Its owner was obviously trying to look nightmarish, but had tried too hard. The basic appearance was that of a chicken that had been dead for about two months, but the unpleasant effect was rather spoiled by warthog tusks, moth antennae, wolf ears and a unicorn spike. The whole thing had a self-assembled look, as if the owner had heard about anatomy but couldn't quite get to grips with the idea.

It was staring, but not at her. Something behind her occupied all its interest. Esk turned her head very slowly.

Simon was sitting cross-legged in the centre of a circle of Things. There were hundreds of them, as still and silent as statues, watching him with reptilian patience.

There was something small and angular held in his cupped hands. It gave off a fuzzy blue light that made his face look strange.

Other shapes lay on the ground beside him, each in its little soft glow. They were the regular sort of shapes that Granny dismissed airily as jommetry – cubes, many-sided diamonds, cones, even a globe. Each one was transparent and inside was . . .

Esk edged closer. No-one was taking any notice of her.

Inside a crystal sphere that had been tossed aside on to the sand floated a blue-green ball, crisscrossed with tiny white cloud patterns and what could almost have been continents if anyone was silly enough to try to live on a ball. It might have been a sort of model, except something about its glow told Esk that it was quite real and probably very big and not – in every sense – totally inside the sphere.

She put it down very gently and sidled over to a ten-sided block in which floated a much more acceptable world. It was properly disc-shaped, but instead of the Rimfall there was a wall of ice and instead of the Hub there was a gigantic tree, so big that its roots merged into mountain ranges.

A prism beside it held another slowly-turning disc, surrounded by little stars. But there were no ice walls around this one, just a red-gold thread that turned out on closer inspection to be a snake – a snake big enough to encircle a world. For reasons best known to itself it was biting its own tail.

Esk turned the prism over and over curiously, noticing how the little disc inside stayed resolutely upright.

Simon giggled softly. Esk replaced the snake-disc and peered carefully over his shoulder.

He was holding a small glass pyramid. There were stars in it, and occasionally he would give it a little shake so that the stars swirled up like snow in the wind, and then settled back in their places. Then he would giggle.

And beyond the stars . . .

It was the Discworld. Great A'Tuin no bigger than a small saucer toiled along under a world that looked like the work of an obsessive jeweller.

Jiggle, swirl. Jiggle, swirl, giggle. There were already hairline cracks in the glass.

Esk looked at Simon's blank eyes and then up into the hungry faces of the nearest Things, and then she reached across and pulled the pyramid out of his hands and turned and ran.

The Things didn't stir as she scurried towards them, bent almost double, with the pyramid clasped tightly to her chest. But suddenly her feet were no longer running over the sand and she was being lifted into the frigid air, and a Thing with a face like a drowned rabbit turned slowly towards her and extended a talon.

You're not really here, Esk told herself. It's only a sort of a dream, what Granny calls an annaloggy. You can't really be hurt, it's all imagination. There's absolutely no harm that can come to you, it's all really inside your mind.

I wonder if *it* knows that?

The talon picked her out of the air and the rabbit face split like a banana skin. There was no mouth, just a dark hole, as if the Thing was itself an opening to an even worse dimension, a place by comparison with which freezing sand and moonless moonlight would be a jolly afternoon at the seaside.

Esk held the Disc-pyramid and flailed with her free hand at the claw around her. It had no effect. The darkness loomed over her, a gateway to total oblivion.

She kicked it as hard as she could.

Which was not, given the circumstances, very hard. But where her foot struck there was an explosion of white sparks and a pop – which would have been a much more satisfying bang if the thin air here didn't suck the sound away.

The Thing screeched like a chainsaw encountering,

deep inside an unsuspecting sapling, a lurking and long-forgotten nail. The others around it set up a sympathetic buzzing.

Esk kicked again and the Thing shrieked and dropped her to the sand. She was bright enough to roll, with the tiny world hugged protectively to her, because even in a dream a broken ankle can be painful.

The Thing lurched uncertainly above her. Esk's eyes narrowed. She put the world down very carefully, hit the Thing very hard around the point where its shins would be, if there were shins under that cloak, and picked up the world again in one neat movement.

The creature howled, bent double, and then toppled slowly, like a sackful of coathangers. When it hit the ground it collapsed into a mass of disjointed limbs; the head rolled away and rocked to a standstill.

Is that all? thought Esk. They can hardly walk, even! When you hit them they just fall over!

The nearest Things chittered and tried to back away as she marched determinedly towards them, but since their bodies seemed to be held together more or less by wishful thinking they weren't very good at it. She hit one, which had a face like a small family of squid, and it deflated into a pile of twitching bones and bits of fur and odd ends of tentacle, very much like a Greek meal. Another was slightly more successful and had begun to shamble uncertainly away before Esk caught it a crack on one of its five shins.

It flailed desperately as it fell and brought down another two.

By then the others had managed to lurch out of her way and stood watching from a distance.

Esk took a few steps towards the nearest one. It tried to move away, and fell over.

They may have been ugly. They may have been evil. But when it came to poetry in motion, the Things had all the grace and co-ordination of a deck-chair.

Esk glared at them, and took a look at the Disc in its glass pyramid. All the excitement didn't seem to have disturbed it a bit.

She'd been able to get *out*, if this indeed was *out* and if the Disc could be said to be *in*. But how was one supposed to get back?

Somebody laughed. It was the sort of laugh—

Basically, it was p'ch'zarni'chiwkov. This epiglottis-throttling word is seldom used on the Disc except by highly-paid stunt linguists and, of course, the tiny tribe of the K'turni, who invented it. It has no direct synonym, although the Cumhoolie word 'squernt' ('the feeling upon finding that the previous occupant of the privy has used all the paper') begins to approach it in general depth of feeling. The closest translation is as follows:

the nasty little sound of a sword being unsheathed right behind one at just the point when one thought one had disposed of one's enemies

—although K'turni speakers say this does not convey the cold sweating, heart-stopping, gut-freezing sense of the original.

It was that kind of laugh.

Esk turned around slowly. Simon drifted towards her across the sand, with his hands cupped in front of him. His eyes were tight shut.

'Did you really think it would be as easy as that?' he said. Or something said; it didn't sound like Simon's voice, but like dozens of voices speaking at once.

'Simon?' she said, uncertainly.

'He is of no further use to us,' said the Thing with Simon's shape. 'He has shown us the way, child. Now give us our property.'

Esk backed away.

'I don't think it belongs to you,' she said, 'whoever you are.'

The face in front of her opened its eyes. There was nothing there but blackness – not a colour, just holes into some other space.

'We could say that if you gave it to us we would be merciful. We could say we would let you go from here in your own shape. But there wouldn't really be much point in us saying that, would there?'

'I wouldn't believe you,' said Esk.

'Well, then.'

The Simon-thing grinned.

'You're only putting off the inevitable,' it said.

'Suits me.'

'We could take it anyway.'

'Take it, then. But I don't think you can. You can't take anything unless it's given to you, can you?'

They circled round.

'You'll give it to us,' said the Simon-thing.

Some of the other Things were approaching now, striding back across the desert with horrible jerky motions.

'You'll get tired,' it continued. 'We can wait. We're very good at waiting.'

It made a feint to the left, but Esk swung around to face it.

'That doesn't matter,' she said. 'I'm only dreaming this, and you can't get hurt in dreams.'

The Thing paused, and looked at her with its empty eyes.

'Have you got a word in your world, I think it's called "psychosomatic"?'

'Never heard of it,' snapped Esk.

'It means you *can* get hurt in your dreams. And what is so interesting is that if you die in your dreams you stay here. That would be niiiiice.'

Esk glanced sideways at the distant mountains, sprawled on the chilly horizon like melted mud pies. There were no trees, not even any rocks. Just sand and cold stars and—

She felt the movement rather than heard it and turned with the pyramid held between her hands like a club. It hit the Simon-thing in mid-leap with a satisfying thump, but as soon as it hit the ground it somersaulted forward and bounced upright with unpleasant ease. But it had heard her gasp and had seen the brief pain in her eyes. It paused.

'Ah, that hurt you, did it not? You don't like to see another one suffer, yes? Not this one, it seems.'

It turned and beckoned, and two of the tall Things

lurched over to it and gripped it firmly by the arms.

Its eyes changed. The darkness faded, and then Simon's own eyes looked out of his face. He stared up at the Things on either side of him and struggled briefly, but one had several pairs of tentacles wrapped around his wrist and the other was holding his arm in the world's largest lobster claw.

Then he saw Esk, and his eyes fell to the little glass pyramid.

'Run away!' he hissed. 'Take it away from here! Don't let them get it!' He grimaced as the claw tightened on his arm.

'Is this a trick?' said Esk. 'Who are you really?'

'Don't you recognize me?' he said wretchedly. 'What are you doing in my dream?'

'If this is a dream then I'd like to wake up, please,' said Esk.

'Listen. You must run away now, do you understand? Don't stand there with your mouth open.'

GIVE IT TO US, said a cold voice inside Esk's head.

Esk looked down at the glass pyramid with its unconcerned little world and stared up at Simon, her mouth an O of puzzlement.

'But what *is* it?'

'Look hard at it!'

Esk peered through the glass. If she squinted it seemed that the little Disc was granular, as if it was made up of millions of tiny specks. If she looked hard at the specks—

'It's just numbers!' she said. 'The whole world – it's all made up of numbers . . .'

'It's not the world, it's an idea of the world,' said Simon. 'I created it for them. They can't get through to us, do you see, but ideas have got a shape here. Ideas are real!'

GIVE IT TO US.

'But ideas can't hurt anyone!'

'I turned things into numbers to understand them, but they just want to control,' Simon said bitterly. 'They burrowed into my numbers like—'

He screamed.

GIVE IT TO US OR WE WILL TAKE HIM TO BITS.

Esk looked up at the nearest nightmare face.

'How do I know I can trust you?' she said.

YOU CAN'T TRUST US. BUT YOU HAVE NO CHOICE.

Esk looked at the ring of faces that not even a necrophile could love, faces put together from a fishmonger's midden, faces picked randomly from things that lurked in deep ocean holes and haunted caves, faces that were not human enough to gloat or leer but had all the menace of a suspiciously v-shaped ripple near an incautious bather.

She couldn't trust them. But she had no choice.

Something else was happening, in a place as far away as the thickness of a shadow.

The student wizards had run back to the Great Hall, where Cutangle and Granny Weatherwax were still locked in the magical equivalent of Indian arm wrestling. The flagstones under Granny were half-melted and cracked and the table behind Cutangle had taken root and already bore a rich crop of acorns.

One of the students had earned several awards for bravery by daring to tug at Cutangle's cloak . . .

And now they were crowded into the narrow room, looking at the two bodies.

Cutangle summoned doctors of the body and doctors of the mind, and the room buzzed with magic as they got to work.

Granny tapped him on the shoulder.

'A word in your ear, young man,' she said.

'Hardly young, madam,' sighed Cutangle, 'hardly young.' He felt drained. It had been decades since he'd duelled in magic, although it was common enough among students. He had a nasty feeling that Granny would have won eventually. Fighting her was like swatting a fly on your own nose. He couldn't think what had come over him to try it.

Granny led him out into the passage and around the corner to a window-seat. She sat down, leaning her broomstick against the wall. Rain drummed heavily on the roofs outside, and a few zigzags of lightning indicated a storm of Ramtop proportions approaching the city.

'That was quite an impressive display,' she said: 'You nearly won once or twice there.'

'Oh,' said Cutangle, brightening up. 'Do you really think so?'

Granny nodded.

Cutangle patted at various bits of his robe until he located a tarry bag of tobacco and a roll of paper. His hands shook as he fumbled a few shreds of second-hand pipeweed into a skinny homemade. He ran the wretched thing across his tongue, and barely moistened it. Then a dim remembrance of propriety welled up in the back of his mind.

'Um,' he said, 'do you mind if I smoke?'

Granny shrugged. Cutangle struck a match on the wall and tried desperately to navigate the flame and the cigarette into approximately the same position. Granny gently took the match from his trembling hand and lit it for him.

Cutangle sucked on the tobacco, had a ritual cough and settled back, the glowing end of the rollup the only light in the dim corridor.

'They've gone Wandering,' said Granny at last.

'I know,' said Cutangle.

'Your wizards won't be able to get them back.'

'I know that, too.'

'They might get *something* back, though.'

'I wish you hadn't said that.'

There was a pause while they contemplated what might come back, inhabiting living bodies, acting almost like the original inhabitants.

'It's probably my fault—' they said in unison, and stopped in astonishment.

'You first, madam,' said Cutangle.

'Them cigaretty things,' asked Granny, 'are they good for the nerves?'

Cutangle opened his mouth to point out very courteously that tobacco was a habit reserved for wizards, but thought better of it. He extended the tobacco pouch towards Granny.

She told him about Esk's birth, and the coming of the old wizard, and the staff, and Esk's forays into magic. By the time she had finished she had succeeded in rolling a tight, thin cylinder that burned with a small blue flame and made her eyes water.

'I don't know that shaky nerves wouldn't be better,' she wheezed.

Cutangle wasn't listening.

'This is quite astonishing,' he said. 'You say the child didn't suffer in any way?'

'Not that I noticed,' said Granny. 'The staff seemed – well, on her side, if you know what I mean.'

'And where is this staff now?'

'She said she threw it in the river . . .'

The old wizard and the elderly witch stared at each other, their faces illuminated by a flare of lightning outside.

Cutangle shook his head. 'The river's flooding,' he said. 'It's a million-to-one chance.'

Granny smiled grimly. It was the sort of smile that wolves ran away from. Granny grasped her broomstick purposefully.

'Million-to-one chances,' she said, 'crop up nine times out of ten.'

There are storms that are frankly theatrical, all sheet lightning and metallic thunder rolls. There are storms that are tropical and sultry, and incline to hot winds and fireballs. But this was a storm of the Circle Sea plains, and its main ambition was to hit the ground with as much rain as possible. It was the kind of storm that suggests that the whole sky has swallowed a diuretic. The thunder and lightning hung around in the background, supplying a sort of chorus, but the rain was the star of the show. It tap-danced across the land.

The grounds of the University stretched right down to the river. By day they were a neat formal pattern of gravel paths and hedges, but in the middle of a wet wild night the hedges seemed to have moved and the paths had simply gone off somewhere to stay dry.

A weak wyrdlight shone inefficiently among the dripping leaves. But most of the rain found its way through anyway.

'Can you use one of them wizard fireballs?'

'Have a heart, madam.'

'Are you sure she would have come this way?'

'There's a sort of jetty thing down here somewhere, unless I'm lost.'

There was the sound of a heavy body blundering wetly into a bush, and then a splash.

'I've found the river, anyway.'

Granny Weatherwax peered through the soaking darkness. She could hear a roaring and could dimly make out the white crests of floodwater. There was also the distinctive river smell of the Ankh, which suggested that several armies had used it first as a urinal and then as a sepulchre.

Cutangle splashed dejectedly towards her.

'This is foolishness,' he said, 'meaning no offence,

madam. But it'll be out to sea on this flood. And I'll die of cold.'

'You can't get any wetter than you are now. Anyway, you walk wrong for rain.'

'I beg your pardon?'

'You go all hunched up, you fight it, that's not the way. You should – well, move between the drops.' And, indeed, Granny seemed to be merely damp.

'I'll bear that in mind. Come on, madam. It's me for a roaring fire and a glass of something hot and wicked.'

Granny sighed. 'I don't know. Somehow I expected to see it sticking out of the mud, or something. Not just all this water.'

Cutangle patted her gently on the shoulder.

'There may be something else we can do—' he began, and was interrupted by a zip of lightning and another roll of thunder.

'I said maybe there's something—' he began again.

'What was that I saw?' demanded Granny.

'What was what?' said Cutangle, bewildered.

'Give me some light!'

The wizard sighed wetly, and extended a hand. A bolt of golden fire shot out across the foaming water and hissed into oblivion.

'There!' said Granny triumphantly.

'It's just a boat,' said Cutangle. 'The boys use them in the summer—'

He waded after Granny's determined figure as fast as he could.

'You can't be thinking of taking it out on a night like this,' he said. 'It's madness!'

Granny slithered along the wet planking of the jetty, which was already nearly under water.

'You don't know anything about boats!' Cutangle protested.

'I shall have to learn quickly, then,' replied Granny calmly.

'But I haven't been in a boat since I was a boy!'

'I wasn't actually asking you to come. Does the pointy bit go in front?'

Cutangle moaned.

'This is all very creditable,' he said, 'but perhaps we can wait till morning?'

A flash of lightning illuminated Granny's face.

'Perhaps not,' Cutangle conceded. He lumbered along the jetty and pulled the little rowing boat towards him. Getting in was a matter of luck but he managed it eventually, fumbling with the painter in the darkness.

The boat swung out into the flood and was carried away, spinning slowly.

Granny clung to the seat as it rocked in the turbulent waters, and looked expectantly at Cutangle through the murk.

'Well?' she said.

'Well what?' said Cutangle.

'You said you knew all about boats.'

'No. I said you didn't.'

'Oh.'

They hung on as the boat wallowed heavily,

miraculously righted itself, and was carried backwards downstream.

'When you said you hadn't been in a boat since you were a boy . . .' Granny began.

'I was two years old, I think.'

The boat caught on a whirlpool, spun around, and shot off across the flow.

'I had you down as the sort of boy who was in and out of boats all day long.'

'I was born up in the mountains. I get seasick on damp grass, if you must know,' said Cutangle.

The boat banged heavily against a submerged tree trunk, and a wavelet lapped the prow.

'I know a spell against drowning,' he added miserably.

'I'm glad about that.'

'Only you have to say it while you're standing on dry land.'

'Take your boots off,' Granny commanded.

'What?'

'Take your boots off, man!'

Cutangle shifted uneasily on his bench.

'What have you in mind?' he said.

'The water is supposed to be *outside* the boat, I know that much!' Granny pointed to the dark tide sloshing around the bilges: 'Fill your boots with water and tip it over the side!'

Cutangle nodded. He felt that the last couple of hours had somehow carried him along without him actually touching the sides, and for a moment he nursed the strangely consoling feeling that his life was totally beyond his control and whatever happened no one could blame him. Filling his boots with water while adrift on a flooded river at midnight with what he could only describe as a *woman* seemed about as logical as anything could be in the circumstances.

A fine figure of a woman, said a neglected voice at the back of his mind. There was something about the way she used the tattered broomstick to scull the boat across the choppy water that troubled long-forgotten bits of Cutangle's subconscious.

Not that he could be certain about the fine figure, of course, what with the rain and the wind and Granny's habit of wearing her entire wardrobe in one go. Cutangle cleared his throat uncertainly. Metaphorically a fine figure, he decided.

'Um, look,' he said. 'This is all very creditable, but consider the facts, I mean, the rate of drift and so forth, you see? It could be miles out on the ocean by now. It might never come to shore again. It might even go over the Rimfall.'

Granny, who had been staring out across the water, turned around.

'Can't you think of anything else at all helpful that we could be doing?' she demanded.

Cutangle baled for a few moments.

'No,' he said.

'Have you ever heard of anyone coming Back?'

'No.'

'Then it's worth a try, isn't it?'

'I never liked the ocean,' said Cutangle. 'It ought to be paved over. There's dreadful things in it, down in the deep bits. Ghastly sea monsters. Or so they say.'

'Keep baling, my lad, or you'll be able to see if they're right.'

The storm rolled backwards and forwards overhead. It was lost here on the flat river plains; it belonged in the high Ramtops, where they knew how to appreciate a good storm. It grumbled around, looking for even a moderately high hill to throw lightning at.

The rain settled down to the gentle patter of rain that is quite capable of keeping it up for days. A sea fog also rolled in to assist it.

'If we had some oars we could row, if we knew where we were going,' said Cutangle. Granny didn't answer.

He heaved a few more bootfuls of water over the side, and it occurred to him that the gold braiding on his robe would probably never be the same again. It would be nice to think it might matter, one day.

'I don't suppose you *do* know which way the Hub is, by any chance?' he ventured. 'Just making conversation.'

'Look for the mossy side of trees,' said Granny without turning her head.

'Ah,' said Cutangle, and nodded.

He peered down gloomily at the oily waters, and wondered which particularly oily waters they were. Judging by the salty smell they were out in the bay now.

What really terrified him about the sea was that the only thing between him and the horrible things that lived at the bottom of it was water. Of course, he knew that logically the only thing that separated him from, say, the man-eating tigers in the jungles of Klatch was mere distance, but that wasn't the same thing at all. Tigers didn't rise up out of the chilly depths, mouths full of needle teeth . . .

He shivered.

'Can't you feel it?' asked Granny. 'You can taste it in the air. Magic! It's leaking out from something.'

'It's not actually water soluble,' said Cutangle. He smacked his lips once or twice. There was indeed a tinny taste to the fog, he had to admit, and a faint greasiness to the air.

'You're a wizard,' said Granny, severely. 'Can't you call it up or something?'

'The question has never arisen,' said Cutangle. 'Wizards never throw their staffs away.'

'It's around here somewhere,' snapped Granny. 'Help me look for it, man!'

Cutangle groaned. It had been a busy night, and before he tried any more magic he really needed twelve hours sleep, several good meals, and a quiet afternoon in front of a big fire. He was getting too old, that was the trouble. But he closed his eyes and concentrated.

There was magic around, all right. There are some places where magic naturally accumulates. It builds up around deposits of the transmundane metal octiron, in the wood of certain trees, in isolated lakes, it sleets through the world and those skilled in such things can catch it and store it. There was a store of magic in the area.

'It's potent,' he said. 'Very potent.' He raised his hands to his temples.

'It's getting bloody cold,' said Granny. The insistent rain had turned to snow.

There was a sudden change in the world. The boat stopped, not with a jar, but as if the sea had suddenly decided to become solid. Granny looked over the side.

The sea had become solid. The sound of the waves was coming from a long way away and getting further away all the time.

She leaned over the side of the boat and tapped on the water.

'Ice,' she said. The boat was motionless in an ocean of ice. It creaked ominously.

Cutangle nodded slowly.

'It makes sense,' he said. 'If they are . . . where we think they are, then it's very cold. As cold as the night between the stars, it is said. So the staff feels it too.'

'Right,' said Granny, and stepped out of the boat. 'All we have to do is find the middle of the ice and there's the staff, right?'

'I knew you were going to say that. Can I at least put my boots on?'

They wandered across the frozen waves, with Cutangle stopping occasionally to try and sense the exact location of the staff. His robes were freezing on him. His teeth chattered.

'Aren't you cold?' he said to Granny, whose dress fairly crackled as she walked.

'I'm cold,' she conceded. 'I just ain't shivering.'

'We used to have winters like this when I was a lad,'

said Cutangle, blowing on his fingers. 'It doesn't snow in Ankh, hardly.'

'Really,' said Granny, peering ahead through the freezing fog.

'There was snow on the tops of the mountains all year round, I recall. Oh, you don't get temperatures like you did when I was a boy.

'At least, until now,' he added, stamping his feet on the ice. It creaked menacingly, reminding him that it was all that lay between him and the bottom of the sea. He stamped again, as softly as possible.

'What mountains are these?' asked Granny.

'Oh, the Ramtops. Up towards the Hub, in fact. Place called Brass Neck.'

Granny's lips moved. 'Cutangle, Cutangle,' she said softly. 'Any relation to old Acktur Cutangle? Used to live in a big old house under Leaping Mountain, had a lot of sons.'

'My father. How on disc d'you know that?'

'I was raised up there,' said Granny, resisting the temptation merely to smile knowingly. 'Next valley. Bad Ass. I remember your mother. Nice woman, kept brown and white chickens, I used to go up there to buy eggs for me mam. That was before I was called to witching, of course.'

'I don't remember you,' said Cutangle. 'Of course, it was a long time ago. There was always a lot of children around our house.' He sighed. 'I suppose it's possible I pulled your hair once. It was the sort of thing I used to do.'

'Maybe. I remember a fat little boy. Rather unpleasant.'

'That might have been me. I seem to recall a rather bossy girl, but it was a long time ago. A long time ago.'

'I didn't have white hair in those days,' said Granny.

'Everything was a different colour in those days.'

'That's true.'

'It didn't rain so much in the summer time.'

'The sunsets were redder.'

'There were more old people. The world was full of them,' said the wizard.

'Yes, I know. And now it's full of young people. Funny, really. I mean, you'd expect it to be the other way round.'

'They even had a better kind of air. It was easier to breathe,' said Cutangle. They stamped on through the swirling snow, considering the curious ways of time and Nature.

'Ever been home again?' said Granny.

Cutangle shrugged. 'When my father died. It's odd, I've never said this to anyone, but – well, there were my brothers, because I am an eighth son of course, and they had children and even grandchildren, and not one of them can hardly write his name. I could have bought the whole village. And they treated me like a king, but – I mean, I've been to places and seen things that would curdle their minds, I've faced down creatures wilder than their nightmares, I know secrets that are known to a very few—'

'You felt left out,' said Granny. 'There's nothing strange in that. It happens to all of us. It was our choice.'

'Wizards should never go home,' said Cutangle.

'I don't think they *can* go home,' agreed Granny. 'You can't cross the same river twice, I always say.'

Cutangle gave this some thought.

'I think you're wrong there,' he said. 'I must have crossed the same river, oh, thousands of times.'

'Ah, but it wasn't the same river.'

'It wasn't?'

'No.'

Cutangle shrugged. 'It looked like the same bloody river.'

'No need to take that tone,' said Granny. 'I don't see why I should listen to that sort of language from a wizard who can't even answer letters!'

Cutangle was silent for a moment, except for the castanet chatter of his teeth.

'Oh,' he said. 'Oh, I see. They were from you, were they?'

'That's right. I signed them on the bottom. It's supposed to be a sort of clue, isn't it?'

'All right, all right. I just thought they were a joke, that's all,' said Cutangle sullenly.

'A joke?'

'We don't get many applications from women. We don't get *any*.'

'I wondered why I didn't get a reply,' said Granny.

'I threw them away, if you must know.'

'You could at least have – *there* it is!'

'Where? Where? Oh, there.'

The fog parted and they now saw it clearly – a

fountain of snowflakes, an ornamental pillar of frozen air. And below it . . .

The staff wasn't locked in ice, but lay peacefully in a seething pool of water.

One of the unusual aspects of a magical universe is the existence of opposites. It has already been remarked that darkness isn't the opposite of light, it is simply the absence of light. In the same way absolute zero is merely the absence of heat. If you want to know what *real* cold is, the cold so intense that water can't even freeze but anti-boils, look no further than this pool.

They looked in silence for some seconds, their bickering forgotten. Then Cutangle said slowly: 'If you stick your hand in that, your fingers'll snap like carrots.'

'Do you think you can lift it out by magic?' said Granny.

Cutangle started to pat his pockets and eventually produced his rollup bag. With expert fingers he shredded the remains of a few dogends into a fresh paper and licked it into shape, without taking his eyes off the staff.

'No,' he said. 'But I'll try anyway.'

He looked longingly at the cigarette and then poked it behind his ear. He extended his hands, fingers splayed, and his lips moved soundlessly as he mumbled a few words of power.

The staff spun in its pool and then rose gently away from the ice, where it immediately became the centre of a cocoon of frozen air. Cutangle groaned with the effort – direct levitation is the hardest of the practical magics, because of the ever-present danger of the well-known principles of action and reaction, which means that a wizard attempting to lift a heavy item by mind power alone faces the prospect of ending up with his brains in his boots.

'Can you stand it upright?' said Granny.

With great delicacy the staff turned slowly in the air until it hung in front of Granny a few inches above the ice. Frost glittered on its carvings, but it seemed to Cutangle – through the red haze of migraine that hovered in front of his eyes – to be watching him. *Resentfully*.

Granny adjusted her hat and straightened up purposefully.

'*Right*,' she said. Cutangle swayed. The tone of voice cut through him like a diamond saw. He could dimly remember being scolded by his mother when he was small; well, this was that voice, only refined and con-centrated and edged with little bits of carborundum, a tone of command that would have a corpse standing to attention and could probably have marched it halfway across its cemetery before it remembered it was dead.

Granny stood in front of the hovering staff, almost melting its icy covering by the sheer anger in her gaze.

'This is your idea of proper behaviour, is it? Lying around on the sea while people die? Oh, very well done!'

She stomped around in a semi-circle. To Cutangle's bewilderment, the staff turned to follow her.

'So you were thrown away,' snapped Granny. 'So what? She's hardly more than a child, and children throw us all away sooner or later. Is this loyal service? Have you no shame, lying around sulking when you could be of some use at last?'

She leaned forward, her hooked nose a few inches from the staff. Cutangle was almost certain that the staff tried to lean backwards out of her way.

'Shall I tell you what happens to wicked staffs?' she hissed. 'If Esk is lost to the world, shall I tell you what I will do to you? You were saved from the fire once, because you could pass on the hurt to her. Next time it won't be the fire.'

Her voice sank to a whiplash whisper.

'First it'll be the spokeshave. And then the sandpaper, and the auger, and the whittling knife—'

'I say, steady on,' said Cutangle, his eyes watering.

'—and what's left I'll stake out in the woods for the fungus and the woodlice and the beetles. It could take *years*.'

The carvings writhed. Most of them had moved around the back, out of Granny's gaze.

'Now,' she said. 'I'll tell you what I'm going to do. I'm going to pick you up and we are all going back to the University, aren't we? Otherwise it's blunt saw time.'

She rolled up her sleeves and extended a hand.

'Wizard,' she said, 'I shall want you to release it.'

Cutangle nodded miserably.

'When I say now, now! *Now!*'

* * *

Cutangle opened his eyes again.

Granny was standing with her left arm extended full length in front of her, her hand clamped around the staff.

The ice was exploding off it, in gouts of steam.

'Right,' finished Granny, 'and if this happens again I shall be *very* angry, do I make myself clear?'

Cutangle lowered his hands and hurried towards her.

'Are you hurt?'

She shook her head. 'It's like holding a hot icicle,' she said. 'Come on, we haven't got time to stand around chatting.'

'How are we going to get back?'

'Oh, show some backbone, man, for goodness sake. We'll fly.'

Granny waved her broomstick. The Archchancellor looked at it doubtfully.

'On that?'

'Of course. Don't wizards fly on their staffs?'

'It's rather undignified.'

'If I can put up with that, so can you.'

'Yes, but is it safe?'

Granny gave him a withering look.

'Do you mean in the absolute sense?' she asked. 'Or, say, compared with staying behind on a melting ice floe?'

'This is the first time I have ever ridden on a broomstick,' said Cutangle.

'Really.'

'I thought you just had to get on them and they flew,' said the wizard. 'I didn't know you had to do all that running up and down and shouting at them.'

'It's a knack,' said Granny.

'I thought they went faster,' Cutangle continued, 'and, to be frank, higher.'

'What do you mean, higher?' asked Granny, trying to compensate for the wizard's weight on the pillion as they turned back upriver. Like pillion passengers since the dawn of time, he persisted in leaning the wrong way.

'Well, more sort of *above* the trees,' said Cutangle, ducking as a dripping branch swept his hat away.

'There's nothing wrong with this broomstick that you losing a few stone wouldn't cure,' snapped Granny. 'Or would you rather get off and walk?'

'Apart from the fact that half of the time my feet are touching the ground anyway,' said Cutangle, 'I wouldn't want to embarrass you. If someone had asked me to list all the perils of flying, you know, it would never have occurred to me to include having one's legs whipped to death by tall bracken.'

'Are you smoking?' said Granny, staring grimly ahead. 'Something's burning.'

'It was just to calm my nerves what with all this headlong plunging through the air, madam.'

'Well, put it out this minute. And hold on.'

The broomstick lurched upwards and increased its speed to that of a geriatric jogger.

'Mr Wizard.'

'Hallo?'

'When I said hold on—'

'Yes?'

'I didn't mean there.'

There was a pause.

'Oh. Yes. I see. I'm terribly sorry.'

'That's all right.'

'My memory isn't what it was . . . I assure you . . . no offence meant.'

'None taken.'

They flew in silence for a moment.

'Nevertheless,' said Granny thoughtfully, 'I think that, on the whole, I would prefer you to move your hands.'

Rain gushed across the leads of Unseen University and poured into the gutters where ravens' nests, abandoned since the summer, floated like very badly-built boats. The water gurgled along ancient, crusted pipes. It found its way under tiles and said hallo to the spiders under the eaves. It leapt from gables and formed secret lakes high amongst the spires.

Whole ecologies lived in the endless rooftops of the University, which by comparison made Gormenghast look like a toolshed on a railway allotment; birds sang in tiny jungles grown from apple pips and weed seeds, little frogs swam in the upper gutters, and a colony of ants were busily inventing an interesting and complex civilization.

One thing the water couldn't do was gurgle out of

the ornamental gargoyles ranged around the roofs. This was because the gargoyles wandered off and sheltered in the attics at the first sign of rain. They held that just because you were ugly it didn't mean you were stupid.

It rained streams. It rained rivers. It rained seas. But mainly it rained through the roof of the Great Hall, where the duel between Granny and Cutangle had left a very large hole, and Treatle felt that it was somehow raining on him personally.

He stood on a table organizing the teams of students who were taking down the paintings and ancient tapestries before they got soaked. It had to be a table, because the floor was already several inches deep in water.

Not rainwater, unfortunately. This was water with real personality, the kind of distinctive character water gets after a long journey through silty countryside. It had the thick texture of authentic Ankh water – too stiff to drink, too runny to plough.

The river had burst its banks and a million little watercourses were flowing backwards, bursting in through the cellars and playing peekaboo under the flagstones. There was the occasional distant boom as some forgotten magic in a drowned dungeon shorted out and surrendered up its power; Treatle wasn't at all keen on some of the unpleasant bubblings and hissings that were escaping to the surface.

He thought again how nice it would be to be the sort of wizard who lived in a little cave somewhere and collected herbs and thought significant thoughts and knew what the owls were saying. But probably the cave would be damp and the herbs would be poisonous and Treatle could never be sure, when all was said and done, exactly what thoughts were really significant.

He got down awkwardly and paddled through the dark swirling waters. Well, he had done his best. He'd tried to organize the senior wizards into repairing the roof by magic, but there was a general argument over the spells that could be used and a consensus that this was in any case work for artisans.

That's wizards for you, he thought gloomily as he waded between the dripping arches, always probing the infinite but never noticing the definite, especially in the matter of household chores. We never had this trouble before that woman came.

He squelched up the steps, lit by a particularly impressive flash of lightning. He had a cold certainty that while of course no one could possibly blame him for all this, everybody would. He seized the hem of his robe and wrung it out wretchedly, then he reached for his tobacco pouch.

It was a nice green waterproof one. That meant that all the rain that had got into it couldn't get out again. It was indescribable.

He found his little clip of papers. They were fused into one lump, like the legendary pound note found in the back pockets of trousers after they have been washed, spun, dried and ironed.

'Bugger,' he said, with feeling.

'I say! Treatle!'

Treatle looked around. He had been the last to leave the hall, where even now some of the benches were beginning to float. Whirlpools and patches of bubble marked the spots where magic was leaking from the cellars, but there was no one to be seen.

Unless, of course, one of the statues had spoken. They had been too heavy to move, and Treatle remembered telling the students that a thorough wash would probably do them good.

He looked at their stern faces and regretted it. The statues of very powerful dead mages were sometimes more lifelike than statues had any right to be. Maybe he should have kept his voice down.

'Yes?' he ventured, acutely aware of the stony stares.

'Up here, you fool!'

He looked up. The broomstick descended heavily through the rain in a series of swoops and jerks. About five feet above the water it lost its few remaining aerial pretensions, and flopped noisily into a whirlpool.

'Don't stand there, idiot!'

Treatle peered nervously into the gloom.

'I've got to stand somewhere,' he said.

'I mean give us a hand!' snapped Cutangle, rising from the wavelets like a fat and angry Venus. 'The lady first, of course.'

He turned to Granny, who was fishing around in the water.

'I've lost my hat,' she said.

Cutangle sighed. 'Does that really matter at a time like this?'

'A witch has got to have a hat, otherwise who's to know?' said Granny. She made a grab as something dark and sodden drifted by, cackled triumphantly, tipped out the water and rammed the hat on her head. It had lost its stiffening and flopped rather rakishly over one eye.

'Right,' she said, in a tone of voice that suggested the whole universe had just better watch out.

There was another brilliant flash of lightning, which shows that even the weather gods have a well-developed sense of theatre.

'It rather suits you,' said Cutangle.

'Excuse me,' said Treatle, 'but isn't she the w—'

'Never mind that,' said Cutangle, taking Granny's hand and helping her up the steps. He flourished the staff.

'But it's against the lore to allow w—'

He stopped and stared as Granny reached out and touched the damp wall by the door. Cutangle tapped him on the chest.

'Show me where it's written down,' said Cutangle.

'They're in the library,' Granny interrupted.

'It was the only dry place,' said Treatle, 'but—'

'This building is frightened of thunderstorms,' said Granny. 'It could do with comforting.'

'But the lore—' repeated Treatle desperately.

Granny was already striding down the passage, with Cutangle hopping along behind. He turned.

'You heard the lady,' he said.

Treatle watched them go, with his mouth hanging

open. When their footsteps had died away in the distance he stood silently for a moment, thinking about life and where his could have gone wrong.

However, he wasn't going to be accused of disobedience.

Very carefully, without knowing exactly why, he reached out and gave the wall a friendly pat. 'There, there,' he said.

Strangely enough, he felt a lot better.

It occurred to Cutangle that he ought to lead the way in his own premises, but Granny in a hurry was no match for a near-terminal nicotine addict and he kept up only by a sort of crabwise leaping.

'It's this way,' he said, splashing through the puddles.

'I know. The building told me.'

'Yes, I was meaning to ask about that,' said Cutangle, 'because you see it's never said anything to me and I've lived here for years.'

'Have you ever listened to it?'

'Not exactly listened, no,' Cutangle conceded. 'Not as such.'

'Well then,' said Granny, edging past a waterfall where the kitchen steps used to be (Mrs Whitlow's washing would never be the same again). 'I think it's up here and along the passage, isn't it?'

She swept past a trio of astonished wizards, who were surprised by her and completely startled by her hat.

TERRY PRATCHETT

Cutangle panted after her and caught her arm at the doors to the library.

'Look,' he said desperately, 'No offence, Miss – um, Mistress—'

'I think Esmerelda will suffice now. What with us having shared a broomstick and everything.'

'Can I go in front? It *is* my library,' he begged.

Granny turned around, her face a mask of surprise. Then she smiled.

'Of course. I'm so sorry.'

'For the look of the thing, you see,' said Cutangle apologetically. He pushed the door open.

The Library was full of wizards, who care about their books in the same way that ants care about their eggs and in time of difficulty carry them around in much the same way. The water was getting in even here, and turning up in rather odd places because of the library's strange gravitational effects. All the lower shelves had been cleared and relays of wizards and students were piling the volumes on every available table and dry shelf. The air was full of the sound of angry rustling pages, which almost drowned out the distant fury of the storm.

This was obviously upsetting the librarian, who was scurrying from wizard to wizard, tugging ineffectually at their robes and shouting 'ook'.

He spotted Cutangle and knuckled rapidly towards him. Granny had never seen an orang-outang before, but wasn't about to admit it, and remained quite calm in the face of a small pot-bellied man with extremely long arms and a size 12 skin on a size 8 body.

'Ook,' it explained, '*ooook*.'

'I expect so,' said Cutangle shortly, and grabbed the nearest wizard, who was tottering under the weight of a dozen grimoires. The man stared at him as if he was a ghost, looked sideways at Granny, and dropped the books on the floor. The librarian winced.

'Archchancellor?' gasped the wizard, 'you're alive? I mean – we heard you'd been spirited away by—' he looked at Granny again, '—I mean, we thought – Treatle told us—'

'*Oook*,' said the librarian, shooing some pages back between their covers.

'Where are young Simon and the girl? What have you done with them?' Granny demanded.

'They – we put them over here,' said the wizard, backing away. 'Um—'

'Show us,' said Cutangle. 'And stop stuttering, man, you'd think you'd never seen a woman before.'

The wizard swallowed hard and nodded vigorously.

'Certainly. And – I mean – please follow me – um—'

'You weren't going to say anything about the lore, were you?' asked Cutangle.

'Um – no, Archchancellor.'

'Good.'

They followed hard on his trodden-down heels as he scurried between the toiling wizards, most of whom stopped working to stare as Granny strode past.

'This is getting embarrassing,' said Cutangle, out of the corner of his mouth. 'I shall have to declare you an honorary wizard.'

Granny stared straight ahead and her lips hardly moved.

'You do,' she hissed, 'and I will declare you an honorary witch.'

Cutangle's mouth snapped shut.

Esk and Simon were lying on a table in one of the side reading-rooms, with half a dozen wizards watching over them. They drew back nervously as the trio approached, with the librarian swinging along behind.

'I've been thinking,' said Cutangle. 'Surely it would be better to give the staff to Simon? He *is* a wizard, and—'

'Over my dead body,' said Granny. 'Yours, too. They're getting their power through him, do you want to give them more?'

Cutangle sighed. He had been admiring the staff, it was one of the best he had seen.

'Very well. You're right, of course.'

He leaned down and laid the staff on Esk's sleeping form, and then stood back dramatically.

Nothing happened.

One of the wizards coughed nervously.

Nothing continued to happen.

The carvings on the staff appeared to be grinning.

'It's not working,' said Cutangle, 'is it?'

'Ook.'

'Give it time,' said Granny.

They gave it time. Outside the storm strode around the sky, trying to lift the lids off houses.

Granny sat down on a pile of books and rubbed her

eyes. Cutangle's hands strayed towards his tobacco pocket. The wizard with the nervous cough was helped out of the room by a colleague.

'Ook,' said the librarian.

'I know!' said Granny, so that Cutangle's half-rolled homemade shot out of his nerveless fingers in a shower of tobacco.

'What?'

'It's not finished!'

'What?'

'She can't use the staff, of course,' said Granny, standing up.

'But you said she swept the floors with it and it protects her and—' Cutangle began.

'Nonono,' said Granny. 'That means the staff uses itself or it uses her, but she's never been able to use *it*, d'you see?'

Cutangle stared at the two quiet bodies. 'She should be able to use it. It's a proper wizard's staff.'

'Oh,' said Granny. 'So she's a proper wizard, is she?'

Cutangle hesitated.

'Well, of course not. You can't ask us to declare her a wizard. Where's the precedent?'

'The what?' asked Granny, sharply.

'It's never happened before.'

'Lots of things have never happened before. We're only born once.'

Cutangle gave her a look of mute appeal. 'But it's against the l—'

He began to say 'lore', but the word mumbled into silence.

'Where does it say it?' said Granny triumphantly. 'Where does it say women can't be wizards?'

The following thoughts sped through Cutangle's mind:

. . . It doesn't say it anywhere, it says it everywhere.

. . . But young Simon seemed to say that everywhere is so much like nowhere that you can't really tell the difference.

. . . Do I want to be remembered as the first Archchancellor to allow women into the University? Still . . . I'd be remembered, that's for sure.

. . . She really is a rather impressive woman when she stands in that sort of way.

. . . That staff has got ideas of its own.

. . . There's a sort of sense to it.

. . . I would be laughed at.

. . . It might not work.

. . . It might work.

She couldn't trust them. But she had no choice.

Esk stared at the terrible faces peering down at her, and the lanky bodies, mercifully cloaked.

Her hands tingled.

In the shadow world, ideas are real. The thought seemed to travel up her arms.

It was a buoyant sort of thought, a thought full of fizz. She laughed, and moved her hands apart, and the staff sparkled in her hands like solid electricity.

The Things started to chitter nervously and one or

two at the back started to lurch away. Simon fell forward as his captors hastily let go, and he landed on his hands and knees in the sand.

'Use it!' he shouted. 'That's it! They're frightened!'

Esk gave him a smile, and continued to examine the staff. For the first time she could see what the carvings actually were.

Simon snatched up the pyramid of the world and ran towards her.

'Come on!' he said. 'They hate it!'

'Pardon?' said Esk.

'Use the staff,' said Simon urgently, and reached out for it. 'Hey! It bit me!'

'Sorry,' said Esk. 'What were we talking about?' She looked up and regarded the keening Things as it were for the first time. 'Oh, *those*. They only exist inside our heads. If we didn't believe in them, they wouldn't exist at all.'

Simon looked around at them.

'I can't honestly say I believe you,' he said.

'I think we should go home now,' said Esk. 'People will be worrying.'

She moved her hands together and the staff vanished, although for a moment her hands glowed as though they were cupped around a candle.

The Things howled. A few of them fell over.

'The important thing about magic is how you don't use it,' said Esk, taking Simon's arm.

He stared at the crumbling figures around him, and grinned foolishly.

'You *don't* use it?' he queried.

'Oh, yes,' said Esk, as they walked towards the Things. 'Try it yourself.'

She extended her hands, brought the staff out of the air, and offered it to him. He went to take it, then drew back his hand.

'Uh, no,' he said, 'I don't think it likes me much.'

'I think it's all right if I give it to you. It can't really argue with that,' said Esk.

'Where does it *go*?'

'It just becomes an idea of itself, I think.'

He reached out his hand again and closed his fingers around the shining wood.

'*Right*,' he said, and raised it in the classical revengeful wizard's pose. 'I'll show them!'

'No, wrong.'

'What do you mean, wrong? I've got the power!'

'They're sort of – reflections of us,' said Esk. 'You can't beat your reflections, they'll always be as strong as you are. That's why they draw nearer to you when you start using magic. And they don't get tired. They feed off magic, so you can't beat them with magic. No, the thing is . . . well, not using magic because you can't, that's no use at all. But not using magic because you *can*, that really upsets them. They hate the idea. If people stopped using magic they'd die.'

The Things ahead of them fell over each other in their haste to back away.

Simon looked at the staff, then at Esk, then at the Things, then back at the staff.

'This needs a lot of thinking about,' he said uncertainly. 'I'd really like to work this out.'

'I expect you'll do it very well.'

'Because you're saying that the real power is when you go right through magic and out the other side.'

'It works, though, doesn't it?'

They were alone on the cold plain now. The Things were distant stick-figures.

'I wonder if this is what they mean by sourcery?' said Simon.

'I don't know. It might be.'

'I'd really like to work this out,' said Simon again, turning the staff over and over in his hands. 'We could set up some experiments, you know, into deliberately not using magic. We could carefully not draw an octogram on the floor, and we could deliberately not call up all sorts of things, and – it makes me sweat just to think about it!'

'I'd like to think about how to get home,' said Esk, looking down at the pyramid.

'Well, that is supposed to be *my* idea of the world. I should be able to find a way. How do you do this thing with the hands?'

He moved his hands together. The staff slid between them, the light glowing through his fingers for a moment, and then vanished. He grinned. 'Right. Now all we have to do is look for the University . . .'

Cutangle lit his third rollup from the stub of the second. This last cigarette owed a lot to the creative powers of nervous energy, and looked like a camel with the legs cut off.

He had already watched the staff lift itself gently from Esk and land on Simon.

Now it had floated up into the air again.

Other wizards had crowded into the room. The librarian was sitting under the table.

'If only we had some idea what is going on,' said Cutangle. 'It's the suspense I can't stand.'

'Think positively, man,' snapped Granny. 'And put out that bloody cigarette, I can't imagine anyone wanting to come back to a room that smells like a fireplace.'

As one man the assembled college of wizards turned their faces towards Cutangle, expectantly.

He took the smouldering mess out of his mouth and, with a glare that none of the assembled wizards cared to meet, trod it underfoot.

'Probably time I gave it up anyway,' he said. 'That goes for the rest of you, too. Worse than an ashpit in this place, sometimes.'

Then he saw the staff. It was—

The only way Cutangle could describe the effect was that it seemed to be going very fast while staying in exactly the same place.

Streamers of gas flared away from it and vanished, if they were gas. It blazed like a comet designed by an inept special effects man. Coloured sparks leapt out and disappeared somewhere.

It was also changing colour, starting with a dull red and then climbing through the spectrum until it was a painful violet. Snakes of white fire coruscated along its length.

(There should be a word for words that sound like things would sound like if they made a noise, he thought. The word 'glisten' does indeed gleam oilily, and if there was ever a word that sounded exactly the way sparks look as they creep across burned paper, or the way lights of cities would creep across the world if the whole of human civilization was crammed into one night, then you couldn't do better than 'coruscate'.)

He knew what would happen next.

'Look out,' he whispered. 'It's going to go—'

In total silence, in the kind of silence in fact that sucks in sounds and stifles them, the staff flashed into pure octarine along the whole of its length.

The eighth colour, produced by light falling through a strong magical field, blazed out through bodies and bookshelves and walls. Other colours blurred and ran together, as though the light was a glass of gin poured over the watercolour painting of the world. The clouds over the University glowed, twisted into fascinating and unexpected shapes, and streamed upwards.

An observer above the Disc would have seen a little patch of land near the Circle Sea sparkle like a jewel for several seconds, then wink out.

The silence of the room was broken by a wooden clatter as the staff dropped out of the air and bounced on the table.

Someone said 'Ook', very faintly.

Cutangle eventually remembered how to use his hands and raised them to where he hoped his eyes would be. Everything had gone black.

'Is – anyone else there?' he said.

'Gods, you don't know how glad I am to hear you say that,' said another voice. The silence was suddenly full of babble.

'Are we still where we were?'

'I don't know. Where were we?'

'Here, I think.'

'Can you reach out?'

'Not unless I am quite certain about what I'm going to touch, my good man,' said the unmistakable voice of Granny Weatherwax.

'Everyone try to reach out,' said Cutangle, and choked down a scream as a hand like a warm leather glove closed around his ankle. There was a satisfied little 'ook', which managed to convey relief, comfort and the sheer joy of touching a fellow human being or, in this case, anthropoid.

There was a scratch and then a blessed flare of red light as a wizard on the far side of the room lit a cigarette.

'Who did that?'

'Sorry, Archchancellor, force of habit.'

'Smoke all you like, that man.'

'Thank you, Archchancellor.'

'I think I can see the outline of the door now,' said another voice.

'Granny?'

'Yes, I can definitely see—'

'*Esk?*'

'I'm here, Granny.'

'Can I smoke too, sir?'

'Is the boy with you?'

'Yes.'

'Ook.'

'I'm here.'

'What's happening?'

'*Everyone stop talking!*'

Ordinary light, slow and easy on the eye, sidled back into the library.

Esk sat up, dislodging the staff. It rolled under the table. She felt something slip over her eyes, and reached up for it.

'Just a moment,' said Granny, darting forward. She gripped the girl's shoulders and peered into her eyes.

'Welcome back,' she said, and kissed her.

Esk reached up and patted something hard on her head. She lifted it down to examine it.

It was a pointed hat, slightly smaller than Granny's, but bright blue with a couple of silver stars painted on it.

'A wizard hat?' she said.

Cutangle stepped forward.

'Ah, yes,' he said, and cleared his throat: 'You see, we thought – it seemed – anyway, when we considered it—'

'You're a wizard,' said Granny, simply. 'The Archchancellor changed the lore. Quite a simple ceremony, really.'

'There's the staff somewhere about here,' said Cutangle. 'I saw it fall down – oh.'

He stood up with the staff in his hand, and showed it to Granny.

'I thought it had carvings on,' he said. 'This looks just like a stick.' And that was a fact. The staff looked as menacing and potent as a piece of kindling.

Esk turned the hat around in her hands, in the manner of one who, opening the proverbial brightly-wrapped package, finds bath salts.

'It's very nice,' she said uncertainly.

'Is that all you can say?' said Granny.

'It's pointed, too.' Somehow being a wizard didn't feel any different from not being a wizard.

Simon leaned over.

'Remember,' he said, 'you've got to have *been* a wizard. Then you can start looking on the other side. Like you said.'

Their eyes met, and they grinned.

Granny stared at Cutangle. He shrugged.

'Search me,' he said. 'What's happened to your stutter, boy?'

'Seems to have gone, sir,' said Simon brightly. 'Must have left it behind, somewhere.'

The river was still brown and swollen but at least it resembled a river again.

It was unnaturally hot for late autumn, and across the whole of the lower part of Ankh-Morpork the steam rose from thousands of carpets and blankets put out to dry. The streets were filled with silt, which on the whole was an improvement – Ankh-Morpork's impressive civic collection of dead dogs had been washed out to sea.

The steam also rose from the flagstones of the Archchancellor's personal verandah, and from the teapot on the table.

Granny lay back in an ancient cane chair and let the unseasonal warmth creep around her ankles. She idly watched a team of city ants, who had lived under the flagstones of the University for so long that the high levels of background magic had permanently altered their genes, anthandling a damp sugar lump down from the bowl on to a tiny trolley. Another group was erecting a matchstick gantry at the edge of the table.

Granny may or may not have been interested to learn that one of the ants was Drum Billet, who had finally decided to give life another chance.

'They say,' she said, 'that if you can find an ant on Hogswatch Day it will be very mild for the rest of the winter.'

'Who says that?' said Cutangle.

'Generally people who are wrong,' said Granny. 'I makes a note in my *Almanack*, see. I checks. Most things most people believe are wrong.'

'Like "red sky at night, the city's alight",' said Cutangle. 'And "you can't teach an old dog new tricks".'

'I don't think that's what old dogs are for,' said Granny. The sugar lump had reached the gantry now, and a couple of ants were attaching it to a microscopic block and tackle.

'I can't understand half the things Simon says,' said Cutangle, 'although some of the students get very excited about it.'

'I understand what Esk says all right, I just don't believe it,' said Granny. 'Except the bit about wizards needing a heart.'

'She said that witches need a head, too,' said Cutangle. 'Would you like a scone? A bit damp, I'm afraid.'

'She told me that if magic gives people what they want, then not using magic can give them what they need,' said Granny, her hand hovering over the plate.

'So Simon tells me. I don't understand it myself, magic's for using, not storing up. Go on, spoil yourself.'

'Magic beyond magic,' snorted Granny. She took the scone and spread jam on it. After a pause she spread cream on it too.

The sugar lump crashed to the flagstones and was immediately surrounded by another team of ants, ready to harness it to a long line of red ants enslaved from the kitchen garden.

Cutangle shifted uneasily in his seat, which creaked.

'Esmerelda,' he began, 'I've been meaning to ask—'

'No,' said Granny.

'Actually I was going to say that we think we might allow a few more girls into the University. On an experimental basis. Once we get the plumbing sorted out,' said Cutangle.

'That's up to you, of course.'

'And, and, it seemed to me that since we seem destined to become a co-educational establishment, as it were, it seemed to me, that is—'

'Well?'

'If you might see your way clear to becoming, that is, whether you would accept a Chair.'

He sat back. The sugar lump passed under his chair on matchstick rollers, the squeaking of the slavedriver ants just at the edge of hearing.

'Hmm,' said Granny, 'I don't see why not. I've always wanted one of those big wicker ones, you know, with the sort of sunshade bit on the top. If that's not too much trouble.'

'That isn't exactly what I meant,' said Cutangle, adding quickly, 'although I'm sure that could be arranged. No, I mean, would you come and lecture the students? Once in a while?'

'What on?'

Cutangle groped for a subject.

'Herbs?' he hazarded. 'We're not very good on herbs here. And headology. Esk told me a lot about headology. It sounds fascinating.'

The sugar lump disappeared through a crack in a nearby wall with a final jerk. Cutangle nodded towards it.

'They're very heavy on the sugar,' he said, 'but we haven't got the heart to do anything about it.'

Granny frowned, and then nodded across the haze over the city to the distant glitter of the snow on the Ramtops.

'It's a long way,' she said. 'I can't be keeping on going backwards and forwards at my time of life.'

'We could buy you a much better broomstick,' said Cutangle. 'One you don't have to bump start. And you, you could have a flat here. And all the old clothes you can carry,' he added, using the secret weapon. He had wisely invested in some conversation with Mrs Whitlow.

'Mmph,' said Granny. 'Silk?'

'Black *and* red,' said Cutangle. An image of Granny in black and red silk trotted across his mind, and he bit heavily into his scone.

'And maybe we can bring some students out to your cottage in the summer,' Cutangle went on, 'for extra-mural studies.'

'Who's Extra Muriel?'

'I mean, there's lots they can learn, I'm sure.'

Granny considered this. Certainly the privy needed a good seeing-to before the weather got too warm, and the goat shed was ripe for the mucking-out by spring. Digging over the Herb bed was a chore, too. The bedroom ceiling was a disgrace, and some of the tiles needed fixing.

'Practical things?' she said, thoughtfully.

'Absolutely,' said Cutangle.

'Mmph. Well, I'll think about it,' said Granny, dimly aware that one should never go too far on a first date.

'Perhaps you would care to dine with me this evening and let me know?' said Cutangle, his eyes agleam.

'What's to eat?'

'Cold meat and potatoes.' There was. Mrs Whitlow had done her work well.

Esk and Simon went on to develop a whole new type of magic that no one could exactly understand but which nevertheless everyone considered very worthwhile and somehow comforting.

Perhaps more importantly, the ants used all the sugar lumps they could steal to build a small sugar pyramid in one of the hollow walls, in which, with great ceremony, they entombed the mummified body of a dead queen. On the wall of one tiny hidden chamber they inscribed, in insect hieroglyphs, the true secret of longevity.

They got it absolutely right and it would probably have important implications for the universe if it hadn't, next time the University flooded, been completely washed away.

THE END

A LIST OF OTHER TERRY PRATCHETT TITLES
AVAILABLE FROM CORGI BOOKS

The prices shown below were correct at the time of going to press. However, Transworld Publishers reserve the right to show new retail prices on covers which may differ from those previously advertised in the text or elsewhere.

12475 3	THE COLOUR OF MAGIC	£6.99
15259 5	THE LIGHT FANTASTIC	£6.99
15261 7	MORT	£6.99
15262 5	SOURCERY	£6.99
15263 3	WYRD SISTERS	£6.99
15264 1	PYRAMIDS	£6.99
13462 7	GUARDS! GUARDS!	£6.99
13463 5	MOVING PICTURES	£6.99
13464 3	REAPER MAN	£6.99
13465 1	WITCHES ABROAD	£6.99
13890 8	SMALL GODS	£6.99
13891 6	LORDS AND LADIES	£6.99
14028 7	MEN AT ARMS	£6.99
14029 5	SOUL MUSIC	£6.99
14235 2	INTERESTING TIMES	£6.99
14236 0	MASKERADE	£6.99
14237 9	FEET OF CLAY	£6.99
14542 4	HOGFATHER	£6.99
14598 X	JINGO	£6.99
14614 5	THE LAST CONTINENT	£6.99
14615 3	CARPE JUGULUM	£6.99
14616 1	THE FIFTH ELEPHANT	£6.99
14768 0	THE TRUTH	£6.99
14840 7	THIEF OF TIME	£6.99
14899 7	NIGHT WATCH	£6.99
14941 1	MONSTROUS REGIMENT	£6.99
14161 5	THE STREETS OF ANKH-MORPORK (with Stephen Briggs)	£8.99
14324 3	THE DISCWORLD MAPP (with Stephen Briggs)	£8.99
14608 0	A TOURIST GUIDE TO LANCRE (with Stephen Briggs and Paul Kidby)	£6.99
14672 2	DEATH'S DOMAIN (with Paul Kidby)	£9.99
14673 0	NANNY OGG'S COOKBOOK (with Stephen Briggs, Tina Hannan and Paul Kidby)	£9.99
14429 0	MORT – THE PLAY (adapted by Stephen Briggs)	£4.99
14430 4	WYRD SISTERS – THE PLAY (adapted by Stephen Briggs)	£6.99
14431 2	GUARDS! GUARDS! – THE PLAY (adapted by Stephen Briggs)	£6.99
14432 0	MEN AT ARMS – THE PLAY (adapted by Stephen Briggs)	£6.99
14159 3	THE LIGHT FANTASTIC – GRAPHIC NOVEL	£9.99
14556 4	SOUL MUSIC: THE ILLUSTRATED SCREENPLAY	£9.99
14575 0	WYRD SISTERS: THE ILLUSTRATED SCREENPLAY	£9.99
13325 6	STRATA	£6.99
13326 4	THE DARK SIDE OF THE SUN	£6.99
13703 0	GOOD OMENS (with Neil Gaiman)	£6.99

All Transworld titles are available by post from:
Bookpost, P.O. Box 29, Douglas, Isle of Man IM99 1BQ.

Credit cards accepted.
Please telephone +44(0)1624 836000, fax +44(0)1624837033,
Internet http://www.bookpost.co.uk or e-mail: bookshop@enterprise.net for details.

Free postage and packing in the UK.
Overseas customers allow £2 per book (paperbacks) and £3 per book (hardbacks).